# SECOND UNIT

### BOOK I OF
## THE BOX OFFICE OF TERROR TRILOGY

# RUSSELL C. CONNOR

Visit us online at

# DarkFilament.com

Contact the author at
facebook.com/russellcconnor
Or follow on Twitter @russellcconnor

Cover Art by SaberCore23 Artwork Studio
For commissions, visit sabercore23art.com

ISBN:
978-1-952968-08-2

Third Edition: 2018

Also by Russell C. Connor

*Novels*
Race the Night*
The Jackal Man
Whitney
Finding Misery*
Sargasso*
Good Neighbors
Between
Predator

*Collections*
Howling Days*
Killing Time*

*The Box Office of Terror Trilogy*
Second Unit*
Director's Cut

*The Dark Filament Ephemeris*
Volume I: Through the Deep Forest
Volume II: On the Shores of Tay-ho
Volume III: Sands of the Prophet
Volume IV: The Halls of Moambati

*eBook Format*
Outside the Lines*
Dark World
Talent Scout
Endless
Mr. Buggins

*Indicates Dark Filament Ephemeris supplementary connection

For David, the only person I've ever known who
can match me film quote for film quote, no
matter how obscure. I can't tell if we've
known each other too long, or just
spent too much of our lives in a theater.

For Cassie, who I think wanted to see me
published more than I did.

For Missy, for growing up Connor with me,
which meant an endless tide of movies
every Tuesday.

For the DFW Writers' Workshop, which listened
to every agonizing page of this novel. You guys
are the best editor a writer could ask for.

For Abbie, for helping me pick up the
pieces. There aren't enough yoodles in
the world to repay you.

# FOREWORD

I can only hope that my love of cinema in general and horror movies in particular shows through in the novel you are about to read; I see a good eighty percent of what comes out in the theaters, plus all the low budget, straight-to-video flicks that catch my eye. The art of filmmaking is something I take very seriously, and, growing up, Hollywood always seemed like a magical place, where movie cameras cast a spell and created the worlds and characters I fell in love with. This is what inspired the largest ideas behind *Second Unit*.

That being said, I want to express heartfelt sincerity in the claim that it was not my intent to malign or insult those in the film industry involved in second unit work. For those unfamiliar with the term, a 'second unit' is a group assisting the main director or filming team with tasks or shots that—due to time or budget constraints—they are unable to finish on their own. In most theatrically released films, if you sit through the credits long enough, you'll eventually see the names of those men and women who toil as hard as the main crew to produce the film you just watched, and it was their somehow forlorn appearance that gave me the inspiration for how I would tell a story set in a city I always wanted to be part of.

Second unit work is (probably) nowhere near as bad or thankless as I have painted it here; that's all in fun. It is a vital part of the film industry that can be found in the early careers of such great directors as Martin Scorsese, Peter Jackson, Guillermo del Toro, and Robert Rodriguez, to name a few.

Then again, everyone hates their job some days.

# SCENE I

(fade in)

# TAKE 1

"Well, does it say 'high rises' or not?" Jared Mane asked, adjusting the zoom on the camera—one of the big Arri 35 millimeters, outfitted with a wide-angle lens—until he zeroed in on the building across the street.

Davis Lowe made no move to check the clipboard in his hand. He just stared out across the expanse of MacArthur Park, toward where downtown L.A. was visible on the horizon.

"Davis? Dave, my man? Mr. Director, you wanna help me out here?"

"Huh?" Davis snorted like a man jolted out of sleep. "Sorry, hold on." He glanced at the clipboard with their shot list. "I don't know, it just says, 'city life scenes.' I guess high rises are part of life in the city, right?"

"God, you make it sound like a *Sesame Street* bit. Which one of these things doesn't belong, boys and girls?" Jared brushed hair out of his face as he readjusted the camera and bent to check the eyepiece. "But Lakewood's just such an *auteur*. I'd hate to disrupt his grand vision for this piece of shit."

Davis shook his head. "He loves to make things complicated, doesn't he?"

They stood at the top of a small, grassy rise with a 360 degree, unobstructed view in the middle of the park, just two guys in khaki shorts, t-shirts and sandals, one of Jared's cameras mounted on a tripod between them. Traffic was stalled below them on Wilshire amid a symphony of honking horns. The sky was smogless today (or as close to smogless as it ever got), the sun perfect, and they'd spent the last five hours on an exhaustive shoot around the city, starting uptown in San Fernando and working their way down.

All for what would be chopped into a thirty-second montage over the opening credits of Dermott Lakewood's newest film, some romantic garbage called *Love Syrup*. Which, to Davis, sounded more like something a pervert poured on his waffles.

He scanned the shot requirements again—a list Lakewood didn't even have the courtesy to furnish himself, but was instead passed along by one of the assistant-assistants-to-whoever—and said, "Just pan up and down a few, and we'll have Otter edit them in, just in case. If Lakewood doesn't like it, he can get out here and do it himself."

"That'll be the day. Christ, can't he use stock footage for this instead of having us bust our asses all over L.A.?"

"If he did that, my friend, we'd be out of a job. However crappy that job might be." Davis grinned at the cameraman. "Besides, what do you think all this will end up as?"

Jared glanced up from the eyepiece. "Hey shithead, I'll have you know, I'm making *art* here."

"Yeah, aren't we all?"

They fell quiet as Jared started rolling, not from necessity—the sound would be edited out later anyway—but from lack of something more enlightening to say on the subject. Davis watched him for a minute and then became interested in a cop that had pulled over a man who appeared to be doing angry jumping jacks behind his car. There was a time when such an image would've sent him scrambling for his own camera—the 8mm or the Sony Digicam Hi-8 or even his old Polaroid, all within a minute's reach at any given second—to record the stark reality of the moment, but such enthusiasm had been chipped away by years of his own 'art' barely yielding enough money to keep him in crackers and cans of Spam.

"You know," he said, leaning an elbow on Jared's hunched back, "we really gotta stop taking these bullshit jobs."

"Not again," Jared groaned, shrugged his arm off, and straightened to face him with an exasperated frown. "You say that every time we catch a gig that's actually gonna pay."

"So?"

"So there's not a helluva lot of other jobs besides the 'bullshit' variety coming our way. I mean, what the hell rubs you so wrong about your current situation?"

"I dunno, maybe the fact that none of this matters in the least? And I could've sworn you were just bitching, too."

"Yeah, about our colleagues, not the job. You know what your problem is?"

"I'm sure you're gonna tell me."

"You look at the future too much. You never just enjoy what you've already earned. Take a look around, Davis. You're outside, you're working in the industry you love, and you don't have to wear a suit to work. Do you know how many of the wannabes in Holly-weird would kill to be in your position?"

Davis waved a hand at the sentiment. "Then let them have it, Jared. I'm tired of doing goddamn montages and close-ups and shitty detail work nobody pays any attention to anyway. I want something more, and don't tell me you don't too."

"Sure I do, and it'll come when it comes. But this pays the bills, and that's enough for me. Sorry if that don't get your creative rocks off hoss, but the most you can hope for in this business is not having to suck some dick for the privilege of cranking out slick, pre-packaged, mass-consumption-ready movies."

"Hey, if Kevin Spacey offered..." Davis laughed and stared up at the one cloud that had managed to form in the dazzling California sky. "Look, I don't need to make my own stuff. I don't have to be another Tarantino or Scorsese. Or even a Kevin Smith. I'm not saying it wouldn't be nice, you understand, but I'd be satisfied with some notoriety for a change. I want to work with actual actors and not stand-in's. I want an audience to know that *I* made the movie for a change, I want my name to appear on screen before they have time to get up and walk out of the theater, I want—"

"A big-breasted girl whose clothes look like they might fall off at any second?"

"Well, now that you mention it..."

Jared nudged him and nodded his head toward the far end of the park. "Check it out."

# TAKE 2

As advertised, a rather well-endowed female strolled across the grass toward them, long platinum blond hair spilling past shoulders bared by a plum-colored spaghetti strap midriff and wearing a pair of denim shorts cut so high they would've shown pubic hair if the region in question was not, most likely, waxed smoother than a bowling alley lane. She looked like the kind of woman who devoured her mate during sex, a woman whose throaty moans—real or not—would set off car alarms, and she didn't appear to be out for a pleasant, midday stroll in the park; there was too much purpose in her stride. She'd probably seen them shooting from one of the apartment buildings across the street.

"Hi there," she gushed. Davis placed her in the late-twenties, probably no more than five years his junior, tanned skin the color of heavily-creamed coffee, face plastic-surgery smooth, breasts so fake they could be used as pool toys. She licked her lips after she spoke, two collagen-injected mounds daubed in an overstated shade of red that seemed unable to stop smiling.

Not one factory-issued part left on her; God's work had been swept aside to a degree that her own mother wouldn't recognize her. Davis wiped his chin to make sure the saliva was imaginary.

"Are you guys making a movie?"

"Why, yes ma'am." Jared tossed his long hair and laid his Texas accent on thick. "Jared Mane. That's 'Mane' just like a lion."

"Are you the director?" she asked, turning to Davis without giving Jared more than passing consideration.

"I am *a* director," he told her. "Davis Lowe, at your service."

She stepped closer, moving her body right up to his, blue eyes meeting his so directly he felt mesmerized. Those bouncy breasts came within inches of his chest. Out of the corner of his eye, he could see Jared smirking. "My name's Candy Donner. Wow, that is *soooo* cool, I've never seen a movie being made!" She held the word 'so' just long enough to purse her lips at him like the oral passage on a blow-up doll. "What's it about?"

"Um, it's a romantic comedy."

"Wow, really?" Her eyes batted, she smiled even wider, and he waited for what he knew must be coming. "You know, *I'm* an actress myself, and I'd do *anything* to get a part in a real movie." Now the breasts actually *were* against him, and oh Jesus, they might be fake but who the fuck really cared, in a city where you were lucky if the women had the original limbs they were born with, who gave a nickel-plated rat's ass? He could have her, he knew he could screw her eight ways to

Sunday and she would beg for more if only to indulge him, she would let him do things to her that would baffle even Dr. Ruth, and all he had to do was just keep his mouth shut.

"*Anything*," she reiterated, and somehow, amazingly, right here before Jared, God, and the inhabitants of General Doug¬las MacArthur Park in Los Angeles, California at 2:30PM on a Monday in June, this gorgeous woman's hand slid down the front of his pants and massaged a member that had already gone stiff from mere proximity.

For one dizzying second he wanted to leap on her like an animal, to begin fornicating with buck wild abandon, the way it always happened in the movies, but then Susan flashed across his mind, and his mouth opened, and he said, "I'd be happy to see what I could do, Miss Donner, but, well...we're on second unit."

A pause of perhaps two seconds while his words registered, and then the hand disappeared from his pants, the luscious, pouting lips moved out of his face, and Miss Candy Donner strolled back the way she'd come with two tan butt cheeks hanging out of the seat of her shorts. Davis heard her mumble, "Second unit trash," over her shoulder before she vanished like a heat mirage.

Jared snickered. "You dope, you don't tell them you're second unit until after you fuck them."

"That's a good way to get drummed right out of town these days."

"You have to be rich and/or famous before anybody would bat an eyelash."

"Do you realize that girl would've been nicer to us if we were making a porno?"

"Shit, she would've been nicer to us if we fetched Lakewood his morning coffee."

"Dude, I really *hate* this job."

# SCENE II

(establishing shot)

# TAKE 1

The Lowe-Mane Production Company sat just off Venice Boulevard east of the 405, part of an innocuous strip mall sharing space with a Latino shoe store and a family-owned Chinese restaurant that couldn't be more thrilled about their neighbor's inadvertent pun. Their last big paycheck—for some light second unit work on a forgettable indie, straight-to-streaming, sci-fi thriller with terrible CGI—went toward a long overdue sign for the front of the building, which Jared claimed had finally stopped the winos from wandering into what they believed to be the abandoned end of the mall. The Lakewood picture would buy them enough cans of paint to overhaul the outside themselves, since they couldn't convince the management company to do it.

But, if the outside wasn't much to look at, it was only because the startup capital (half borrowed from Jared's parents and the rest a sizeable loan taken out by Davis) went into the interior of the company. They couldn't refurbish the entire suite, so they closed off the rooms at the rear and fully furnished an office for Davis, Jared's studio, a conference room ("just in case a client ever actually comes in," Davis insisted), Otter's editing room with a computer bank that looked like the leftovers of a NORAD garage sale, and a reception area for a receptionist they couldn't afford to hire.

Not exactly Skywalker Ranch, but it was *theirs*, and the three of them had fought and clawed for every inch of it.

They pulled Jared's van into a space between Otter's elderly Civic and Davis' battered Mazda. The storefronts were quiet, the entire shopping center tucked up behind an abandoned chicken shack and a strip of city-maintained grass and palm trees. The area had started out as a target for urban development, but the city abandoned the project at some point, which was the only reason they could pay the rent. At least the neighborhood was buffered against the sounds of the freeway. Mr. Chang stood outside sweeping his front walk and waved to Davis, who raised a hand in return.

"I'm telling you, that girl had more open positions than a Wal-Mart," Jared said, as he pulled equipment out of the van's rear doors and tossed a metal suitcase of used film to Davis.

"Let me reiterate—for the hundredth time, I might add—I feel no urge to hear about your deviant fantasies," he said, low enough that the little Asian man couldn't hear.

"Oh, don't be so repressed."

They pushed through the glass front door and into the empty reception area. A few padded chairs occupied the room along with a semi-circular reception desk, the walls and carpet a deep ocean shade of blue. They headed down a hallway to the left of the desk, past Davis' office and the conference room on the left, Jared's studio on the right, and stopped at another closed entry just past this. The only other door in the short passage led to the interior of the suite at the end of the hall, an area untouched since the day they moved in.

Jared tried the knob at their destination, found it locked, and rapped on the door, which rattled on its hinges.

"Who is it?" came a voice, muffled more from the cruller surely shoved in its owner's mouth than by the cheap, faux-wood door.

"Who do you think it is Ot?" Jared shouted. "Open the door before I drop this!"

There was the sound of wheels scraping across the carpet followed by the click of the door latch. By the time Davis could open the door, their film editor, Terrence Ottman the Third, had already rolled back across the office to his usual place in front of his wall of computer monitors and editing equipment.

# TAKE 2

From behind, the man resembled a giant beanbag shoved into a rolling office chair. His head squashed out his neck almost entirely, forming a perfect convexity from the top of his balding head to his shoulders, and down to his Humpty-Dumpty-shaped body. The arms of the chair cut into his sides, forming a roll of flab oozing off his ribs and dripping down his hips, but he never noticed the constriction. His legs were little more than fleshy cones dangling off the front of the chair, broad thighs tapering to surprisingly small ankles and feet. He was pudgy and awkward, out of place on land or sea, a man going the wrong direction on the evolutionary ladder.

But, oh, his fingers were another story.

Despite the girth of his arms, the width of his hands, and the bulbous sausages on the ends of them, he could move his digits across a keyboard like lightning. And that was good, considering he worked on three of them, currently hooked up to monitors simultaneously streaming an episode of *Buffy the Vampire Slayer*, playing a pirated mod version of some first-person shooter, and editing home movie footage of a high school play whose lead actor hired them to create a video résumé.

Terence Ottman the Third, or 'Otter' as Davis had called him since the fifth grade, was the best unknown film editor in the land of digital wizards. Davis had seen him put together works of visual art without so much as glancing up from one of his precious japanimation DVD's.

"You shouldn't lock yourself in here, Otter," Davis set the film suitcase inside the door. "How are you gonna know if any clients come in?"

"Because I'll feel the draft when hell freezes over," he said over his shoulder, his round-frame glasses winking light off the computers in the otherwise dim room.

Jared snorted. "He's got you there."

"Did you get it done?" Otter asked.

"Read it and weep." Jared hoisted two cameras onto the jutting shelf surrounding the monitors next to Otter and removed the film canisters. "About two-and-a-half hours worth of footage. I'll convert it tonight and have dailies for you in the morning. Have fun sorting through it."

"Davis?" Otter stretched up to turn off one of his monitors. His chair creaked in protest as he settled back down. "Any instructions for arrangement?"

"I don't know how Lakewood wants it. Stick with longer cuts and we can pare it down later if we need to. But no sound; I think he wants some kind of sappy Celine Dion crap playing over it."

"Hey, I like Celine Dion!"

Jared clapped his hands on Otter's thick shoulders and gave them a hearty shake. "I'm sure you do, my man. Make me a separate tape of any hot girl footage, especially the one that gave Davis a hand job in the park." Otter's head whipped toward Davis. "I'll catch you guys later. I'm setting up for my shoot tomorrow and then I'm outta here."

Otter's piggy eyes scrutinized Davis as Jared walked out. He raised one bushy eyebrow, wrinkling his entire forehead.

Davis could feel warm guilt creeping in. What would Susan say if she knew about Miss Donner's 'audition' in the middle of the park? "It's nothing, don't listen to him. Did we get any calls?"

"Yes, one from a girl named *Susan*," Otter said, peering over the rim of his glasses. "Do *you* know anyone named Susan?"

Davis sighed. Otter's tendency to mother hen was almost pathological. Considering his mother, that was no surprise. "Nothing happened, Otter. Just some desperate actress sniffing around for a role."

The suspicion in the editor's fleshly face disappeared. "She blow you off when you told her you were second unit?"

"For Christ's sake, what did Susan say?"

"Well, first she complained that you weren't answering your cell again and probably wouldn't hear her message."

"I forgot to charge it!"

"Then she told me to tell you that she can't make it to the restaurant because she heard about a casting call. Said she'd see you at her place tonight and you could eat there."

"Okay, fine. Anything else?"

Otter swiveled around to shovel through paper scraps on the far side of his keyboards. "Let's see…yeah, Lakewood's assistant called about the crowd scene you're filming tomorrow. He's having forty extras meet you at the studio tomorrow at one. Oh, and someone named Phillip Reilly called, real official sounding, just said he wanted you in his office Wednesday morning."

Davis was halfway out the door when the name grabbed him by the throat. "Wait a minute, *Phillip Reilly* called?"

"Yeah, I think so." Otter checked his note again. "Who's Phillip Reilly?"

Davis tried to answer, tripped over his tongue, and sputtered, "Otter, that's the head of Trimax Studios!"

"Trimax?" Jared shouted from down the hall. "Holy shit, someone from *Trimax* called?"

"Yeah, don't you remember, we met him at James Kincaid's party two months ago, the one we crashed? Or wait, maybe you'd already gone home with that toothpaste commercial girl by then." It was the only time Davis had met the man in person, and all he could remember through the haze of alcohol was a long face anchored by a huge, shining grin, the kind of smirk only producers could afford.

Jared reappeared in the door. "What does he want with you?"

"Trimax has this slasher movie they're getting ready to hire a director for—."

"Oh yeah, *Open Arteries*!"

"No, *Arterial Slice*, but thanks for trying, 'tardo. I talked to him about it at the party, sent him a copy of the documentary we did on the homeless shelters. Then, out of the blue, he sends me a script last month, we trade emails, I give him my take on it, and he says he'll keep me in mind, etcetera, etcetera, etcetera, and I never heard anything back. What the hell did he say, Otter?"

"Nothing. Just said to be in his office Wednesday around ten." He blinked owlishly. "What does that mean?"

"What does it mean?" Davis leapt across the short distance in one bound, put his palms on either side of Otter's loose jowls, and squeezed them together until his lips puckered. "I'll tell you what that means, you wonderfully fat bastard! *He's giving us this movie!* He's gonna let me direct it!"

"You really think so?" Jared asked behind him.

Davis released Otter and spun to face his partner. "Of course, what else could it be? This is big, this is really big! I mean, Trimax isn't a blockbuster studio, but this is a real step up! This will be *our* movie! Ours, the three of us! This is exactly what we've been waiting for!" He pushed past his cameraman and took off down the hallway toward the reception area.

"Where are you going?" they called after him in unison.

"To tell Susan! If this doesn't get me laid, nothing will!"

# TAKE 3

Davis reached Susan Campbell's apartment around 5:30, as the bulk of the traffic clogged the freeways like a cholesterol-choked artery. Her place was closer to the office than his—on Olympic, on the cusp of Beverly Hills, where the cloying scent of money, power, and fame was both a distraction and a motivator. It was on the fourth floor of a fifteen-story building, modest but more upscale than the roadside motel address he kept in South Venice Beach, where the pool usually contained large quantities of vomit from the college kids' all night parties. Susan paid for this comparative Eden with a much steadier paycheck from adjusting claims at an insurance company while she searched for on-screen work along with the other two bazillion souls unfortunate enough to be bitten by the acting bug.

She'd been after him to move in for some time and he wanted to—it only made sense at this point in their relationship—but something kept him from selling off his flea-infested furniture and telling his Iranian landlord to take that lease and shove it.

Davis changed out of his shorts and searched through the various clothes that had collected at her apartment for something more formal as he pondered this problem yet again. Susan was sweet and innocent and wholesome, all qualities elevated in his mind because he hadn't met her at another tired party full of deviants and suck-ups, and he'd never been happier in his life.

*So why the fuss then? Kiss the random sex scene goodbye, and hang up your testicles at the door.*

He would, it wasn't like he got Jared's kind of action even when single, so nothing about monogamy scared him (although a few more like the one in the park could definitely get his imagination working overtime; he'd have to take that frustration out in a marathon with Susan tonight).

No, any hesitation was strictly his problem, and he didn't like to admit the reason to anyone, not even himself.

The bottom line was this: Davis Lowe believed he was a failure, and until the world did something to show him otherwise, he would remain a deer dazzled by the headlights of elusive success, unable to make any changes in his life indicative of 'growing up.' There was an order to things, a specific course the events in his life should follow just like the board game suggested, and he remained stuck on the square where you picked a career path.

Jared was right. He was just too obsessed with what was coming down the line three months from now, a year from now, a decade from now. If life was what happened while you made other plans, then he really needed a personal organizer so he could enjoy it.

But all of that was about to change. Mr. Phillip Reilly would see to that.

He had time to throw on jeans and a blue chambray shirt, run out for a moderately-priced bottle of wine, cook a linguini dinner for two, spin a John Mayer CD, and set a candlelit tabletop before she arrived home. He waited for her at the table in her cramped kitchen as the door opened.

# TAKE 4

He felt that curious uplift in his chest that always happened when he saw her. On the CD player, Mayer was singing about how a woman had his only heart, and Davis thought he'd never identified more with any sentiment in history. She paused in the doorway, giving him an appreciative smile as she swept her sandy blond, shoulder-length locks out of her face. "Isn't it a little early to be celebrating? I haven't gotten the part yet."

"Do we need a reason to celebrate?"

She gestured at the bottle of wine in the middle of the table as she closed the door. "For something that expensive, we sure as hell better."

"We do."

"Tell me."

"You first. What was the audition for?"

"Just something I heard about through the grapevine. Bit part in an independent film about lemmings or something."

"Lemmings?"

"I think the writer must've seen *March of the Penguins* one too many times. Anyway, I got off early to go, but the casting people herded us through like cattle. I can't see that I stood out any more than the three hundred other girls there."

She put her purse down beside the door. She wore a low cut green top to showcase her cleavage and a pair of hip-hugging black slacks. "Not even with that outfit?"

"I'll never go to my knees for a role, but it doesn't hurt to look like I might." She slid into the seat across from him, and he reached for her hand.

"You're beautiful and talented. You'll get it. It takes time."

Susan grinned, turning her sculpted lips into a work of art. She had worn lipstick for the audition, and he wanted to suck them clean. "Cheer me up, babe. What's all this about?"

"I got a directing gig. A real one, for a studio."

Her jaw sprung open in comical surprise. She could emote naturally, another reason he remained sure she would rise above the acting sewage in this city. "You're kidding! What is it?"

"That horror movie I told you about for Trimax."

"Oh, don't tell me…something about bleeding veins?"

"Close. *Arterial Slice*. The studio head over there, Phillip Reilly, wants me in his office Wednesday morning."

She beamed now, scooting her chair around the table closer to him. "What did he say?"

"I don't know, I didn't talk to him. He just left a message with Otter."

"Well, what did he say to Otter?"

"Just what I said, to be in his office Wednesday morning."

The smile on her lips slowly melted into a frown. "How do you know you got it then?"

The question was so far from what he expected he could only grunt, "What?"

"How do you even know that's what he was calling for?"

"Jesus, Suze!" He pushed away from the table and stood up. There had been no malice in her question, no conscious attempt to break him down, but he felt wildly defensive all the same, as eager to prove himself as though she'd just questioned his bedroom prowess. "Do you have to be so negative here? Why else would the guy want to meet with me?"

"I don't know, it just seems like the kind of thing he'd leave in a message. If you had an agent, wouldn't he call and tell *him*?"

"But I *don't* have an agent. He probably just wants to meet and go over some specifics."

She remained silent for a moment, her eyes drifting to the tabletop, and then she nodded. "I guess you would know better than me. I'm not officially in the 'industry.'"

The last of his anger melted away, leaving him guilty and embarrassed. He came back and knelt in front of her. His palms caressed her cheeks, gently turning her to look at him. "I'm sorry, I didn't mean to snap. It's just that, this is it Suze, the big time. I've been dreaming about this since the first time I saw—"

"Yeah, yeah, *E.T.*, I know." She rolled her eyes.

"Laugh all you want, but that movie is what made me want to become a director. And now I'm on the verge of something really huge. Me, calling the shots for an entire movie; me, getting to tell some other second unit schlubs what to do." He grinned and raised his eyebrows. "Me... having a huge say in casting?"

It took a fraction of a second for her to see what he was hinting at, then she jerked her head away and smacked him on the shoulder with her palm. "Oh right Davis, because that's how I wan to get all my parts, in my boyfriend's movies!"

"Hey, Tim Burton does it all the time!"

"I don't care. I want my own career."

This time he got to his feet and leaned over her, rubbing his lips against her ear and down her neck. "I didn't mean to start a fight with any of this. I just wanted us to have a little dinner, and a little wine," his hand roamed across her breasts, "and see where the night takes us."

She grabbed his shoulders and held him at arm's length. "What makes you think I'm gonna have sex with a guy on second unit?"

"You're dating me. You're sort of obligated."

"Not good enough."

"Well babe, I *am* a director now."

"In that case, let's skip dinner."

It was, indeed, a marathon.

# SCENE III

(perspective change)

# TAKE 1

*Arterial Slice*, as far as Davis could determine from the script, was a low-budget bloodfest drafted by some unknown writer undoubtedly forced to hack out such drivel while he tried to sell his own version of *Good Will Hunting*. Ostensibly, it told the story of three young nurses (to be played by busty, leggy vixens, no doubt) who were terrorized, hunted down, and butchered one at a time in the mental ward they worked in. Chesterfield Hospital, it was called, the killer an inmate that expired during intensive shock therapy years before but now back from the grave to seek revenge.

Trimax obviously wanted to start up a franchise, but if they wanted it to succeed, they needed a director with enough fresh ideas to turn what was otherwise video store discount bin trash into a slasher with enough punch to get it on the radar of critics and cult lovers. There was a precise science to making movies like this, one few people in the industry took the time to learn or appreciate.

The studio couldn't be expecting a huge take on grosses—the movie houses turned out dozens of low-profit films each year just to keep the wheels greased—but with any luck, he could give them a return profit-to-budget ratio that would put *The Blair Witch Project* to shame, and forever stamp his name on the Hollywood map.

And he ignored a sniping voice in his head when it asked if he could even recall the names of the two guys who directed *Blair* in the first place.

# TAKE 2

The city's smog respite ended the day he left to meet Phillip Reilly, and the sky crusted over with a layer of wispy gray. A stiff breeze came off the hills just heavy enough to make the heat pleasant. He dressed in black slacks and white shirt, deciding at the last moment to forego the tie; sometimes hip and youthful was more valuable than professionalism in this business. He left straight from Susan's place, trying not to let his hands shake as he pulled into midmorning traffic.

He'd considered having Jared come, but besides the fact that the man possessed no subtlety, Davis felt possessive of the opportunity and a little resentful that he was the only one out there working the clientele and networking like mad these past few years. Technically, as a full partner, the decision to take on the project was as much Jared's as his, but the cameraman was mostly satisfied to do his thing and let Davis steer the Lowe-Mane ship.

This first moment of glory would be his and his alone even if he showed up with vomit on his shoes.

Trimax Motion Pictures was on Sunset, squarely in the middle of studio alley, just up the street from MGM and NBC's L.A. offices. When he reached the gates on Wednesday morning, he pulled his clunking Mazda onto a short strip of driveway and stopped next to a guard shack bigger than his apartment.

The guard dragged himself away from a rerun of the Jerry Springer show being played on a multi-thousand dollar flat screen television and leaned out the window, sneering at his car from beneath his triangular brown cap, and said, "Studio tours are through the west side gate, and only on the weekends. Private entrance only."

He tried to look inflated and important. "My name is Davis Lowe, I have a meeting with Mr. Reilly this morning."

The guard lifted his eyebrows as if he thought this as likely as finding out his testicles had turned to gold overnight and withdrew into his booth to check a computer screen. When he came back, his demeanor changed.

"Yes, Mr. Lowe, I'll open the gates for you immediately."

"Mind telling me where I need to go?" he added with just the right amount of haughty poise.

"Yes sir, go straight and take the second left, follow it all the way down till you see the main building. Parking's on the right."

"Thank you," Davis said, enjoying the look of humble servitude sweeping the guard's face. This was something he could get used to.

The gates opened and he followed the directions through the lot, passing several open studios where filming was taking place. He parked in the lot of the headquarters and entered an immaculate reception area that made the one at Lowe-Mane look like a McDonald's. The receptionist was a pretty young thing with bulging muscles and thighs that could crack a walnut. She sent him up three floors where another grinning receptionist that looked like a twin of the first asked him to have a seat on a leather couch. He was there for ten minutes before Phillip Reilly entered from the same door Davis had just come through.

"Davis Lowe!" he shouted cordially, holding out his hand. "Just the man I wanted to see, sorry to keep you waiting, my team had to play a game in the Porcelain Bowl if you know what I mean, walk with me to my office, why don't you?" The man had a habit of running his sentences together in a boisterous, overbearing way. Davis thought it was the alcohol at the party that caused it during their first meeting, but maybe not. At the mention of his bathroom habits, Davis saw the receptionist blanch.

Davis launched off the couch, shaking the offered hand and trying not to imagine where it had been. The man passed him without a pause, and he quickened his pace to keep up. They started through the door on the opposite end of the waiting room and into a long hallway decorated with the bland prints only people with no taste in art put up.

Phillip Reilly couldn't be more than seven or eight years older than Davis himself, his build wider and squatter. His face was as long and horse-like as Davis remembered, with blinding white teeth and a jaw like a bear trap. He dressed casually also—dress shirt open at the throat, slacks and loafers—but the ensemble still probably cost more than the car Davis drove here in.

It seemed he should say something, but the meeting was so informal he had no idea what direction to go in. "Sir, I wanted to thank you for calling me in."

"Uh huh," Reilly returned noncommittally over his shoulder. He power-walked down the hallway, Davis struggling to keep up. "You read the script for *Arterial Slice*, Lowe, what'd you *really* think? No more bullshit now, be honest."

"Wellllll, I mean, it was a little derivative, and the dialogue could use some punching up..."

Reilly stopped his power walk so abruptly Davis walked on a few paces without him. "My nephew wrote that."

"Oh. Oh god, no, I didn't mean—"

He gave an obnoxious snort. "Joking, Lowe."

"Right. Yes. Very amusing, sir."

"Anyway," Reilly resumed his thunderous pace, "this movie isn't a project the studio is pinning its hopes on, but it's still a film we'd like to see take off, a franchise we'd like to see grow. You know, have our own Frankie Krueger, or whatever the hell his name is. For that to happen, we need a director that's really gonna pitch himself into the work, not go by the numbers just because this thing doesn't have five star talent. I always say the best way to get that sort of approach is to bring in a fresh perspective. Find somebody not afraid to break rules, don't you agree?"

They reached the end of the hallway, where a large, ornate oak door was embossed with the executive's name. Davis' chest swelled, and he felt like he would never stop smiling. "Yes, I agree completely."

"And I think we may've found that perspective, someone to take this picture in a whole new direction, grab the American audience by the throat."

They stopped at the door, and Phillip Reilly pushed it open to reveal the oak paneled office beyond. His desk stretched across its length with the presence of an aircraft carrier, two tall-backed Gothic chairs positioned neatly in front of it. "I'm honored, Mr. Reilly. I won't let you down."

Reilly's hand pounded him between the shoulder blades. "Glad to hear it, Lowe. In that case, let me introduce you to the director of *Arterial Slice*, acclaimed German filmmaker Torsten Gross."

# TAKE 3

At this point in the conversation, the proud swelling in his chest deflated like a popped balloon, and Davis began to feel like he was in an elevator whose cables had snapped somewhere near the thirtieth floor.

*Say something*, he told himself. *Something that shows you understand what's going on even though you couldn't be more clueless if he were speaking Mandarin Chinese.*

"Wha?" The word came out as a low grunt. Before he could make a further ass of himself, there was movement within the office.

A figure climbed out of the large chair on the left and turned to face them. A gaunt, balding scarecrow dressed like a patron from a beatnik coffeehouse. His head looked like a shiny, flesh-colored bowling ball, a bald runway of liver-spotted flesh stretched taut over his skull and surrounded by a thinning roll of dark gray hair. Lumps of coal in his eye sockets glittered mutely from under a single, thick, bushy eyebrow. He looked lean and lanky, somewhere in his mid-to-late sixties, but still healthy, vital, and alive. Dressed in all black, from neatly polished wingtips to turtleneck sweater, and square tinted glasses perched on the end of his abnormally thin, long nose. All he needed was a black beret and a scarf to look like the stereotype of a Hollywood director.

"*Guten morgen*, Mr. Lowe," were the first words Davis heard Torsten Gross say, and 'mister' came out a deeply slurred 'mishtah' from his accent. "Mr. Reilly has told me you are also quite the talented filmmaker."

He didn't really care what Mr. Reilly had told him. At this point the elevator in his head plummeted past the twentieth floor.

The man came forward crisply, each step a military march, and jabbed a hand at Davis. He found himself shaking it out of instinct more than a real desire to meet the man, and the hand pressing against his was strong but oily, with another underlying quality—

*Fake*, his ever-vigilant inner voice chimed in, whispering the word uncomfortably. *Like a rubber glove pulled over a skeleton frame of a hand.*

"I-I don't understand," he stammered, pulling his hand quickly away to part with that flesh. The elevator hurtled past ten, reaching terminal velocity.

"The studio has persuaded Mr. Gross—."

"Please, no 'Mister,' I simply go by 'Gross,'" the scarecrow insisted, drawing back thin lips at Davis in a ghoulish grin.

"Yes, I'm sorry, 'Gross' was talked into coming overseas for his American debut. Trimax feels this would be a great project for him to cut his teeth on, bring some of his style and edge to a film that would otherwise, frankly, be lucky to go straight to video."

And the elevator hit bottom, exploding like a trash can on a cherry bomb, shredding the remains of Davis Lowe's dignity. He wanted to ask a thousand questions, the most prominent being if this sprocket was directing *Arterial Slice*, then—

"Um, why am I here, exactly?" he asked.

"For second unit work, of course," Reilly answered. He smiled as if Davis should be thrilled. "The studio decided to give it to you based on that documentary. Cute piece of filmmaking, it really was."

Davis nodded numbly, but couldn't shake the doped expression slipping across his face.

"Perhaps I should explain further," Gross cut in, a hooded twinkle in his eye making Davis suspect he already had a bit more of an idea what was going on than he should. At least that awful smile finally disappeared. "I am a quite…ah, *exzentrisch* filmmaker. How would you say, ah, very strange, unusual…?"

"Eccentric?" Davis offered.

"Ah, yes, 'eccentric,' thank you Mr. Lowe! My habits are quite eccentric, and many do not find it easy to work with me. I am demanding and must have…precision…at all times. I often do most of the special effects, the filming, the editing myself, because so few people measure up to my strict standards. I have never worked with one of these 'second units,' but with the timetable Trimax is imposing on this project," his hard eyes flicked to Reilly, "they feel it would be beneficial to have someone aid me with the work. They have recommended you, and I have acquiesced. It is quite an honor for you, rest assured."

"I, well, thank you," Davis stammered.

"So whaddaya say, Lowe?" Reilly asked. "Your company up for something like this? Gross is gonna need some extensive second unit work and the fee," he handed Davis a piece of paper produced from somewhere like a magician with a bundle of flowers, "is quite fair, I think you'll see."

Davis glanced at the figure and felt his mouth dry up. It was quite fair, and he would be insane to refuse out of some half-baked idea of pride. "I think we can make it work."

"Excellent!" Gross exclaimed. "Trimax and myself have several stars in mind from which we will make a final decision by week's end. Filming will start immediately thereafter and maintain a fairly brisk pace. I will furnish you with a list of my needs on a daily to weekly basis. If we are to survive this experience, we will have to work closely, Mr. Lowe, and I expect you to be at my—what is the American saying?—'beck and call?'"

"Sounds…good. Let me give you a number to reach me at."

"I have your information, Mr. Lowe. We will be in touch." *Ve vill be in touch,* like something from a bad spy movie. Gross turned to Reilly and sketched a brief, jerking bow of his head. "And now, if there is nothing further Mr. Reilly, I must immerse myself in the making of this picture, beginning with the awful excuse for a script I have been provided."

Without waiting for a dismissal, acclaimed German film-maker Torsten Gross slipped between the two of them and started back down the long hallway with his staccato steps.

# TAKE 4

Davis continued to stare after the director, the piece of paper with his fee wilted in his hand. When Gross was completely out of the office, Reilly's face changed, expressing the sour look of a kid after his first and last Brussels sprout. "*Eccentric,*" he snorted. "Christ, *Manson* was eccentric. That guy…" He rubbed his forehead as if to erase the wrinkle forming there.

Davis tried to smile but had trouble getting his mouth to make the shape.

Reilly turned and went into his office, leaving Davis in the doorway. "I like you, Lowe. You're my kind of guy. That's why I'm going to drop the whole cheerleader routine and level with you: Gross was not my choice. I know you wanted the director spot and, to be honest, I wanted to give it to you."

"Um…thanks."

Reilly lit up a huge cigar and puffed, sending mini smoke signals into the air. "Personally, Gross gives me the creeps.

But the other execs think he's going to perform Hollywood magic. I don't know, maybe he will. They say he's a genius. And just because he has a lot of strange working habits doesn't mean anything, right? They say Kubrick used to sit around in Jell-o before he started a new film."

"I hadn't heard that one," Davis mumbled.

"Look Lowe, you're a professional, you know this business, and he's gonna make a lot of weird requests, but just humor him. He's the type that goes on and on about how art can't be rushed, but it can if it's on my dime. Keep an eye on him, keep him on target, and if anything goes too far astray or you see something that sets off an alarm in your head, give me a shout. If things go all right on this…well, no promises, but I'll see what I can do about getting you a directing spot on a future project."

"Thank you," Davis said again.

"Great. Just so we're square." He stubbed the barely-smoked stogie into a gold ashtray. Davis wondered if the man would be kept up at night between his satin sheets if he knew just how far from fucking square they were.

"There's going to be a studio kick-off party Friday night so we can announce the stars of this thing. Everyone will be there. Bring your unit so they can meet Gross and have a good time, okay?"

"Sounds good."

"All right, talk to my secretary. She'll give you the info on the party and work out the contract details. See you Friday."

Davis nodded and left. Cowardly, humiliated, and useless, he walked away from Phillip Reilly's office wishing with his entire being that he'd told the man to screw his fee, and for more reasons than the fact he'd led him on like a donkey with a carrot.

Something—some nagging, fearful intuition—told him it was a monumentally bad idea to work under, above, or anywhere in the near vicinity of Mr. Torsten Gross.

# SCENE IV

(extreme close-up)

# TAKE 1

He was thankful to find an empty parking lot when he arrived back at Lowe-Mane. He prayed Jared was off on a shoot the rest of the day and Otter had gone to one of his numerous doctor appointments for his bad back or chronic allergies, all symptoms forced upon him by his mother. If Davis turned his cell phone off, he should be safe. He felt no rush to face the same defeated stare from them that he'd been giving himself in the rearview mirror all the way back.

*Yeah, and imagine what it's going to be like telling Susan.* His stomach churned as he recalled everything he'd said to her two nights ago. Once again, she was the realist, and he the dreamer. God, had he actually offered to get her a part?

That wasn't optimism, it was sheer naivety. You'd think he was one of the starry-eyed girls fresh off the bus from Indiana or Michigan, sure that a multi-million dollar part would be hers by week's end.

The door was locked and the lights off, and he left them that way while he walked down the hallway to his cramped office. As he pushed open the door, the fluorescents blazed on and he was hit with a concussive boom that sounded vaguely like the word, "Surprise!"

Davis staggered back. Jared was up against the wall to his left so he could reach the light switch. Otter hunkered in the chair behind his desk with Susan hovering over him, both beaming and holding up plastic glasses of champagne. The bottle sat on the corner of his stringently clean desk; a banner stretched from wall to wall that read, "CONGRATULATIONS!" A congregation of multi-colored balloons hung from both ends.

He wanted to throw up. A lot.

"Surprise, babe." Susan came around the desk to plant a kiss on his cheek. "Gary gave me the morning off so I could arrange this little soirée."

Jared slung an arm around him and pushed a glass of champagne into his hand. "Congrats, partner. You worked a long time for this, and I can't think of a single soul in this fucked up 'burg that deserves it more."

"Okay, okay, I can't take it," Otter howled, jiggling all over. "When do we start and how much are we getting paid?"

They all pressed in on him in the close quarters; he felt a wave of claustrophobia settle around him like a giant boa constrictor.

Davis shrugged out of Jared's arm, slid past Susan and put the glass down on his desk in front of Otter before he could drop it. "We're not. At least, not directing. Reilly wanted us for second unit work, that's all. Expensive second unit work, but nothing more."

And there it was, the crestfallen look on the faces of those most important to him in the universe. Suddenly their eyes were everywhere but on him, the excitement in their face shriveling up like salted slugs.

This is probably what Columbus' men looked like just before they attempted mutiny.

So how much longer before they keelhauled him?

Susan came forward to hug him. "Oh Davis, I'm so sorry."

No recriminations, no I-told-you-so's. It felt good in her arms, and horrible at the same time. He hated feeling dependent on her, financially or emotionally. He pressed his face into her hair and said, "No, *I'm* sorry. I got everyone's hopes up. I guess I just misunderstood the situation."

Otter looked like he might cry. "I-I don't understand. I thought he'd been talking to you about it. About directing. I thought...he wanted you to do it. Wanted *us*."

"Yeah, well, apparently not."

"Bastard," Jared grumbled. "Doesn't know what he's missing."

"He said he might have something for us after this."

"Yeah, well fuck him. He can shove it up his ass."

Davis mustered a grin. "I'll let you tell him that."

"Man," Otter whispered. "I already told my mother. She's gonna try to make me move home again." He leaned over far enough to put his forehead on the desk.

"Aw, God Ott, I'm so sorry."

"Who'd they hire?" Jared asked.

"Some weirdo German they imported named Torsten Gross."

Otter's head shot back up. "Wait a minute, you're not serious. Trimax got *the* Torsten Gross? You *met* him?"

"You've heard of him?"

"Um, *yeah!* He's only the king of the underground German horror movie market!"

"That supposed to mean something?" Jared muttered.

"It's certainly big business over there! His films have topped their box office charts for thirty years! He's a legend! From the way I always heard it, people can't get enough of them!"

"From the way you always heard it?" Davis frowned. "Is he a legend, or is he an *urban* legend?"

"Well, he only makes a movie about every five years or so. And he's very selective about who he casts." A dreamy expression came over Otter's thick features, reminding Davis of the look the tourists got when they spotted their favorite celebrity on the street. "To think that the three of us are going to see how he operates! I just...I can't believe it!"

"But Otter," Susan put in, "if he's so big, how come *we've* never heard of him?"

"It's illegal for his films to be imported to America. Some religious groups have been lobbying to get them outright banned for years. But I think I have some of his stuff downloaded somewhere from my webgroup. Come on, it'll just take a second!"

Davis shared a look with Jared and Susan and then the three of them followed Otter as he waddled back to his cubbyhole and waited while he settled himself behind his computer. He worked the keyboard and began searching through meticulously neat directories for the proper file.

Susan's arms were still draped around Davis, her head on his shoulder. He planted a kiss at her hairline. She turned to give him a smile, but he couldn't find the strength to return it.

Jared squeezed in beside them, still shaking his head in disgust. "So how much is Mr. Phillip 'The Shithead' Reilly paying us to work on this heap?"

"You know our fee for the Lakewood film? Triple it."

"Like I said, I always liked that guy."

"Okay, here it is, check this out!" Otter cried. He punched a few more keys and the image came up on the middle monitor. He tilted this one to face them.

"What are we watching, Otter?" Davis asked, as the three of them crowded closer behind his chair.

"It's from one of his films called *Tote Jetzt, Stirb Spater*. It means *Kill Now, Die Later*. I don't have the whole thing downloaded though. The guy I got it from found the murder scenes spliced in with some other stuff on a German fetish website."

On the monitor was a grainy picture of a very voluptuous and very nude woman. She was the picture of German statehood, blond hair cut short and curled around her strong jaw, face attractive in a harsh way. Her blue eyes stretched wide open, the look of fear in them unmistakable. She appeared to be stepping out of a shower and reaching for a towel hanging to her left in a bathroom dim and dirty enough to be part of a condemned building. Otter hit a button and the film lurched into motion.

"Tell me that's download corruption and not the camera work," Jared said.

"Actually, this is a pretty clear copy. Gross is notorious for intentionally using unfinished film."

"Davis, look at the camera angles he's using. Where did the guy learn to direct, from a home security company?"

Davis nodded, but he was quickly becoming engrossed in the static technique the man employed. As the girl emerged from the shower and covered herself with a towel (black, as everything else in the film; he hadn't seen such a drab piece since film school), the camera switched from various high and low corners of the room. It reminded him of the perspective of many of the old third-person video games, where the scene didn't change until the player directed the character to a point off screen. Almost as if Gross had installed cameras in the selected positions so the actress could work unfettered, without cameramen or dollies in the way.

And then the action started, and thoughts of color and camera blew away like smoke.

# TAKE 2

The young girl, frightened from hearing something that interrupted her shower, took a cautious step out of the bathroom into a hallway that stretched forever in both directions. The wallpaper was torn and fading, the drywall showing through in ragged patches, and Davis couldn't tell if it was intentionally part of the film's décor or if a cracked-out slum was just the best they could do on budget. She shouted something in German he couldn't understand, but had to be something along the classic lines of, 'Who's there?' She breathed hard, panting, her breasts heaving beneath the towel, the realism of the moment startling.

"She's terrified," Susan whispered. He glanced down at her. "That's good acting, Davis."

He had to agree. The girl seemed as completely unsure of what was coming as they did. She stood frozen in the doorway, looking both directions down the hall, and the fear coupled with the innocuous angle, the raw footage, and the complete lack of musical score made for a picture so genuine it was like watching a documentary. As the perspective switched, she remained on the threshold, swinging her foot indecisively, as though scared to leave the safe confines of the bathroom.

The image abruptly skewered past her to a huge silhouette blocking the light from the far end of the hall.

"That's Lars Krieg," Otter said. "He's the killer in all of Gross' films. It's kind of a running joke."

"That guy doesn't look like a joke," Davis whispered.

The exact details of the man got lost in the shadows, but his dimensions were enhanced by them. The actor was tall and wide and thick, arms as big as telephone poles and a chest that reminded Davis of the grill of a big rig. He stood silently at the end of the hallway, unmoving, the hulking demeanor reminding Davis of Michael Myers in the old *Halloween* movies. The classic supernatural serial killer pose.

Davis knew exactly how this would go. The girl would see him and run, and he would calmly walk after her, taking slow, measured steps, and, somehow, would still catch up with her.

But the scene didn't follow the formula at all. The man charged forward, bearing down on the girl, footsteps booming like fireworks in the narrow hallway, making no effort to muffle his approach. It was barbaric, and far more frightening than the norm.

The girl spotted him and shrieked. The angle was perfect, across the hall and low, cutting up close to her stretched eyes and gaping mouth. She hurtled awkwardly out of the bathroom, her foot slipped on the tile, and she went down on one knee. She regained her feet, lurching into a run. Her neck craned around to a nearly impossible degree so her eyes could stay rooted to the figure barreling at her. Her head and body worked against one another, causing her to stumble again.

She picked up speed, but she also loped sideways in order to keep her attacker in sight, flattening her upper body against the filthy wall. Davis understood her fear, and god, it was *realistic*, but he found himself more afraid for the character than in awe of the acting and silently encouraging her to just move her tight ass instead of trying to watch the behemoth stalking her.

"C'mon girl, *run*," Susan commiserated, echoing his thoughts.

On the other side of him, Jared shifted his weight from foot to foot unconsciously.

Then it was too late.

Lars Krieg caught her.

All four people in the room jumped as though fifty thousand volts had slammed through them. Even Otter, who'd seen this before. The camera switched to another high position—nearly overhead—as Krieg's hand swiped out and gave the girl a brutal chop across the throat, producing a wet *thwak* audible even on the video clip's poor sound. The girl came to a sluggish halt, eyes bulging and hands going up to clutch at her throat as she made a gurgling noise. The point of contact on her neck rapidly turned red and swollen.

The girl struggled to stay on her feet, still making a noise like someone deep-throating a capful of mouthwash, and Krieg—just a lump of shadow, the wan light in the hall fleeing from him—sidled up behind her, close, like a lover, and took her gently in his arms as she collapsed. The look of fear and pain on the girl's face was disconcerting, but as she clutched at her throat she allowed herself to be laid gently back in the floor. He cradled her in his lap, his thick legs stretched out along her sides and reaching nearly to her hips, her head on his crotch. At some point her towel had flapped open and lay in a heap beneath her, revealing a smooth, taut expanse of belly and breasts that stood a bit too rigid. Krieg made a complacent, "Shhhhh," noise, like a mother quieting her upset baby.

The killer produced a knife from somewhere and brandished it in front of the choking girl's face. His teeth glittered dully behind her, the only thing visible in that nest of darkness. Her struggled renewed at the sight of the blade.

"Shhhh," he repeated, and then spoke to her rapidly in German, repeating some of the same syllables over and over and interspersing them with that soft shushing sound.

The camera stayed high overhead as the knife slid slowly into her taut stomach. Blood flowed, first darkening the black towel under her and then spreading over it to pool on the floor. He removed the blade and put it back in, higher up, directly between her breasts, and then brought it down to connect to the first incision.

Eviscerating her.

And all without a single cut, without a single break in the crackly footage. Davis realized there hadn't been a cut since the brute first bashed the girl across the throat, and even before that the action had been so seamless it must've been done in one take. This was why Gross positioned the cameras the way he did; otherwise, the actress wouldn't be able to perform the scene all the way through without stopping.

But, if it was done all at once, where did the blood come from? How had Gross created the ultimately realistic gaping hole in the woman's stomach, in which organs were now visible?

"Jesus, that's some incredible special effects work."

"Aw, he did it with a computer. You know as well as I do you can manipulate any image these days," Jared countered.

"That doesn't look CGI'ed."

"Yeah, and this is thirteen years old," Otter said.

"*Thirteen?*" he and Jared echoed together. They leaned in closer behind Otter, Davis dragging Susan with them.

The girl's face was a study in pain, and Davis didn't know if Germany held the equivalent of the Academy Awards, but if so, this girl deserved to win ten times over. She thrashed, bucked, and wailed, all signs easily identifiable with a convincing orgasm if not for the terrified look still in her eyes and the pain twisting her mouth. Her hands flailed at Krieg, trying to push him away, but their waning strength was no match for his girth. He still repeated his ghoulish, soothing litany, only occasionally drowned out by the screams she managed to squeeze through her bruised trachea.

Susan shuddered and looked away from the monitor, pulling out of Davis' arms. He was so hypnotized by the brutality, he let her go without objection. This was beyond car-wreck rubbernecking; mankind's insatiable attraction to violence. This was hypnotism, hypnotism without medallion or coin but hypnotism all the same. No wonder his films did so well overseas.

The girl remained alive as Krieg pushed the knife into the side of the wound, turned it, and brought it out sideways, coring her out like a pumpkin. A grayish bulge of entrails slipped out of the wound to coil on the floor beside her. Somewhere in the middle of the grisly operation, her last feeble movements had ceased.

"I'm gonna be sick, I swear to God," Jared growled.

And then it ended, the computer's video player freezing the last second as the clip finished. The final image showed Krieg turned halfway to the camera that caught the majority of the action, his face a lumpy relief map of mountainous, bad terrain. In his lap, the girl's mutilated body was visible in a spreading puddle of her own blood.

# TAKE 3

Otter swiveled in his chair to face them, his eyes unfocused behind his glasses. "What'd you think?" He didn't seem to know whether to be proud or embarrassed that he'd showed them such an abomination.

Susan made a gagging sound. "It was awful."

"Was that a snuff film we just watched?" Davis asked.

"No...but there are rumors he's done those too."

"I hope Trimax doesn't think that sicko is gonna try some of that shit over here," Jared said. "I'd like to see something like that slip by Jack Valenti's lapdogs without an NC-17."

"More like X," Davis added. He meant it as a joke—no way a movie without any sex would get the dreaded rating—

but the words fell flat because, actually, there *was* something disgustingly sexual in the sensuous and loving way Krieg had butchered the girl. That feeling from earlier in Reilly's office, that he'd made a bad mistake in agreeing to work on *Arterial Slice*, no matter what the pay, increased.

"I could find some other stuff if you guys wanna check it out."

"Ot, I'd rather take in the matinee at a slaughterhouse." Jared strode from the room. Davis wo

Susan took Davis by the arm and pulled him toward the door. "Thanks for the great time Otter, but we'll be hitting the road now."

He allowed himself to be lead into the hallway, giving Otter a half-hearted smile on his way out. The film editor hung his head and turned back to the keyboard.

Outside, Susan dragged him down the hall until they reached his office. The banner stretched across the room looked sad and lonesome now, the balloons mocking him with their cheerful colors.

"That was truly *vile*," she said, emphasizing the last word in a way that made her sound like she was fresh out of the valley. "Disgusting. Revolting. Loathsome."

"Want me to find you a thesaurus?"

She crossed her arms and glared at him.

"Don't look at me, I didn't hire the guy."

"But you're working for him."

"I didn't know he did that kind of work until just now."

"You know now."

"Yeah, so?"

"So call Trimax and quit."

"I'm sure that would go over real well. 'Uh, yes, Mr. Reilly, I can't take the job after all. How come? Oh, because my girlfriend thinks Torsten Gross is an icky-face.'"

She stared daggers at him.

He rolled his eyes. "Suze, you can't just call up and quit in this business. Do that sort of thing too much and pretty soon you're a pariah. And do you understand how much we're getting paid for this? We might actually get this place into the black for a change."

Susan kept her arms crossed, rubbing her shoulders. He knew what was running through her head: the image of the pretty German girl being turned inside out. "Is it worth your morals? Your sanity?"

"Oh, don't be so dramatic. The guy's just a filmmaker, with a very graphic style." He came forward to wrap his arms around her. A true actress, through and through, and that was his one dilemma with her and their relationship: he never knew how much was real and how much her natural talent. His own fear, reflected by her panic, felt stupid and childish. "Besides, if I'd gotten this gig, what do you think *I* would be filming?"

"Not that," she said quickly. "You're not capable of creating something like that." She relaxed in his arms. "Just promise me you're taking this job because you believe in the movie or even because you're desperate for the money and not because some weasel-in-a-suit said he might think about proposing to nominate you for a directing job at some point in the vague future."

"I promise," he said, the lie rolling off his tongue so smoothly he could almost believe it himself. "Who knows, maybe we'll still even be able to get you a role."

"Right. The day you see me acting in a piece of filth like that is the day you can tear up my SAG card."

He smiled and kissed her, and they both laughed at how silly a notion it was.

# SCENE V

(off camera)

# TAKE 1

The end of the week passed uneventfully as the day of the party rolled around. They finished work on the Lakewood picture—and received a bland thank-you note from the man's personal assistant—and then…nothing. They floated in limbo while they waited for contact from Gross or the studio.

None of them wanted to admit it, but there was a growing exhilaration as Friday arrived, the excitement of belonging to the real Hollywood. Except Otter, they'd all gone to the typical parties full of bottom feeders, always held at some wannabe's split-level ranch in the valley, but this was an actual, studio-sponsored event. Even Susan caught the fever, as she would be going as Davis' date.

Trimax rented a hall on Santa Monica for the filming party and the secretary only told Davis the event was 'formal,' leaving them all with the agonizing decision of what to wear. He and Otter decided on tuxedoes, rented hastily from a men's wear shop, Otter taking the biggest size available and still looking like a snake about to burst through its old layer of skin. They dressed at the office, buttoning each other's various accoutrements as they waited for Susan.

Otter quivered as Davis helped him with his cufflinks. "Are they…gonna make us go on stage or introduce us or anything?"

"Not us," Davis assured him. "The studios don't usually make a big deal over us third class citizens."

They heard the door open as Davis finished smoothing Otter's collar, then he stepped into the hallway to check out his date.

Her outfit was top secret, kept from him as stringently as a Disney script. She came around the corner in an elegant white evening gown with no back and a front revealing enough cleavage to sink a fence post in. She wore the gold necklace he gave her the past Christmas and her hair was piled on her head like spring coils. She looked gorgeous, and he told her so.

"Thank you, babe. You look pretty great yourself. Otter, can you breathe?"

"Oh, who needs to breathe?"

She leaned her head carefully on Davis' shoulder to keep her hair coiffed. "Well my prince, did we get a limo for this occasion, or are we taking our chances in your car?"

"You can always walk, you know."

"And you can always be single. Where's Jared?"

"He's meeting us there," Otter said darkly.

"It's kind of like when you're a teenager and you don't want anybody to know your mom drove you," Davis explained. "We cramp his style."

"Because he has so much of it."

"He better have found a tux or I'll cramp more than his style."

They piled into Davis' car and arrived at the hall about a half hour later. It was how he always imagined arriving at a big premiere would feel, except for the fact that the engine of his car sputtered. The building's front was tall and narrow, neo architecture with a large corporate art sculpture squatting in the middle of a fountain pond like an alien relic. The bushes along both sides of the walk were immaculate and as tended as an L.A. housewife's nails, perfect globes announcing man's intent to make nature tame and manageable. Outdoor lights cast large beams of luminescence from the ground onto the building like some kind of Gothic temple, and a red carpet—*a red carpet!*—extended from the curb to the double glass doors at the front of the building. It made him hungry, actually physically hungry, as though walking down that maroon rug would satisfy an urge in him akin to eating or breathing. Otter practically bounced up and down in the backseat, anxiety forgotten. Davis smiled at Susan beside him in the passenger seat and could see the same eager excitement in her eyes.

Tonight, they were somebodies, part of the glitterati. He couldn't remember feeling something this intense—something this starkly gleeful—in years, not since outgrowing the concept of Christmas morning. Once the apathy of adulthood sets in, such moments as these were few and far between.

Fuck Reilly and Gross; fuck Trimax and the paycheck; it was worth taking the job just to feel this tingle of accomplishment. It might be gone in the morning, but for this one night they were stars, and Susan was Cinderella of the ball.

A valet took the car (Davis ignored the look of disdain on his face as he slid behind the warped steering wheel), they were asked to check their phones at the door, and then they were swept into the vestibule with a throng of other arrivals all dressed equally formal. A bouncer checked their names on a list and granted them access into the party.

# TAKE 2

The interior of the hall contained one big, rectangular room, decorated in somber blacks and reds. The Trimax emblem—three point-to-point red triangles overlaid by a black tiger's face with muzzle frozen open in an eternal roar—was placed prominently about the room, with a monstrous flag incarnation of the same above the grand staircase. These stairs rose from the far end of the room, flanked by two open bars and headed by an ice sculpture of the snarling tiger. The place was already packed, some of the partygoers moving on a dance floor to music performed by a band playing eighties and nineties pop and the rest milling around the room, sipping champagne brought around by actual waiters. Together the three of them pointed out a plethora of B-list celebrities in the crowd. Davis wondered if any of them were cast.

"Is this a press party?" Otter whispered to Davis. Press parties were more fake than some of the schmooze flings Davis had been to, all show and no heart, basically a big commercial.

"Nope. Employees and producers only. This is the real thing, Otter." He turned to Susan and cocked out an elbow. "Care to dance, my lady?" he asked.

"Why, thank you sir," she accepted.

"You're leaving me?" Otter asked, horrified.

"Just for a minute. Be cool. Mingle." He swept her onto the floor, leaving Otter to gape after them.

Davis wasn't as graceful as she was, but he managed to get through several songs without stepping on her and received a look of pure love for the effort.

*She's beautiful,* he thought for the zillionth time since

meeting her, amazed at the statement's simple truth. He loved her, truly and deeply, would kill for her if necessary.

*You don't have to kill for her. You just have to put an itty-bitty little ring on her finger.*

If this relationship with Trimax proved a long and fruitful one, he might do just that.

*And if it isn't? She doesn't want a miracle. And she's not the type of girl that will wait forever on hope. Just because she's tactful enough to never bring it up, doesn't mean she doesn't want it.*

They stepped back off the dance floor during a Wang Chung cover and got glasses of champagne. On the way back, he spotted Jared against the far wall, long hair pulled back in a ponytail, chatting with two girls whose collective breast size must be somewhere near the end of the alphabet. He wore a tux all right, but one that looked like the seventies had thrown up all over it. Polyester, oversize lapels and pants legs, material a glittering maroon, exactly the sort of kitsch-retro style Jared used to ensure every woman's eyes lingered on him. Anyone else would look like an idiot, but he pulled it off somehow. Davis knew better than to interrupt the man while he worked, but he and Susan passed close enough for him to hear, "That's 'Mane,' girls. Just like a lion, if you know what I mean."

They finished their drinks and another glass each in front of a huge picture window looking out on a rose garden, and then grabbed thirds as they headed back to regroup with Otter, who sat all alone at a table with his four chins held in his hands.

"So where is this Gross guy?" Susan asked.

"Are you using that as noun or adjective? Because both are appropriate." He shrugged and sipped champagne. "I don't know, I haven't see him. You, Ot?"

"I wouldn't know him even if I did. I have no idea what he looks like. Do you think we'll get to talk to him tonight?"

"I sure as hell hope so. They start shooting on Monday, and Trimax wants this thing wrapped up in two months. Enjoy this now boys and girls, because the ride will be over before you know it."

"But the memories will last a lifetime," Jared said as he came up behind them. "Jesus Ot, they shrink-wrap you in that thing? You look like a sausage with a defective casing." Otter flushed a deep shade of red and drew into himself like a turtle. Jared hopped into the seat next to him, his own suit flashing, and rubbed his palms together. "Did you see some of the talent in here? We're moving up on the food chain, boys! This here cowpoke ain't seen so many stars since he was back home in good ol' no-light-pollution Texas!"

"Oh yeah, every reality TV star right here in the same room," Susan said. "Let me get my autograph book."

"Well, it's a higher caliber of film bunnies, anyway."

"Your attention please," an amplified voice boomed across the gallery, cutting the band off in the middle of a rendition of Eagle Eye Cherry's "Save Tonight." Davis looked around, trying to find the source, and saw a tiny Phillip Reilly at the top of the grand staircase on the far side of the room. A small podium was set up at some point while he and Susan tripped the light fantastic, and they were using the area as an impromptu stage. Reilly was dressed in a tux tailored to him like a second skin. He raised his hands for silence as the band wound down and the revelers found seats or paused to listen.

"Thank you all for coming. Trimax likes to keep its family close, and when one of us is honored, we all share that honor. And like many of your agents, we only ask for ten percent." A smattering of groans at this awkward attempt at humor. Reilly either ignored it or was so accustomed to such a response he didn't care. He continued. "The studio has decided to take a risk on a rather unique piece of horror filmmaking called *Arterial Slice*, which starts filming this week. We decided we needed a unique director to helm such a project, and we found one. A man with an artistic vision for such pieces, whose very name will soon be synonymous with terror, and, most importantly," Reilly paused and gave what Davis was sure he thought was a suave grin, "whose films have made so much in his own country, they could've bought me a new Porsche for every day of the year if I'd produced them." Genuine laughter at this, but most of it had that *ha-ha-you-asshole* undertone. "It is my proud honor to introduce to you, straight from Germany, Mr. Torsten Gross."

# TAKE 3

Now came genuine applause, quite a bit of it, enough to make Davis think perhaps more than just Otter had heard of the man. Gross entered the room from the upper right side of the staircase, sweeping down on Reilly in slacks, a solid black shirt, and an impeccable pinstriped black suit jacket. The executive stepped aside, relinquishing the microphone podium.

"Hey, you remember *Seventh Seal*?" Jared hissed across the table to Davis.

Davis frowned as he strained to remember the Bergman classic. "Distantly. Why?"

"Because this guy seriously reminds me of Ekerot as Death."

Davis tried to look at Gross from a fresh perspective. He could see Jared's point. Bengt Ekerot's portrayal of Death perfectly mirrored the pinched, gaunt, and pale aspects of the elderly man's face, his hawk-like nose and glittering, deep-set eyes, the bald cranium, all except the roll of white hair stretching from the ears to the nape of the neck.

Though the comparison felt close, Gross was somehow still scarier than even Death.

*Ve vill be in touch*, Davis thought, and shivered. Susan raised a sculpted eyebrow at him.

"Good evening, ladies and gentleman. Thank you for your generous welcome. Mr. Reilly flatters me with his accolades. When Trimax contacted me with this offer for *Arterial Slice*, I thought, *mein Gott*, what a hopeless pile of excrement."

The effect on the crowd was like a blast of hot air in their faces. Jaws dropped in amazement and necks pulled heads back as though showing the slightest bit of amusement would melt their eyeballs. Reilly, a few steps back and to the left of Gross, actually put two fingers in his collar and tugged.

Gross relished the effect. "But what is all horror but excrement? Is it not still art thought, just as much as a Bach symphony or a da Vinci painting? Art can evoke precious few emotions in us, when reduced to basics. Anger, happiness, sadness and, more rarely…fear. Fear is a base, loathsome emotion; it encompasses disgust and revulsion and everything that makes us want to turn our heads away, and that is why horror movies are one of the lowest grossing genres worldwide. That is why such films are a rarity at the

Academy Awards. Because people don't want to be scared." Gross stepped toward the microphone, and even from across the room, Davis could see the fever in those crow's eyes. "But scaring is my job. I will rewrite this script and make a film that will have audiences slavering whether they want to or not. They will *beg* me to stop terrifying them."

This time it was Susan that shivered against Davis. He heard Jared mutter, "Jesus Hitler, calm down."

"And now, on to the business at hand," Gross said. No hesitations or mental word-searches in his speech now; this had all been prepared in advance. "The director is only one component in these affairs, so let us unveil the other. Allow me to introduce those that will star in the picture." He turned to the left, facing the same staircase he'd come down moments before. His hand sliced upward, beckoning. "After an extensive talent search, Trimax and I have agreed on the three stars of our film. First, the lead role of Terry Yancy will be played by Miss Tonya Werdner."

Applause around the room, steady but reserved, reminding Davis of one of those applause-o-meters popular on seventies game shows. Susan caught his attention and rolled her eyes. Otter lifted his glasses, pushing them to his bulging eyes for a better look. Jared made cups of his hands and held them a foot out in front of his chest, nodding his head approvingly.

Tonya Werdner descended the staircase toward Gross, showing enough leg and cleavage in her skimpy gold-sequined dress to be modeling lingerie. Her blond locks were tied back in a neat ponytail, and her huge grin flashed down on the assemblage like a searchlight. Davis never paid much attention to the specifics of her career, but was familiar enough with her resumé to know it read like any typical Cinemax after-dark lineup. She was next in line for the cable-rated porn queen title previously held by such stars as Shannon Tweed. And now here she was, breaking off to do what she surely considered 'legitimate work.' Just as he suspected; a trio of fuckable starlets to turn this flick into a glorified T-and-A fest. Werdner came down and affected a pose like a Miss America contestant behind Gross.

"And the role of Julie Knight will be played by Miss Samantha Cox."

Another attractive female, but a more accomplished actress. She started down the stairs in a somber, dark blue number, her black hair lying across the fronts of her shoulders. More applause, this time heartfelt, at least a seven on the applause-o-meter, and Susan whispered to Davis, "I thought she was in rehab."

Davis nodded. He'd heard the same, but when you were in and out of the clinics as often as Samantha Cox, it was hard to keep track. If she was as hooked on painkillers and alcohol as the tabloids recently claimed, the last stint had done her good. She looked as fresh as when she'd starred in *The Pains of the Heart* at eighteen, a long decade before.

Gross waited until Cox took her place beside Werdner. "And, last but not least, the role of Nancy Dubose will be played by Miss Katherine Wickersham."

Another of those brief, shocked pauses as when Gross had called the script 'excrement.' The applause came soon on its heels, and when it came, it was thunderous. Susan stood up to clap, and Otter did the same. Davis found himself standing only to squint at the stage to see if the rumors were true.

Even from his seat, even through a deepening haze of alcohol-induced blur, he could see the extensive scarring on the familiar face as it came down the stairs. Katherine Wickersham had blasted onto the silver screen eight years ago from nowhere at the age of twenty-four, but that was the way it always went with the greats. She had acted legitimately since, in every genre, been nominated for two Academy Awards, and starred in some major blockbuster vehicles, including the most recent Bruckheimer flick the summer before last.

This was her downfall.

While performing a particularly dangerous explosive stunt that she insisted on doing herself, she'd received a face full of burning pyrotechnic sulfur and was rushed to the hospital, where she remained for nearly three months. Reconstructive surgery could do little. Her husband, the renowned French director Jean du Vaulier, had left her after the prognosis. She'd not been in a film since, had dropped out of the public eye almost completely. A tragedy, many said, to lose one so talented.

*Why here, why this movie*, Davis asked himself. The woman would be able to get work somewhere. Not everyone in Hollywood was as caught up in looks as the stereotype purported. Here was a young woman with real, raw *talent*, and she was making her comeback in a cheap slasher? Not only that, but if Davis was remembering the script correctly, her character was the first to die.

She came down the stairs to Gross, who received her more warmly than the other two, with a smile and a pat on the shoulder. Her face was indeed a twisted snarl of scar tissue, eyes peering out from eyebrow-less sockets, nose just visible and mouth no more than a slash. Her brown hair was cropped high and close on the sides of her skull, beautiful but professional. She smiled at Gross—but Davis thought he saw a grimace at his touch on her shoulder—and went to stand beside her fellow cast members.

Maybe he'd been looking at this movie all wrong. It wasn't just another phony-bologna, cat-jumping-out-the-closet-for-the-cheap-scare film. It might be, under another director, but Torsten Gross was making it into an affair.

"Take a good look at these three, because two of them will be dead before the end of the month," Gross said with his savage grin. He about-faced, turning to the other staircase and raising his hand in the same militant, slicing gesture. "But of course, what would a horror movie be without its villain? The particular villain in Arterial Slice is a supernatural mental patient, but it is his portrayal that will be vital. Those of you who know my work are already familiar... with Mr. Lars Krieg!"

"Oh my God," Susan gasped. "Please tell me that... man... is not gonna be in this movie! That you're not gonna be *working with him!*"

Davis shrugged, but already the familiar, hulking figure from Otter's internet download was thumping down the stairs. Gross was thin and gaunt, and Krieg easily four times his size in comparison. He wore a simple tux as he marched down to stand on the opposite side of the director. The actresses maintained their smiles but shrank away from the behemoth.

Gross placed a hand on Krieg's upper arm, which his bicep swallowed. "That is all I have to say about the film until its completion. I will relinquish control to Mr. Reilly."

Reilly took the microphone as Gross, Krieg, and the trio of women descended the last flight of stairs to the party and got lost in the crowd, all except for Krieg's head, which floated at least a foot above everyone else. Reilly hurriedly said, "Please enjoy the rest of the evening, courtesy of Trimax."

He turned and hurried back up the stairs, disappearing into one of the upper rooms to snort coke or fuck young starlets or maybe just take a dump. The band started up and the dancing resumed, life flowing back into the party like a lawnmower engine revving up to an even throttle.

# TAKE 4

Otter shoved his chair away from the table and began the laborious process of getting to his feet. "C'mon!"

"Where are we going?"

"To meet Gross, of course!" He said it with determination, which must be taking real bravery on his part.

Davis downed the last of his champagne. "You go ahead, I've already had the dubious pleasure."

"But you have to introduce us!" Otter whined. "C'mon Jared, you too! I have to talk to him. Do you think it will be okay if I ask for Krieg's autograph?"

"Show some professionalism, will ya Ot? We're colleagues, not groupies."

"Look, they're making for the door! You guys will see them everyday, but this could be my only chance to meet them!"

"If you're lucky," Davis said, but he stood. The alcohol had hit him harder than usual, and the room did a little dance of its own in his vision. He expected Susan to stay at the table, but was pleasantly surprised when she slipped her arm through his. The flat sheen in her eyes told him that she was a bit tipsy as well.

Otter was right about the duo's destination. The three stars had gotten themselves lost in a sea of congratulations, but Gross was making for the exit, followed closely by Krieg. No one tried to talk to them; in fact, the crowd parted faster than Heston at the Red Sea. Davis leapt into the crush of bodies, leading the four of them on a path to intercept Gross' hasty departure.

Davis pushed through the last wave of party-goers, passing between the star of a freshly-cancelled sitcom and one of the kids from the last installment of *The Real World*, and stepped into the director's path. The elegantly dim overhead lights caused Krieg's shadow to fall over him, making him think of the poor victim from the Otter's download. He was conspicuously aware of how the space around him had cleared, how the eyes of so many crawled over him with pity, suspicion...and envy.

Gross' pace was so fast he was forced to skid to a halt on the tile hall floor to avoid a collision. His deep-set eyes registered instant anger (no alarm, Davis noticed; he might look old, but his mind was as sharp as aged cheddar) followed by recognition.

But the split second it took for him to make the mental connection was almost too long.

With a speed Davis wouldn't think possible for one so big, Krieg sidestepped Gross with a piggish grunt, shielding the man with his body and reaching for Davis' neck with hands the size of melons.

His face—seen clearly for the first time as it bore down like the wrathful Almighty—was a nightmare.

Scarred patches mottled his skin, but its repugnance went far beyond old acne. The muscles beneath the skin looked lumped and twisted, forming obscene hills and valleys that pushed the facial structure in unnatural directions. The nose was lumpish, probably broken several times; the eyes above it slit, with just enough of the pupil visible to show Davis they were empty and dead. His mouth was no more than a lipless hole in the lower half of his face, hemmed by an iron skillet jaw.

"Lars! Halt! *Komm zuruck!*" Gross barked.

Davis was so shocked by the eerie silence of the aggressiveness, he probably would've stood there mesmerized as the great German lug throttled the life out of him, but the giant halted like a programmed robot at the director's words, and resumed his position behind Gross.

"Lars, have patience, you almost killed our second unit director." Gross favored Davis with a quick nod, like Barbara Eden doing her genie thing. Davis wasn't sure if the ever-so-faint note of condescension in his voice was part of his intoxicated imagination. "You must excuse Lars, Mr. Lowe. I have many enemies in Germany, and Lars has become quite protective of me over the years."

"That's all right, the same thing happened when I met my girlfriend's father the first time." He tried on a grin, but Gross looked at him curiously, not understanding or just not finding him amusing. Boy, he was worse than Reilly. "My crew wanted to meet you before you got away."

"Aw yes, your...crew." Gross' withered lips pursed. "They're more than welcome to meet me, but I'm afraid they'll get little out of my associate. He understands English but refuses to speak it. He feels it is a language of degeneration."

Davis glanced up at the pockmarked face, found the dead eyes burning holes in him, and lowered his own quickly, remembering advice from an old documentary about dealing with charging gorillas. The man crossed his immense arms and grunted again. Davis looked back and found the others cowering on the edge of the crowd and another pop culture reference buzzed through his head: Dorothy Gale and her gang of misfits stepping before the Wizard.

"Right, well…this is Jared Mane, my cameraman and partner."

Jared came forward with an amiable smile and hand extended. Gross gave it a puckered frown. Davis at first thought it was the garish suit that put him off until the director said, "Cameraman? I must admit, I've never had much use for them. They filter out too much of the director's…"he paused to search for the word and finished in German, "*vorstellung*. The…'vision.' No one is able to capture what I see in my head. I always control the camera myself."

Jared's face went stony, mouth hardening, and Davis awaited the tirade of expletives that would lose them this job. But instead he cleared his throat and said, "It shows," then stepped aside just in time so Otter didn't bowl him over as he launched out of the crowd.

Otter sucked in air and gushed, "Mr. Gross, hi there, my name is Terence Ottman, I'm a huge, huge, HUGE fan of yours and Mr. Krieg's, your work is just genius, and I do some editing work myself, so we're sort of equals you and I, well, maybe not equals, but you know, contemporaries I guess, and my work has been greatly influenced by you—!"

"This is my film editor," Davis broke in before Otter offered to have the man's baby. "He showed us some of your work."

"It's always nice to meet a fan," Gross said. His eyes darted over Otter's rotund shoulders and he asked, "And who, might I ask, is this lovely maiden?"

The director had a pick of them in this kind of company, but when all three of their heads swiveled, Davis found Susan hovering on the fringe of the crowd in her ball gown, eyes darting from him to Gross and then to Krieg. Davis held out a hand, which she took as she came to his side. "This is my girlfriend, Susan Campbell. She's an actress."

"An actress?" Gross's left eyebrow arched. "Which films have you graced, my dear?"

"Oh well, I'm afraid Davis exaggerates," she answered with a flustered grin. One hand had become plastered to her exposed chest, an endearingly self-conscious gesture. "I've never actually been in a movie."

"I see. And did you also see a sampling of my work?"

"Yes, I did."

"And what were your thoughts?"

"It was…original. Unlike anything I've ever seen, certainly."

Gross leaned closer, reaching out a palsied hand, and Davis was amazed when Susan pressed one palm to it and allowed it to be covered by his other. He had a flash of what that flesh felt like, rubberized and slick and phony. "My dear, confidentially speaking, there is another role that needs to be filled. Quite minor, but an amazing death scene. I would love to have you audition."

Davis couldn't tell who was more shocked between the two of them. Susan stammered, "That…that would be w-wonderful. I would be honored."

"Come downtown to the filming site on Thursday. We'll be shooting Miss Wickersham's final scenes. You can watch my methods and decide whether or not you would even be interested." Gross straightened, businesslike and firm again. "And now, gentlemen and lady, if you will excuse me, Lars and I have some work to do before we begin shooting on Monday." And with that, he stepped between them with Krieg close on his heels.

# TAKE 5

"That didn't go like I imagined," Otter said. "He's not much for goodbyes."

"Or hello's," Jared added. "Uppity Euro-trash. The guy was raised by wolves."

"What are you doing?" Davis hissed at Susan. He felt a surge of jealousy and hated himself for it. "You're going to *audition* for him? What happened to him being disgusting and revolting?"

"I don't know, it must be the alcohol! I just…couldn't say no!" Her face was flushed…but couldn't he see excitement behind the indignation? "God, he's creepy! You're right though, I have to tell him that I can't!"

She bolted away from them before Davis could say more. He shot a look at Jared and Otter and the three of them simultaneously dove back into the crowd after her. The colors of the party swirled together behind his inebriated eyes. She reached the vestibule two steps ahead of them and three behind Gross and Krieg, and they all stepped outside on the red carpet together.

Gross strolled away from them, that aura of royal dignity still about him even with no one around to witness it. The valet had already pulled up and parked a metallic blue Mercedes Benz at the curb at the end of the red carpet. As Gross and Krieg moved toward it, Susan raised her hand to call after them.

Davis wasn't sure whether he wanted to stop her or not, but before he could decide, three people popped out of the immaculate bushes on the right side of the path like the distorted plastic heads in a Whack-a-Mole game. Bright flashes of light flared in the night, chasing shadows all across the walkway, and Davis realized that he was witnessing his first live paparazzi attack.

"Bah!" Gross screamed, flinging his hands violently over his face and stumbling away. For a moment, he was eclipsed from their view by Krieg's bulk, until the giant realized what was happening and moved between him and their attackers to block the director with his body.

The three individuals—all in jeans and t-shirts, out of place after the night of fancy festivities—maneuvered around the hedges, cameras popping constantly as they tried to shoot around Krieg, one of them hollering, "Mr. Gross, Mr. Gross, look this way please! One picture, Mr. Gross!" and another asking, "How does it feel to be shooting your first film in America?"

"No pictures!" Gross howled. It was the first time the man had ever lost control of his cool demeanor, and it didn't make for a pleasant sight. He turned so far away from the paparazzo that his face was in profile to the four of them, and Davis could see every time a new flash went off that it was drawn up in a snarl of rage, teeth bared and eyes wide.

Krieg gave up his previous tactic and got violent with the cameramen, one of whom Davis recognized as part of E.L. Woody's posse. Krieg shoved one of the assailants backward, causing him to trip off the concrete lip of the fountain and splash into the water, camera and all. One of the others used the opportunity to try and jump around the actor and was lifted into the air by the scruff of his neck like a baby kitten for his efforts. Krieg flung him back into the bushes.

"You can't do that!" the last one bawled. "You can't touch us, Gross! I'll sue your ass if you wrinkle one hair on my head, Krieg!"

Jared moved forward to get involved—on whose behalf Davis had no idea—and he and Otter both held him back by the sleeves of his ridiculous jacket, the front of Otter's skin-tight shirt losing several buttons in the process. Susan turned and ran back inside to get help. Davis realized he was holding his breath as he waited to see what Krieg would do, thinking all the time of the knife sliding through pink flesh like butter.

The man *growled*.

It was like listening to an enraged dog. The growl started low and built into a roar of rage that exploded from Krieg's mouth. He tore the camera out of the last man's hand as the other two scrambled away. The photographer made a feeble attempt to snatch it back before realizing escape might be the more prudent option.

Krieg turned and launched the camera past Gross like a quarterback sending one downfield. It didn't so much shatter against the steel façade of the banquet hall as it liquefied. Pieces of glass and plastic sprayed everywhere and a last feeble flash burst from the device.

Gross cursed at the three men in German, and then he and Krieg strode down the path to the idling automobile. The valet, a kid all of sixteen who had watched events from the opposite side with a dumbfounded look, gave a small, mousy squeak of terror and jumped out of their way. They wasted no time in getting in and pulling away from the curb, leaving the paparazzo to lick their wounds and look around bewildered.

Davis glanced at his partners. The look of horror on Otter's face would be comical if he didn't feel the same way. Jared's face was a dark mask of disdain. Davis shook his head as Susan came running back outside with several members of security.

"Guys," Davis said, "we may have a problem."

# SCENE VI

(interior shot)

# TAKE 1

Despite what Gross had told Davis in Phillip Reilly's office, they heard nothing from the director in the days following the party. He couldn't get Phillip Reilly on the phone anymore, and the low-level associates he could reach at Trimax had no idea what was going on with the filming. They didn't even know where the set was, or whether filming was taking place on or off the premises of the studio.

He was beginning to feel a bit unwanted. They had, after all, been forced on the director by the studio, but that didn't mean he had to make use of their services. Perhaps his 'beck and call' comments were merely for Reilly's benefit. In any case, it would be hard to keep tabs on Gross if he didn't know where the director was.

His only ray of hope came in the form of a small article in the *Hollywood Reporter* which told of Gross' involvement with the film and—wonder of wonders—actually mentioned Davis by name on a short cast and crew list. It wasn't long after that a reporter from *Variety* named Sidney Spitzen called and left a message on the machine in the office, wanting his thoughts on working with the German director. Davis was too afraid he was trolling for quotes about the paparazzi incident after the party and, as hard as it was to do, he deleted the message.

Finally, some confused secretary at Trimax got tired of his daily calls and mentioned she'd heard something about a full cast and crew call scheduled for Tuesday. He and Jared, dressed in conservative (for them, anyway) jeans and polos, entered the studio lot on the morning of the call, the guard giving him more respect than on his previous entry, and they were directed to a smaller building far from Reilly's office. They walked down hall after hall until they found their destination, an acoustics lined soundstage resembling a high school band hall. A sign on the door ordered them to leave their cell phones in bins just outside. There was nothing in the room besides a semi-circle of five director chairs, three of them occupied by none other than the stars of the film themselves.

A thrill went through Davis at the sight of the actresses. The last star he'd worked with had been eleven and the star of her own Nickelodeon show.

Tonya Werdner, Samantha Cox, and Katherine Wickersham had their noses buried in copies of the Arterial Slice script, reading their lines aloud to each other. They glanced up for all of two seconds when he and Jared entered, regarding them with as much interest as a waiter, and then back down at their scripts. Only Cox's gaze lingered, and she favored them with a broad, friendly smile.

"Hi," Davis said, striving not to sound awkward. "We're supposed to meet Mr. Gross here today. I'm Davis Lowe and this is Jared Mane. We're second unit." Wincing inside as he admitted it, like a drunk at an AA meeting.

A snort from Werdner, who wore just enough clothing so as not to be mistaken for a stripper. Her breasts (large and beautiful but starting to take on that sagging weight of the middle-aged; *don't get too haughty yet, Miss Orgasm*

*Queen*) strained against the light cotton of her braless top. "Gross," she said, emphasizing the uni-moniker, "had to leave for a moment. If you'll stop bothering us, we're running lines."

"You'll have to forgive Tonya," Samantha Cox said with a drawn-out shake of her head. She was dressed in pajama bottoms with Spongebob on them, and a sleeveless top. Her voice held a bouncy Jersey accent that she must've hidden for all of her roles. "She loses all sense of decency when she's not filming on her back with her legs splayed."

Werdner made a sound through her lips like a can of carbonated soda opening. "Whatever, boozehound."

Cox got up and offered her hand to both of them. "Pleasure to meet you guys. I'm Samantha Cox. You already had the misfortune of meeting Werdner. And this, of course, is Katherine Wickersham."

"Howdy, ma'am," Jared said, raising a hand in greeting to the third actress.

She gave a curt nod but kept her head down. Such a snub coming from Werdner would be rude, but with Wickersham it appeared to be from studious concentration. She was the only one of the trio not dressed comfortably; she wore a black pantsuit and pointed heels. From the angle of her tilted head, the edge of the disfiguring scars was just visible around her perfect ear.

Cox sidled closer to Davis and whispered with a wink, "You'll have to excuse her too, she's very 'driven.'" The last word received the two-fingers-as-quotations gesture. "Her role is just soooo important, you know, she dies in the first half-hour."

"I heard that," Wickersham sang without looking up. "There are no small parts, just small actors. Or small brains, in your case."

Cox giggled. The girl had more energy than a platoon of sugar-hyped four-year-old's. *Easy to be so upbeat when you're on every drug known to man*, Davis thought, and was instantly ashamed at thinking ill of the first person that had been nice to them.

Jared had drifted over near Werdner. Davis heard her mutter, "Dream on, lowlife," before he turned back to Cox.

"Where is everybody?" he asked. "I thought this was a full cast and crew call."

"Oh, I think it is. It's going on all day. Plus, you're looking at pretty close to everybody that has anything to do with making this film."

"What? No way, you can't run a production without any support! I mean, there's more parts in the script than what's here!"

"Yeah, well, Gross met with the extras playing asylum inmates and cops separately this morning. I heard he hired some outside set designers, which has the union in an uproar, but the studio is negotiating something because he's foreign. God, they better not pull us off this shoot or I'm gonna lose it!"

"But what about you three? Who's doing costumes and makeup?"

Cox frowned and shrugged. "We really don't have much in the way of wardrobe, and Gross insists that we do our own makeup for the sake of realism. Said he wants to see us blemishes and all." She glanced at Wickersham as she said this. "Anyway, that's about it. And you guys, of course." Cox giggled again. "Isn't that crazy? I mean, the man is a total control freak!"

For a moment, Davis said nothing. She was wrong, had to be. This room should be packed with people during a full cast and crew call. The director might not believe in cameramen, but what about the stand-in's, the film editors, the lighting techs, and key grips...fucking *craft services?* That list of credits at the end of a movie wasn't just impressive padding.

Then again, indie filmmakers did it all the time.

"So I hear," he said finally. "What about Krieg?" The name brought back the episode with the photographers. He, Jared, and Otter had decided the best course of action was to say nothing about what they'd seen. They'd escaped before the paparazzo could collect their names as witnesses.

"He'll be here. I think there's also one other role they're casting for."

"Yeah, Gross is having my girlfriend audition for it."

"Really? Cool!"

"If you say so."

"Sam, do you think you could finish up the slumber party gossip? We're filming this afternoon." Werdner juggled her breasts absentmindedly as she scolded.

"Gotta go," the actress said, and bounced away.

When Jared returned to his side, Davis asked, "What do you make of this?"

"Definitely Werdner. She's bitchy, but I think I can crack her."

"No, not them. The meeting."

"What about it?"

"There's a skeleton crew filming this thing. I thought Gross was exaggerating, but he really does everything himself."

"Maybe that's the way they do things in German Hollywood."

"*German Hollywood?* You pull that one out of your ass?"

"Yeah, and it hurt too, so appreciate it."

"C'mon, no support whatsoever? No technicians, no designers, no one to run errands?"

"So you're saying we shouldn't expect craft services."

"I'm seriously worried here," Davis insisted. "Everybody knows what they're supposed to be doing except for us."

"Relax man, that's what we're here for."

But he couldn't relax. It felt like the first day of high school, when no one would tell him where to go or what to do. All the makings of a panic attack tugged at him. He realized that despite everything, his misgivings, his resentment at not getting the job himself, he still wanted to please Gross.

A squeak came from behind them as the door swung open. Krieg—no more pretty in bright light—lumbered into the room with the gait of a grizzly bear, and Davis heard nervous rustling from the ladies. They may be three very different personality types, but they were all reduced to the same emotion by a very simple denominator. The trio stared up at Krieg with wide eyes, even Wickersham, scripts forgotten in their hands. The hulk strode around behind them and stood silently.

Gross breezed in next. "Now ladies, I hope you are prepared to..." He trailed off midsentence when he saw Davis and Jared. "Mr. Lowe, what are you doing on my set?"

"I thought...I was told...this was a full call."

The director placed a hand on their shoulders and guided them toward the door. More memories of high school came flooding back: the embarrassment of being asked to leave the room by a teacher. "I'm sorry, but I don't have time to deal with your incompetence. Please understand, when your services are needed, I will tell you directly."

"Yes, but—"

"Good day, gentlemen."

With that, he left them standing in the hall and closed the door. Davis stared at it like a puppy awaiting its master's return.

Jared put a hand on his shoulder. "Man, forget it. It's not worth it. If Gross doesn't wanna work with me, then I don't wanna work with him. We're still getting paid."

Davis nodded, but he recalled what Reilly said about keeping an eye on the director. How was he supposed to do that when the man kept him at arm's length?

He was also quickly coming to realize one other important fact: the more that was taken away from him on this movie, the more eager he was to reclaim it.

# TAKE 2

Susan left Davis sleeping on Thursday morning and crept into the bathroom to get ready for the audition.

She showered, doused herself with body spray, and applied makeup in the mirror, giving extra attention to the accentuation of her eyes and lips, two of her best features, if she said so herself. Her focus kept drifting, and she made a concerted effort not to look into the accusatory eyes of the reflection staring back at her.

Yes, *technically* she'd told Davis that she wouldn't go, yes, he told her she should, and yes, she could read that look behind his eyes that said he really meant just the opposite but pride prevented him from saying it. And yes, she'd assured him she had no intention of auditioning for Torsten Gross.

And yes, she'd lied.

In all fairness, it was the first lie she ever told him, but it was enough to make her feel like a criminal in her own apartment as she skulked about, slipping on heels and grabbing a granola bar as quietly as possible to keep him from waking up and asking her why she was going to work dressed like a hooker from the classy end of Santa Monica. Half of her was positive she wouldn't get the part anyway, and then he would never have to know about it.

*But this is not your typical dogpile casting call, you know. You received a personal invitation from the director. You're getting that part. This is that BIG BREAK! everyone in this city talks about so endlessly, all capital letters and an exclamation point, the whole reason you moved out here, and then what are you gonna tell him?*

Why should she have to tell him anything? It was her life and her career, her beating the streets for going on five years and turning up nothing more lucrative than ten-dollar-an-hour background characters and five-dollar-an-hour crowd scene fill-in's. And porno offers. Jesus, some days she thought if she heard one more proposition for a triple-blow-hole or a Chinese-finger-cuff or a rotating-all-digit-Taliban-whammy, she would go ape shit.

And other days, she was tempted.

But she knew Davis didn't want her to go out of selfish ambition. She knew the way guys thought, but better yet, she knew how *his* mind worked; they'd been together long enough for the beginnings of relationship psychology to set in. The near panic on his face when Gross had asked her to come in said it all. He craved success, needed it like some people need their booze or heroin. It would be fine if he got her the role and she looked like the big screen harlot sleeping her way to the top, but once the movie and decision were out of his hands, she was suddenly honing in on his action.

Davis was obsessed, and part of her knew it would kill him if she made it in this business before he did, if the exclamation point on that BIG BREAK! fell on her before it did him.

Torsten Gross scared her, and that was a stone cold fact.

Lars Krieg scared her even more, and the thought of acting with him, of having him touch her, made her skin crawl.

Hell, she didn't even like the genre. She could never stomach the more graphic horror movies—the likes of Eli Roth and Rob Zombie should be tied up in a burlap sack and dropped in a well, in her humble opinion—and the clip Otter showed them of Gross' movie repulsed her. But after being offered the audition, the memory of it underwent a sort of beautification, like a convict who starts thinking prison isn't so bad after being released, and she began to wonder if Gross would be able to get a similar performance out of her.

So you see, this was really about her. Her part, her career. Her BIG BREAK! Her facing her fears and triumphing through adversity and all that other shit people saw in the movies and believed happened in real life.

Not a betrayal of Davis.

*Keep talking girl. I'm the only one here, and you ain't convincing me.*

She grabbed her car keys and left.

# TAKE 3

She'd gotten the filming location from the studio the afternoon before. Unlike when Davis called, she was put through to someone who knew what was going on, her name obviously on some kind of accepted list, and she couldn't deny the prickle of smug pride that accompanied this fact.

The set itself, however, was downtown in South Central— on West 29th Street, just off Crenshaw, if you could believe it. She felt like she should bring an armed guard.

She missed the building on her first sweep, turned around in the parking lot of a burned out gas station, and soon realized why she'd bypassed the place. She rechecked the address while she stared at it.

A warehouse looked down on her, one probably abandoned since before the Crips and Bloods redecorated the neighborhood. It was a huge rectangular building hunkered on the corner with walls the gray color of light thunderheads. A factory at some point, judging from a small, solitary smokestack on the far side. The few windows not broken were soaped, painted, or crusted over; a veritable palace for the discerning, refined crack addict. It was surrounded by a chain link fence and most of the doors boarded up.

Then she spotted a Trimax sign next to the fence's only point of admission. The tiger roared at her, and beneath it, in polite black lettering, the sign said, FILMING IN PROGRESS, CAST AND CREW ONLY. ABSOLUTELY NO CELL PHONES PERMITTED! The parking lot faced the wide side of the rectangular building, but there were no cars parked anywhere she could see.

She glanced across the street and found three tough-looking *hombres* regarding her from the shade of an apartment breezeway. One grinned when he saw her looking and flicked a cigarette in her direction.

Her mouth went dry. No way was she going in there to get cornered. She had a sudden mental image of gang members flooding out of the building, like something from a Michael Jackson music video, except they wouldn't want to tie one of her hands to one of theirs and knife fight in dazzling 80's fashion choices.

Susan looked away from the leering me and pulled her car through the fence. She parked close to one of the few doors not boarded up, then turned off the ignition and jumped from the car before she could talk herself out of it. As tough as that was, leaving her cell phone behind was even harder. She spared one final glance at the fellows across the street to make sure they hadn't moved; bravery looked great on paper, but when you were a woman alone at the wrong end of L.A., carelessness was not an option.

The parking lot was little more than gravel, and her sharpened heels crunched across it as she headed to the door on the corner facing the street. She reached out for the metal of the handle, sure it would be locked, but the door swung open easily and she was admitted into a stuffy, dark hallway.

She stood uncertainly for a moment, peering down the dim hallway with one hand on the door, unwilling to let it close behind her because that was the way it worked in horror movies; they were always opened and unlocked until the nightmare within revealed itself and then suddenly they sealed tight.

*Yeah, but this isn't a horror movie.*

Actually, it was. Kind of the point, wasn't it?

The hallway, as far as the sunlight could illuminate, was filthy and litter-strewn, the detritus of years of adventurous youths, winos, and addicts collected in the narrow passage. A few of the broken windows allowed milky light in further along the hall, and she saw several doors set into the wall on the right. A sudden flash of the girl from the Gross movie popped up in her head, and she clamped down on the thought before it could percolate.

"Hello? Mr. Gross?" she called. No reply for a long minute, and then she heard something from far off, echoing off the building's cinderblock walls: a high-pitched, abrupt squawk. She stepped further into the hallway, footfalls clacking smartly, and allowed the door to swing shut.

Susan took two steps before a feeling came over her. She recognized it even though she'd never experienced it, only seen it described in books whose writers were too lazy to build tension effectively.

She was being watched.

Susan looked around quickly even though she knew the idea was ridiculous. The hall was too dark to see anything and besides, there was no place for someone to hide in the narrow passage. All the same, she felt eyes on her, keeping track of her every movement.

Now that she was in the building and committed, she tried to move faster, but the heels slowed her down. She bent, removed them and continued on in her pantyhose, taking odd comfort that her progress was now quieter. The feeling of being watched remained with her every step of the way. She reached the first of the doors on the right and found it locked. The second was the same, with something greasy smeared on the knob. The trend went on until she reached a set of double doors about halfway down.

She was almost in a panic now, afraid she would be lost or locked in, the walls closing in like a booby trap from an Indiana Jones movie, and all the time those eyes pressed on her. She expected these doors to be locked also, so she pulled too hard and flung them open with enough force to send them crashing into the walls on either side. She winced as the explosion echoed around her, startling a bird settled somewhere in the low ceiling. The opening revealed a staircase. She started up, taking the steps one at a time and feeling her way along the grimy wall.

The doors closed behind her, choking off the last of the light.

# TAKE 4

This was stupid, she knew, wandering around in the dark in an abandoned warehouse that smelled like urine, and wasn't this the time when you yelled out how stupid the heroine was in the horror movie for doing the same thing? The panic leeched into full-blown fear, and she was ready to turn and run, BIG BREAK! not withstanding, when she realized there was light somewhere above her, getting brighter as she climbed. She went faster now, her eyes gulping it up like an out-of-breath swimmer coming up for air.

Susan continued up a few steps more and could finally see the end of the stairs, terminating in a platform with a railing that gave her the sensation of climbing into the middle of the stands at a baseball game. The effect was so similar that, as her head poked over the level of the last stair, she half expected to see an open-air diamond field despite the corrugated metal roof above.

Somehow, the real contents of the room were far more startling.

Susan had a momentary loss of reality where she thought— for just a split second really *believed*—she was looking at a portal into another world. The rusted railing in front of her did terminate the platform, ending in at least a one-story drop. The room below had probably once been the factory floor, rectangular and stretching out a hundred feet. The rickety platform stretched out to either side but she could see no way down, so she just held her shoes and looked out, fascinated with the scene beyond, the feeling of being watched forgotten.

The dingy cinderblock walls ended almost even with the platform, and turned into gleaming, perfectly placed tile.

The roof above her, made of rusted pipes and metal support struts, became a low-hanging, bleached white fiberboard ceiling, like an office building. The light came from bright fluorescents casting clean light and glittering reflections on every surface. Freshly made beds marched all the way across the space below her in two rows, five on each side, the headboards squared off tidily against the wall. Several strange machines stood in various locations, some glowing, some beeping, some standing only as silent guardians. Another pair of padded double doors faced her on the far side of the room, each with a tiny circular window looking out into the area beyond.

The entire set-up assaulted her senses at once, bringing with it a heavy wave of déjà vu...

The solution hit her, and she felt like a moron. She'd seen such rooms before, rarely in real life but often in television and movies.

This was a set, a stage, a facsimile of any generic hospital room in the world. For Christ's sake, she'd seen them every week for years on *Grey's Anatomy*. Part of her disorientation was the fact that there was no one in it when she was used to seeing them bustling with people, but mostly it was the shock of suddenly coming upon one in the middle of all this filth.

*Arterial Slice* was set in a hospital, right? Well, she'd stumbled right into one of the completed sets, closed down and waiting for the actors to take their places.

But why, she wondered, fix up such a craphole rather than just film in an already camera-friendly location? They could just build a set on the studio cheaper than what it must have cost to turn this roach-motel into a working diorama of a hospital. Then again, she wasn't in that area of the business, she got paid to act (or would someday), and for now she would be happy just to find Gross. She turned away, looking for some other path out of the room.

A scream echoed through the rafters, causing her to jump and bump into the railing with her hip. Pain, bright and biting, flared down the length of her leg.

As she turned back to the sparkling room below, the double doors on the far side crashed open. A woman careened into the room, her feet skidding on the slick tile and sending her sprawling across one of the beds.

The illusion of unreality was only sustained by this new addition. The woman was dressed in a spanking white nurse's outfit complete with a white cap bearing the red cross emblem. The getup ended in a rather short skirt, revealing an expanse of bare leg.

Susan watched, on the verge of calling out, until the woman's head came up as she scrambled over the bed.

# TAKE 5

Susan recognized the face, if not from the party last week than from the many times she'd seen it blown up to two-stories in height and projected onto a movie screen. The intense scars only served to make the face that much more recognizable.

It was Katherine Wickersham.

Susan had followed most of the woman's career before her accident, even used some of her techniques. She was cool and composed in all of her films, playing the roles that empowered women. Davis described her much the same in real life, when he'd told Susan about the brief meeting at Trimax.

Perhaps that was why she had so much trouble recognizing the actress now. After she got over the initial shock of seeing one of her idols this close, Susan was struck by how unlike this behavior was from anything else in her repertoire. The woman clawed her way frantically across the bed, eyes as big as saucers filled with steaming cups of fright. Her lipless mouth hung askew, the muscles in her neck standing out in stark relief as she pulled herself over the bed and tumbled into the floor.

The doors on the far side of the room flew open again. Lars Krieg leapt into the room.

Susan's hands clenched at the sight of him, one of her heels dropping from her hands to plop softly on the platform beside her toe. Her breath gave a ragged hitch.

Krieg wore a tan, one-piece jumpsuit made of some sheer material. His face no longer resembled the dead mask from the party. Those eyes were alive now, dancing, his mouth pulled back into a predatory grin that showed most of his teeth, more like the brutal killer in Otter's clip. The animation made him a different person. His chest heaved as he sucked in lungfuls of air—not from exertion, she realized, but excitement.

He had a very large hunting knife in his hand.

Katherine Wickersham shrieked.

*Only that's not Katherine, that's Nancy Dubose,* Susan assured herself. *No matter how real all of this looks, it's all just an act, a sham for the cameras, and if you want to pick up some pointers from a great actress you won't miss a second.*

*Oh really? Well, if that's true, then where are the cameras?*

This thought stumped her for a moment. It could be a dry run, a dress rehearsal to get the lighting and cues right, but it was too continuous, too intense a performance to be all practice for the technical side of things. If she knew one thing about the pros, they didn't waste their energy if the film wasn't rolling. That's what stand-ins were for.

Then she spotted the large power cable running in from the corner of the room and splicing off in different directions and she understood. The cameras were there; in fact, now that she'd seen through their camouflage, she realized the cameras were *everywhere*. Hidden inside the hospital machines, placed in the corners of the room and looking out through tiny circular holes in the tile, one in the ceiling and one in the air-conditioner vent. They were hidden from view because they needed to be hidden from each other. This was how Gross achieved his static style, angles, and smooth flow of action.

Another cry centered her attention back on the drama below.

Wickersham came around the bed she'd tripped over and into the center aisle in an attempt to escape Krieg. He stomped after her, and she tried to flee just like the woman in the internet download: head craned around nearly 180 degrees in a pretty good impression of a certain split-pea-soup-spouting screen legend. She ran forward, coming right toward Susan, but didn't see her watching from the platform above while looking over her shoulder. In just a few seconds she would be beneath her, crossing over the threshold of the room, the fourth wall where the 'stage' ended, where the fantasy stopped and the grim realities of the building took over.

But surely she wouldn't come that far. She would stop if she did, drop the scared persona, and laugh at her folly. Even if that didn't happen, even if she were so into her performance that she didn't notice, someone would yell 'cut,' and they would go back to their markers and start again, because that's the way making a movie worked, wasn't it?

*Wasn't it?*

But Krieg caught her, as he'd caught the poor girl in the grainy footage, and Susan watched as he spun her around and smacked her with the back of a hand that seemed the size of a three-ring binder. The crack that issued from the point of connection sounded like a snapped bullwhip, and Susan had only a moment to wonder how, exactly, they'd created such a noise. A cry escaped the actress, wordless and high-pitched, and she collapsed against one of the hospital bed railings.

"Help me!" she bawled, and God, was she convincing. "He's gonna kill me!"

*I think that's the idea.* Susan had the sudden urge to giggle at all of this, the way she usually did when she watched horror movies that got under her skin. *Better you than me.*

Below, Krieg came at the actress, and she tried to duck under him. His hand, the one without the knife, shot out like a piston, clamping down on her right arm just above the elbow. He twisted sharply. There was a stout *crack!*, and then Katherine Wickersham shrieked like a fire siren.

Again, Susan marveled at how real it all seemed. This wasn't a finished product, after all the editors and computer manipulators and foley artists took their turns at perfecting the image and adding the effects. This was behind the scenes, the rough sketch that would eventually become the movie, even in a movie where the director handled all that himself. In other words, this wasn't Memorex folks, this was a *live* show, and how were they creating this illusion with her right here, watching…?

"*Tod ist vertraulichkiet,*" a voice whispered in her left ear, and Susan's teeth came together with an audible click, missing her tongue by millimeters.

# TAKE 6

Gross stood at her side, bent over so his withered lips could murmur in her ear. That voice was like sandpaper, and the skin of his face, viewed this close, was as apt for the analogy. She suppressed a shudder.

"It's a German phrase," he continued, low and confidential but still loud enough to be heard over Wickersham's cries of pain below, "meaning 'Death is Intimacy.' I find it quite insightful. I live my life by it, Miss Campbell. It means that death is the only true way to know someone, the only true way to become close to them. Not by love or friendship, or any of those other uplifting notions. They are all too…fleeting, too dependent upon others. Wouldn't you agree?"

Susan opened her mouth and out came a small squeak. She was scared again, an irrational fear that flooded her mouth with the taste of copper and locked up her muscles like taut violin strings. This always happened when she was really, *truly* terrified. When she was ten she'd locked up from a crazed dog that tried to attack her; it had taken three hours before her parents could get her to move again.

She managed a shake of her head that approximated a nod.

Gross stepped up beside her on the platform, resting his hands on the railing and looking down at the action. "There is no guarantee, no requirement that we must love or be loved," he said. "But all of us die, Miss Campbell. That is the one thing all of humanity shares, and it is beautiful for its simplicity. Keep that in mind."

Susan stared at the German Confucius for a few moments longer and then looked down with him.

The actress' cries had trickled down to the pathetic whimpers of a cowed dog. She'd gotten out of Krieg's grasp somehow—or rather, Susan realized, he'd *let* her out. He toyed with her as she tried to escape, her broken right arm hanging limp at her side. She wept, tears that washed off the minimal makeup on her tortured face, and made half-hearted attempts to run.

Krieg again spun her to face him and slapped her over and over, swift, brutal and methodical, back and forth, like a pendulum. The white nurse's cap went flying. She became a little more bruised and bloody with each blow, hellish time-lapse photography, until her already scarred face looked like something hanging in a deli window. The blows began to not just leak but *spray* blood, each swing of the mammoth hand followed by droplets of maroon like ice particles behind a comet, falling on the crisp white linen of the bedsheets around them. Her eyes were swelling shut, she appeared to be missing teeth, and blood flowed from her face to coat her nurse's uniform. She swooned and Krieg caught her deftly with his knife hand so he could continue his barrage, turning the blade so it lay against her skin rather than penetrating it.

Where were the blood packs? How did they make those awful flesh-on-flesh cracking sounds? Something in Susan's head tried to explain to her, calmly and rationally, that this could not be fake, could not be special effect.

She was watching them kill this woman.

"More *lebhaft!*" Gross screamed down at them. "More…" he stopped to hunt for the word, "*vivacious!*"

Krieg held Wickersham at arm's length, and, at the sound of Gross's voice, her battered head fell back. Half-lidded eyes slipped upward to the balcony. They connected squarely with Susan's.

"Help me," she rasped, and then louder, "Please help me!"

She was speaking directly to Susan and asking for help. And if *that* was in the script, she would start filming *Lord of the Cock Rings* tomorrow.

Gross turned to her. He looked brittle enough to be snapped in half by a stiff breeze, but his eyes bore a hardness that would rival the strongest steel. "Very realistic performance, ya? Miss Wickersham truly outdid herself for me. I usually do not allow people to watch these scenes being filmed—it distracts the actors—but I wanted you to see my work in action."

"No, no, this isn't part of it! I don't want to do this anymore!" Wickersham called. "Let me go, let me go, letmegoletmegoletme—"

Krieg cut off her chant by finally putting the hunting knife to use and shoving it directly into her belly. A puff of air escaped Wickersham's lips, no more than a soft sigh, and she doubled over in Krieg's grasp. The uniform around the knife began to stain a creeping red. Wickersham's mouth twisted in pain, and when she looked back up at Susan her eyes glistened with tears.

"Heeeelp," she wheezed. She glanced at Krieg angrily, something about the face like a wounded cat.

Krieg jerked the knife back out, the serrated back of the blade taking a shred of the white nurse's uniform with it. Blood soaked her costume and flowed in rivulets down her side and onto her legs. She pulled one arm up, the good one, and cradled the wound.

Krieg stepped in closer, performing a maneuver that looked like it was from a salsa routine, and jammed the knife into her midriff, just above the other wound. His muscled forearms bunched as he twisted and pulled, slitting her skin and dress upward in a ragged, gaping hole. He grinned and snorted those huge gasps of air.

Katherine Wickersham whined against the giant's chest and crumpled to the floor in a leaking heap.

Susan's stomach did a lazy flip-flop, and she understood how close she was to vomiting.

# TAKE 7

"Annnnnd cut!" Gross cried, startling her out of her shock. "Excellent work, both of you. Miss Campbell, if you'll follow me, please." He started away without waiting for her, heading toward a door behind them and to the right of the staircase she came up to reach the viewing platform.

She bent to get her shoe.

The eyes.

There was no logical reason for Wickersham to look at her. She knew zilch about the nuts and bolts of directing, but she knew it would make no sense on film for the star to ask someone off screen for help.

Correction: *plead* for help.

Susan looked over the edge one last time. Krieg was already halfway across the room, his gigantic strides carrying him to the door. Wickersham lay in the floor, a blood pool spreading outward from her broken form.

She couldn't really be dead, could she? It was a movie, just a stupid horror movie, and if she made it into something more, something *real*, than she was losing it.

This was not a snuff film.

In her head, she heard Otter saying, *There are rumors he's done those too.*

When you made a snuff film, you killed drifters or runaways, not someone who would be missed.

Not actresses.

And, sure enough, the woman began to stir on the floor. Her limbs flapped, clearing swatches in the pristine surface of the blood puddle around her, and she rose jerkily to her feet. She took one dazed look around as if unsure where she was, then walked toward the door that both she and Krieg entered the set through. Her steps had a hesitant, ginger quality that reminded Susan of someone sleepwalking.

Air flooded Susan's lungs from a breath she didn't know she was holding, washing away that queasy feeling.

"Hey," she called out softly. "Miss Wickersham, are you all right?"

Katherine Wickersham turned back and gazed up at her. Her face was still a puffy, swollen, bleeding mess (*but all just special effects, right? all part of the show, so take no look at the man behind the curtain on your way to the egress*), and she stared at Susan as though she didn't understand the question. That blind fear was gone now, but in its place was nothing, no emotion; she was as wrung out as a dishrag after her performance. Finally, she mumbled something and continued out through the double doors.

Susan tried not to notice that her right arm still hung at a crooked angle.

Gross had left the room, and Susan hurried through the door he went through. Another narrow, dim corridor here, and she stepped out just in time to see the director disappear through another door down the hall. She ran to catch up, not wanting to be alone with Krieg's whereabouts unknown. Susan ran through the open door and stepped into a large loft converted into a makeshift office/soundstage with a baffled interior, skidding to a halt only after the decor registered with her. A small desk sat in the corner, and Gross waited for her beside it in a leather chair, bony legs crossed at the ankles and ancient fingers steepled on his chest. He looked at her expectantly, the way an impatient audience member might watch the bear at the circus, waiting for him to ride the little tricycle.

She couldn't think what to say, mainly because she couldn't stop thinking about what she'd just seen.

"It shocked you, did it not?" he asked, reading her. He stood up, unfolding his lean frame from the chair, and started across the room toward her. She nodded. "This was the intent, of course. My films must be as realistic as possible if the…brutality?…is to be properly portrayed."

"It certainly was realistic," she agreed as he came to stand in front of her, and then added hastily, "and brutal."

"Good." He leaned forward with a satisfied grin, taking her agreement as a compliment. "So you would be interested in acting in the film?"

No, she wouldn't be interested in 'actink in ze film.' She could think of nothing she wanted less. She couldn't do what Katherine Wickersham had done, couldn't put that much effort and emotion into a scene that would make her this uncomfortable, and if that was a sign she wasn't meant to be an actress, then so be it.

"You are hesitant." Gross circled her slowly, chin held in one bony hand, eyeing her sidelong. She spun a little bit to keep him in sight, not wanting him behind her.

"Noooo, it's not that."

"You did not like what you saw."

"Well, I wouldn't—"

"I understand, my dear. Not every actress can work within the boundaries of my methods. Most of the charlatans working today must be coached and directed exhaustively through each scene by directors with more time on their hands than myself. As you can see, I typically turn the cameras on, set the actors free, and record the only things that convey true power on screen: life…and death. I have never filmed more than one take on a death scene."

"You mean, that, back there, was their *first time through?*"

Gross was still grinning his gruesome little smirk. His appraising stroll ended, and he now stood next to the entrance to this room, one hand on the sound-baffled padding on the inside of the door. "Absolutely. You get only one death in life; why should film be any different? It is a challenge, but if you are not up to it," he held the other hand up in an invitation to exit, "please waste no more of my time."

Her insides surged desperately at the idea of having the part taken away. She wanted it, she wanted to challenge herself, and how would she know she couldn't do it if she never tried? If she started down this road now, there would always be some excuse. "No, no, I'm very interested. I-I would be honored, in fact."

Gross nodded as though he expected this, despite what he'd said. The hand on the door moved, slamming it shut with a hollow *whump*, and she felt as though the action knocked the air out of her. She became acutely aware that she was alone with him now, closed off in a soundproofed room.

He moved across the short two feet of space between them, eyes drilling into her, closing to an uncomfortable distance. Shit, why had she worn this dress? She fought the urge to cover herself with her arms. "The part is quite simple, Miss Campbell. In the finale of the picture, Krieg is to take one of the hospital inmates, a woman named Denise Hutson, and strap her to a gurney in an effort to lure out the last surviving nurse: Terry Yancy, played by Miss Werdner. This character is ultimately tortured to death during the climax," Gross ran his tongue through his lips as though this idea excited him in ways she didn't want to think about, "but it should be quite a spectacular role for an up-and-coming actress such as yourself."

Susan forced herself to laugh, and was amazed at how natural it sounded.

And then the director—who was, without a doubt, one of the creepiest individuals Susan had ever met—raised his liver-spotted hands and placed them on her bare shoulders, squeezing and kneading her skin with the disgusting flesh on those palms. She wanted to shiver, wanted to pull away and jump in the nearest shower, but she only stood there, meeting his direct gaze pound-for-pound. "There is just one thing I would ask you to do for me. In the name of auditioning, you understand."

Here it was, the invisible attached string. Gross had all the power, and he was willing to use it. Another Weinstein. But how far would she be willing to go for the part? Just the thought of her lips wrapped around his shriveled, old—

"It's quite simple, you see," he continued, a mirthful glint in his eyes. "I need you...to scream."

"Scream?"

"That is the most essential line you will have. Perhaps the most essential line you will *ever* have. A scream must be pure, from the soul. I want you to scream like you have just seen Death's dark shroud standing over your bed in the night, scythe poised for the killing stroke."

"Scream?" she asked again.

He released her, stepping back a half foot. "When you are ready."

She understood exactly what he was asking, and it did make perfect sense; screaming was what made any horror movie worth seeing. But suddenly it seemed as alien an act as walking up the wall to the ceiling.

The first sound out of her mouth started like a hum and became a squeaking dog bark.

"No, no, too timid." Gross sounded disgusted by the effort. "More, *scream!*"

She tried again, thinking about Katherine Wickersham's wail when she flew into the room. Now *that* had been acting. Susan's attempt this time bounced off the far padded walls of the room and returned to her as ululating gibberish.

"Not enough," the director said. "This is the end of your life, it's the last sound you will ever make! Now, *SCREAM!*"

She did this time, thinking about how much he scared her, she sucked in and pushed air out of her lungs as though she would never fill them again, and produced a shriek that rattled her voice box and tore her throat like barbed wire. This time it didn't just echo, it *reverberated*, a radio speaker whose bass has been turned up far too loud. She let the scream go, the act liberating in a way, and continued until she was hoarse and her breath ran out and still she screamed until she was red in the face and the only noise she produced was a high, reedy whistling sound.

Gross nodded and held up a hand. "Good, my dear, that's quite good. The part is yours. We won't be filming the finale for several weeks to come, but you'll have a few scenes before then, so stay in touch. If you'll excuse me now, I must go and see to Miss Wickersham."

He opened the door and strode back out of the room, leaving her standing alone, the straps of her heels still intertwined through her fingers.

And though the prospect of working with these people still terrified her—and she would have to admit to Davis that she'd lied—she still felt an undeniable kernel of excitement blossoming deep within her chest.

# TAKE 8

She debated on how best to broach the subject, even after she arrived back at the apartment. Davis was still there, just out of the shower and freshly shaved, those baby cheeks stretched into a smile upon her entrance.

"What are you doing home from work?"

"I didn't go," she said, not pausing on her way to the kitchen. "I went to audition for Gross."

She poured herself a glass of soda and could feel his gaze crawling over her ensemble as he realized its significance. When she turned back to him, his smile stayed in place, but it faded from his eyes. "I thought you weren't going."

"I changed my mind."

"Well then...how'd it go?" A perfunctory question. She applauded his effort, even though it must be eating him alive inside.

"He gave it to me. I'll be in the movie. We'll be working together, isn't that great?"

He nodded, undoubtedly thinking of one thing only: the order of the credits. Her name would be on that screen long before his. "So...what made you decide to go?"

"Davis, don't."

"What?"

"Don't do this."

"I'm not doing anything!"

"Yes, you are! I know you're upset."

"I'm not. At all. But I *do* think it's a little strange that you—who had nothing but complaints and disgust for his filmmaking—are now a staunch supporter because a role was waved in your face, that's all."

"I admit, I was childish about it."

"I also don't know why you chose to hide the fact that you were going from me."

"I didn't lie to you, you know," she said, a bit too fast. She wanted to be angry—because what did it say about their relationship that she felt the need to hide something this big from him in the first place—but still felt too guilty. "I just wanted to surprise you."

"Oh, I'm surprised all right."

"Can't you just be happy for me?"

The question seemed to throw him, and they stared at one another across the kitchen for a long minute. Then he rubbed the back of his neck with one palm, and said, "Of course I'm happy for you. So, did he like you? Did he say anything else?"

"He just made me scream. Don't be jealous Davis, I'm just some unknown final victim, I may not even have lines."

"I'm *not* jealous!"

She paused, smiled at him, and said, "I got to see them film Katherine Wickersham's death scene though."

His eyes swelled. "You did? What did it look like?"

"Awful. Way worse than the thing Otter showed us." She described her day in detail, from the condition of the building all the way to her audition.

"They did it all on the *first* take?"

"Yep. It was…it was…" She searched for the right words, trying desperately to convey the sense of urgency she'd felt while watching without divulging her fright. "So real," she finished lamely. "Krieg butchered her and...I've never seen anything like it."

"Are you okay?" Apparently she'd communicated *something* to him, because he studied her with concern. Her gratitude caused one of those brief moments of shining love for him that blossomed out of nowhere, the kind that made her warm and light-headed and fearful all at the same time.

"Yeah," she said, and then the tears came, spilling over her eyelids and down her cheeks.

Davis held her. "Suze, what's wrong?"

"Nothing, nothing," she said, trying to staunch the flow. "Are you sure you're not mad at me?"

"No, I'm not mad, don't be ridic—"

He was cut off by the shrill tweet of his cell phone from the table in the living room. He gave her a last squeeze before going to retrieve it. She heard him talking for several minutes before he returned with a large grin on his face.

"Who was that?"

"Gross. We start tomorrow."

# SCENE VII

(f/x shot)

# TAKE 1

The script supervisor's name was Douglas Pickerill, and he was a royal pain in the ass.

Davis knew what to expect. Script supervisors were anal retentive, nit-picky bastards; their job was to supervise every minute detail of a script and insure consistent filming. They treated screenplays as strictly as Baptists treated the Bible, and if God called for a 'close-up' rather than a 'zoom' they brought down the fire and brimstone. They could be useful, when they pointed out a character's hair changed from one scene to the next, but mostly they stood around and whined, 'You're not doing that right,' like some know-it-all in the first grade.

With Douglas Pickerill, it was far worse than even that. He must've been younger than forty, but he dressed and acted like someone ready for retirement. His chestnut hair laid perfectly against his skull, a pair of round frame glasses perched at the tip of a pug nose, and he wore a suit Pee Wee Herman might be missing, with an ancient Polaroid dangling around his neck. Oh, and a clipboard. These guys had clipboards surgically attached to their hands.

The script supervisor introduced himself to Jared and Davis at the studio but refused to ride with them, which irked Davis because they could've saved time and met the scrawny guy at the site.

Jared gave him a pointed look in the van on the way there.

"Not a word," Davis cautioned. "I'm not in the mood. Just...think of the money."

"I'm always thinking of the money, baby."

"Frankly, I'm kind of surprised there even *is* a script supervisor. Just doesn't seem like something Gross would want on his film."

"Maybe he didn't have a choice in that one, either."

"What do you mean?"

Jared reached behind his seat and fumbled for a cigarette, which Davis knocked out of his hand. "You said Reilly wanted us to make sure Gross doesn't implode, right? Maybe this census taker is another insurance policy."

"If that's true, I can't say I'd be sad."

They arrived at the film site as the afternoon heat cranked up. He saw what Susan meant immediately; prime gangland real estate.

The thought of Susan brought a little black cloud over his already dark disposition.

They piled out as Pickerill arrived in a Cutlass, a car he was at least twenty years too young for.

"Jesus, I've never met anybody in such a hurry for a senior citizen discount," Davis mumbled.

Jared pulled metal crates from the rear of the van. "Hey, Pick, give us a hand, grab a few of these camera cases."

Pickerill's upper lip curled back in a sneer. "If I wanted to do manual labor, I would've become a roofer. Perhaps you can hire one of the locals."

"That's all right, we got it." Davis hoisted more of the cases than he could safely manage. Right now he would do anything to avoid an argument with this prick.

Pickerill marched toward the door and Jared glared at his backside before picking up the last of his equipment. The man called back over his shoulder, "Can we hurry this along, gentleman? I do have other projects today."

"If you let me kill him, I swear no one will find the body," Jared grunted.

Davis was so out of breath he didn't try to banter.

They went in through the main door, different than the one Susan used but the same interior she described. He couldn't believe his girlfriend—the same woman who once called him over to kill a spider in her kitchen—navigated this place alone, in the dark.

She *really* wanted that part.

*And she got it*, he thought bitterly. *Hurray for her.*

"Ugh." Pickerill paused at the door to peer inside. "It certainly is a ghastly place, isn't it?"

"Lead the way, Pick," Jared said, and Pickerill shot him a look. "Well, you *are* the supervisor, after all. So supervise." Pickerill straightened his suit jacket, and entered the building with his clipboard clutched as a shield.

They didn't get nearly as lost as Susan. They entered through the correct doorway, and found neat white signs pointing them in the direction of the filming stages. They passed through several rooms totally remodeled to look like a mental ward and through a set of double doors into the one Susan described. Davis saw the railed platform where she watched Nancy Dubose's demise.

"Looks like this is the place." Pickerill checked his clipboard. "I trust you fellows know how to set up."

"Where are you from, Pick?" Jared asked as he squeezed by.

Pickerill frowned. "Santa Barbara. Well, Seattle, originally. Why?"

"Just wondering where you picked up that not-quite-British accent. You and Madonna take classes together or something?"

"Jesus, Jared, would you cut it out and let's get this done?" Davis put down the other equipment beside the door and led his partner away. If he let this go on much longer, fists—or in Pickerill's case, open palms—would start flying.

Most of the lights were turned off on the set to conserve energy. Pickerill went about turning them all on so the shots would have the same quality as Gross' the day before, and then took Polaroids from different angles around the room as a 'back-up copy' of the set, just in case they moved something and needed to replace it. Jared unpacked his equipment. Davis walked down the row between the beds, trying to envision how the murder had looked. He only had what Susan told him to go on; Gross had given him nothing to work with. Today's assignment was a short montage of crime scene close-ups to be interspliced when the investigating officers in the movie came to pick up Nurse Dubose's body.

For some reason, he still found himself wanting to please Gross, to match the man's style so his footage would be deemed acceptable for the director's next dazzling work of art. If only he could just see the dailies from yesterday, to get some idea of his approach. It would be easy; according to Susan there was only one.

What kind of director only did one take?

A visionary, of course. A genius. If the wrinkled old bat came naked to the set and made the actors run their lines while standing on their heads, they'd give him the key to the city.

He sighed, a forlorn sound on an empty set.

# TAKE 2

Davis found the cameras Gross used, spread around the room and camouflaged. All of them would make for those characteristic odd angles and skewed perspectives. He moved to the end of the row, where the murder took place, and almost stepped in the puddle of congealed blood on the floor. Pickerill would surely tear a chunk from his ass for screwing up scene continuity. Dried maroon was splashed across four of the beds, the majority on one to his left. He came up with a few general ideas of how he wanted the shots to look (how *Gross* would want the shots to look), and went back to get Jared.

"When you get the blood sprays on the bed," Pickerill called, "he wants a zoom-*out*, not in. No panning."

"Got it," Davis said. And to Jared, "You say no one will find the body?"

Jared grinned and began to set up, while Pickerill harangued Davis on the sequencing, order, and nature of each shot. He nodded his way through, pretending to drink it all in, but was grateful when Jared called out, "Davis, could you come here?"

Davis left Pickerill by the exit—the man hovered there as though ready to run if the dust got too thick—and went to Jared, who hunkered down with a lowered tripod. He expected another complaint about their script-supervising friend, but instead his partner whispered, "Did you take a look at this?"

"Take a look at what, the shot?"

"No dingus, what we're *shooting*. Did you actually look at this stuff or just daydream about sucking Gross off?"

He let the insinuation slide without comment (maybe because, as crude as it was, it was somewhere in the ballpark, if not the neighborhood, of truth) and studied the mess at their feet. A dried maroon puddle, one that glistened with stickiness, like a soda spill left out in the sun. A few scuffle marks in it, interruptions in its glass surface, and the vague outline of the body it was supposed to have drained from. "Yeah, so?"

"So, what is it?"

Davis shrugged, not understanding. "I don't know, corn syrup?"

Jared shook his head. "Corn syrup doesn't look like this when it dries. Besides, the reason the F/X people use it is because the color shows up the correct shade on film. I know, because I worked with it when that goth chick hired me to do her photo shoot. So I ask you again, what *is* this?"

"I don't know, fake Hollywood blood! Red dye number 8 and shit, for all I care! Who do I fucking look like, Rick Baker?"

Jared recoiled from his anger. "Are you...okay, man?"

"I'm fine," he lied. The thing with Susan loomed large in his mind. She'd lied to him, but, he had to admit, it was the fact she'd stolen his thunder that really got to him. Petty, sure, but that was Davis Lowe in a nutshell. "I guess I just want you to get to the point."

"Okay, I'm getting there, don't pop a hernia. Take a look at this."

Jared bent even further down, pressing his face nearly against the puddle of blood while holding his long hair up and away from it, like Tonto listening for approaching hoof beats, and pointed into the darkness under the bed closest to them. "I spotted it when I was examining the puddle here by sheer chance."

Davis bent low, beside Jared, now a couple of Muslims praying toward Mecca, and followed the direction of Jared's finger. In the darkness under the hospital-style bed, he saw nothing...at first. After several seconds of hunting, his eyes picked it out, a blip of white in the darkness.

"It's a tooth," Jared whispered.

With that, the image locked. He could see the object clearly: a tooth all right, complete with roots, chipped on its crown and with a bit of red, shriveled matter clinging to its base.

"So what?"

"So what? Man, it's a tooth! A *human* tooth!"

"...yeah, aaand...?"

Jared scrunched his face in frustration. "You got a tooth there, you got a puddle of very suspicious looking red stuff on the floor here..."

At last Davis understood, and his face flushed in anger. "What are you saying, that it's real? Newsflash retard, we're making a *horror movie* here!" His voice rose at the end of the pronouncement.

Jared shot a look over his shoulder at Pickerill, frowned in exasperation, and then smiled patiently, as though talking to a slow child. "I'm not saying anything. Just follow the logic with me here, man. What kind of sense does it make to throw part of the scenery under the bed here, away from the blood or anything else we'd be shooting?"

"'*Maybe that's German Hollywood.*'"

"First of all, fuck you. Second, if you take the time to make a prop tooth—and that one looks pretty damn good to me—you don't want to waste it by hiding it. You leave it out, leave it visible, you know that."

"It's a crime scene, the elements are supposed to be random!"

"Yeah, but it's also a movie, which means it's ordered chaos, and these elements are too random."

"Jared, I don't have time to listen to this."

"If you can listen to Otter go on and on about Bigfoot, you can hear me out for two minutes. Look at it, Davis. Does this picture not look off to you?"

Instead of looking back at the scene, Davis stared at *him*, trying to gauge his seriousness. If this wasn't Jared's warped sense of humor, if he *truly* believed they were squatting next to a big puddle of blood and a tooth popped from someone's head like a kernel of corn…well, what? It was all ridiculous and yet…

*And yet it's not just him suddenly going coo-coo for Cocoa Puffs. Susan broke into goddamned tears when she told you about the death scene. You didn't dwell on it because you were too busy begrudging her a little fame and notoriety, but what if…?*

He cut the thought off brutally.

Had everyone gone insane since Torsten Gross came to town?

"You really think this is blood?" He was the one who performed a Pickerill check now. The last thing he needed was for the suit to report back that his crew was losing their minds. They must look like two giggly school girls.

He watched them with a persnickety frown on his face. "Are we okay, gentlemen?"

"Fine, just setting up."

Jared whispered, "Look, do we really know Gross? We only know what we've heard and that he's a first class weirdo—"

"You're competing for that title yourself right now!"

"—and that Krieg has no qualms about violence on or off camera. For all we know, the two of them are murdering people under the guise of filming a movie! Some kind of sick

German thing, like those videos where the girls step on frogs wearing nothing but high heels!"

Davis swallowed but lack of spit almost caused him to choke. The room felt stuffy now, the heat too much, and his thoughts swam. "Have you lost your fucking mind? It's...it's a *movie*, for Christ's sake!"

"Exactly my point! It's the perfect cover. Everyone would say the same thing you just did. They could kill someone right in front of you, and you'd pass it off as effects, as Hollywood magic."

"But Susan was here when they filmed it, Jared! She was in the room! She saw Katherine Wickersham get up and walk out of here!"

"I'm not saying they killed an actress; *that* would be stupid. But for all we know they're strangling hookers and using their internal organs as props. Mr. Realism wants this thing as authentic as possible, right? And just tell me you don't think Lars Krieg is capable of it after what we saw him do to those paparazzo!"

Davis clenched his fingers into a frustrated fist. "I know you don't like the guy, okay, fine, we have plenty of reasons not to, but this insanity goes beyond grudges."

Jared regarded him calmly. "I'm telling you, I just have this feeling. I may not be 100 percent correct, but...something's wrong here, Davis. Wrong the moment we stepped into this building, and more wrong now that I look at this set-up. Can't you feel it?"

He said nothing, because he didn't trust himself to speak. Of course he felt it, ever since meeting Gross, when his intuition told him this job was a bad idea. He hadn't spoken up because it felt like giving voice to those feelings was the first step on the way to the nuthatch.

*Something's wrong here.*

They had said the same thing in every horror movie since the beginning of time.

The walls of reality blurred, and he had to remind himself he was *making* a horror movie, not in one.

Jared broke the lapse in conversation, making Davis realize he'd been staring off into space for a few seconds. "All right, do me a favor and distract Buckaroo Banzai over there."

"Why, what are you gonna do?"

"I'm gonna prove it to you. I'm taking that tooth and some of this blood to that guy I know over at the LAPD."

"What guy? You don't know any guy!"

"Yes I do, I fucked his wife at that party! Oh, wipe that look off your face, you prude, *he* doesn't know that! Just get rid of Pickerill for a minute, will ya?"

He put his hands on Davis' shoulders and shoved, nearly bowling him backward from his precarious kneeling position. Davis took a few awkward, unbalanced steps and then headed to the script supervisor.

"Can I talk to you outside?"

Pickerill scowled, his sculpted eyebrows coming together, but stepped out into the hall without protest. "Are we having a problem, Lowe?"

"Just something with the camera lens." He struggled to find something else to say and decided to kill two birds with one stone. "Say, how well do you know Gross?"

Pickerill sniffed. "I've never met him in person. I talked to him on the phone once."

"So the studio hired you?"

Pickerill favored Davis with a scorching look. "Yes, Mr. Gross made it quite clear that my presence wasn't needed. The man would run the entire production himself if the studio let him. Hasn't quite come to terms with the fact this isn't Nazi Germany."

"Just curious," he said, dismissing the conversation. He reentered the studio ahead of the script supervisor and Jared gave him a circle with thumb and forefinger. He was already shooting.

"Let's hurry this along, children." Pickerill gave them his snidest tone. He muttered, so low Davis barely caught it, "I'd like to go back to where I'm appreciated."

*You and me both*, Davis thought.

# TAKE 3

Gross asked Susan to report to the set for the first time on Monday, three days after having her witness the death of Katherine Wickersham's onscreen persona. The weekend was uncomfortable, things with Davis strained and tense. He tried to stay busy at the office, editing footage with Otter, but when he came home after his first day, he was sullen and…well, weird.

She refused to dwell on any of it, though; no, not on this, her first day as a real actress. She called her parents and sister in Colorado and every girlfriend she ever had to tell them the news. She took a leave of absence from the insurance company until further notice; between the money she was making for her portrayal of Denise Hutson, ill-fated inmate from cell #17, and the money she'd saved the last few years (in anticipation of the BIG BREAK! that was happening with the dreamy speed of a snow avalanche) she would have enough funds to float through until the end of the shoot or—even better—she found another role to take after this one.

The building was just as creepy the second time around, but she was far less scared entering it. This time she went in the correct door, and followed the signs. That feeling of being watched was gone, if it was ever really there in the first place.

Before she knew it, she'd found her way to the set. She eased into the room where she'd watched the slaughter. Only half the overhead fluorescents were on, but she could see the blood was cleaned up, the sheets on the beds changed, presumably so the set could be used in another scene. She stood examining it for a moment, and wondered what she was so freaked out about.

She heard voices behind her, further down the hall, and pressed on until she came to the door from which they issued. She pushed it open and stepped through into another sparklingly clean room, this one with a table in the middle and chairs around it, and a refrigerator against the far wall beside two vending machines.

Samantha Cox and Tonya Werdner were inside. Cox wore a nurse's outfit identical to the one Susan had seen on Wickersham, and stood hunched over a waist-high hand sink built into the wall to Susan's left, applying makeup in a mirror set over the little basin. A bulletin board beside her was filled with safety posters and a sign that read, PROPERLY DISPOSE OF ALL MEDICAL WASTE. Werdner stood on the other side of the room, her nurse's skirt on but nothing except a bra up top. She pulled her hair back into a ponytail and turned toward Susan as she came in. Her large breasts bobbled precariously on the edge of escape.

"Oh, I'm sorry," Susan said, backing out of the room. "I didn't know this was a dressing room."

"That's cause it ain't, sweetheart." Werdner seemed unfazed by the sudden intrusion of a strange woman while half naked. "This is part of the set. The break room at good ol'

Chesterfield. But it's the closest thing to a dressing room we got." She reached out and pulled open the refrigerator door. The outside of this appliance looked used and cheerful, covered with magnets and drawings from the hospital employee's children, but the interior was dark and empty. "See? We don't even get a working fridge. I've been on porno sets with more accommodations."

Cox finished applying eyeliner and turned to her. "Hi!" she said cheerfully. Susan had a sudden flash of the look on her face in the papers the night the police had hauled her off someone's front lawn up in Pasadena. That was just before the court-ordered detox began. "I'm guessing you're the other actress? The one that's playing…uh…uh…the final victim?" she asked in her Jersey accent.

"That's me. Susan Campbell." She shook hands with the actress. Werdner watched but didn't offer the same.

"Yeah, I think I met your boyfriend. Tall guy, cute, sandy blond hair? Works on second unit?"

"Sounds like Davis."

"Blah, second unit?" Werdner slipped on her nurse's top. "How can you stand to be seen with that? Must be murder on your career."

"Actually, this is my first film."

"Too bad it had to be this one. This ain't exactly the glamorous life. We don't even have hairstylists or makeup artists. Gross says he wants us to look natural, but I think he's just cheap. Oh, and whatever you do, don't let him catch you with a cell phone within a hundred yards of him."

"First film and a juicy death scene like this?" Cox asked, ignoring the other woman. "You really lucked out!"

"I don't know about that. Especially after seeing Katherine's scene being filmed on Thursday."

As soon as the words were out, the two of them fell completely silent, staring at her, and then attacked her at once with a barrage of questions.

"You saw the death scene?"

"Was it scary?"

"How'd Wick do?"

"It was pretty intense," she said, when she was able to get a word in.

"We don't know anything about it," Cox said. "Gross took all the information about the death scenes out of our copies of the script after he rewrote it. He wants us to do it totally cold, no rehearsals or anything."

"Gross won't even let us see the film." Werdner picked up where the other actress left off, rubbing one of her breasts distractedly while she spoke. "Says that part of the film doesn't concern us cause our characters weren't there. And we haven't heard from Kathy since she filmed it. Someone told me she was sick. Don't know why *you* were so privileged though."

"What did it look like?"

She gave them a more abbreviated version, worried she might be committing some breach of etiquette that would get her reprimanded, or worse, fired. She was careful to keep whatever alerted Davis to her unease out of her voice. "I just don't know if I can do something like that," she said when she finished. "Especially with no direction or rehearsal."

"Me too." Cox turned back to the mirror. "I guess I'll find out pretty soon though. My big moment is week after next."

"Didn't agree too well with Miss Workaholic of the Year," Werdner said. "I'm certainly not envious of you two. *I* get to survive."

"Just the thought of Krieg touching me..." Cox shuddered.

"Better than Gross," Werdner said.

Susan nodded, and felt a bit better that these two, both accomplished actresses, felt the same way she did. She waited while they finished getting ready, and then, as if he knew when they were fully dressed, Gross breezed into the room without knocking. He reminded her of a drill instructor, coming to get the troops for a grueling day of training.

"Miss Campbell, thank you for joining us. I have new scripts for all of you." He held out a thick sheaf of papers to her, which she accepted reverently, and then he gave the same bundles to the other two.

"Jesus, more rewrites?" Werdner grumbled.

"Originally, the vast majority of Miss Campbell's part was the torture scene in the climax, but I have rethought the character and written her deeper into the film." He flashed his toothy, gruesome grin at them. "So her death will have more emotional impact."

Susan tried to keep her jaw from swinging open. She could feel Cox and Werdner staring at her from behind, probably wondering how many times she'd screwed this prune to be graced with a new and improved role. "Th-thank you."

"Doing the character justice is the only gratitude I require. Today we will be filming with the extras as well as several of your first scenes, which take place after Nurse Dubose's death. That is, if you think you can run your lines cold."

"Absolutely," she said. *Scenes*, she thought in awe. *I have scenes!*

"All right then, ladies," he said, his hard eyes fixed on each of theirs in turn, "let's get down to business."

# TAKE 4

Two days had passed since their film date with Pickerill, and Jared had come no closer to convincing Davis something was amiss with Germany's favorite son. He was no longer sure if he wanted to prove Gross stunk like week-old sushi to vindicate himself, or just to wipe that moony hero worship off his best friend's face. Sure, his theory sounded like the concept for a Mel Brooks comedy, and it might've been enough to make him feel a little stupid.

If not for a certain phone call.

This call came while he was on his way to visit Katherine Wickersham herself, to take a series of close-ups and stills the studio wanted to digitize and manipulate for one of their ad campaigns. Jared suspected they wanted to see for themselves how her scars would play out on film. Phillip Reilly contacted Davis directly with the assignment, bypassing Gross, and Davis passed it on to him while he worked with Otter on some of their other footage, trying not to be too obvious about the fact he was avoiding him.

"Hello?" Jared answered on the first ring, while cruising down 170 in his van. He turned down a blaring Slipknot CD. The number was unknown, but he made it a point to give his digits out to at least five women on any given day.

"It's Vandergriff," the voice on the other end said. That would be Sergeant Ken Vandergriff of the famous Los Angeles Police Department, a man friendly and dopey enough that Jared almost felt bad about sleeping with his wife who, at the time, was a model for some perfume line.

"Oh, hey. Didn't expect to hear back from you so soon." This was the man he'd turned the samples over to mere hours after scraping them from the floor of the set, giving a version of events not so far from the truth: he wanted to know what a colleague used for his very realistic special effects. Vandergriff told him the cops weren't funded by curiosity, and the samples would have to wait until the lab techs got good and bored.

"Jesus, Mane, what're you involved in?"

The question floored him for the span of three seconds. "They're real, aren't they?"

"Did you really not know that when you brought them to me? Or is this a joke?"

"Are you sure it's not animal blood or some kinda new synthetic? Or maybe—"

"We're not idiots, Mane. It's human blood. The tooth is real too. Medical examiner says it was knocked out rather than pulled. Take a few more days to get the full report, but preliminary DNA tests say they both came from the same person." Those friendly, dopey tones were gone, replaced by a hard edge that distracted Jared so much he had to jerk the steering wheel at the last second to avoid colliding with a Honda in front of him already traveling ten miles over the speed limit.

"What's with the attitude?"

"The attitude is because I turned in some samples for analysis that were supposed to be for a friend, just some innocuous bullshit from his make-believe Hollywood world, and now I've got a ton of questions coming from my superiors that I don't know how to answer. Which means I expect to start getting them from you right fucking now."

"Ken, man…I don't know what to say."

"How about the truth?"

*Yeah, Jared, tell him the truth. If you really believe anything you said to Davis—and don't get me wrong, this up-*

*date from your good friend at the LAPD certainly proves you're not completely crazy—then why don't you turn this whole thing over to the cops?*

The answer to that was as easy as a valley girl.

Because it still *sounded* crazy, that's why. Vandergriff wouldn't believe a word he said without proof, and then the cop would just press him harder for information he couldn't give. He couldn't even take them back to the set; it had already been cleaned for future shoots, destroying any link to the evidence and pitting his word against the esteemed director's.

"C'mon Ken, you can't think I did anything wrong! I brought that stuff to you!"

"I know, and that's the only thing you have in your favor right now."

"Are you telling me I'm a fucking suspect in all this?"

"Mane…how the hell can you be a suspect? I don't even know what 'this' is! All I know is, you waltz in here and give me human blood and a tooth and tell me it's special effects shit. And now I have no choice but to bring you in for questioning till I get a clearer understanding of where it came from. Where are you?"

Jared's hands shook while the officer spoke. He kept the phone wedged against his ear with one shoulder—he'd always had a knack for that—and leaned over to the glove compartment to fumble out a cigarette from a stale pack. He lit it with a lighter also in the glove box, and inhaled. "Tell me one thing: what was the blood type?"

"I'm not telling you shit until—"

"JUST TELL ME THE GODDAMN BLOOD TYPE!"

"AB negative, all right? What the hell does that matter? Now, where are you?"

"I...I can't tell you that just yet."

"Mane," Vandergriff said, turning the word into a full-blown warning. "I could've just put out an APB on you, but I called you because I thought we were friends. This is gonna look a lot better for you if you bring yourself in. I don't believe you did anything wrong, I really don't, but if you're withholding information on a crime, it can go just as badly as if you did it yourself."

"Do what you have to do." Jared closed the phone and dropped it into his lap.

He was still shaking, but he forced himself to breath deep from the cigarette until he felt steady. He had to be able to think right now, plan a strategy, let his instincts work. First and foremost, he harbored no real intention of running from the police, not when he was completely innocent, but he also couldn't just stroll into the nearest station with nothing more interesting than his dick to show them (as interesting as that might be) and try to answer their questions. He considered calling Davis, but decided it would just be a waste. He had to use the time available to get some further evidence.

Torsten Gross or Lars Krieg or *someone* working on *Arterial Slice* knew the blood and tooth were from a real person. The 64,000 dollar question was, who was that unfortunate person? Just the fact that it was human was bad—it sure-as-shit proved Gross wasn't going down to Jack's Joke Shop to get his supplies—but if all that blood on the floor came from one human body, chances were that it was, at this very second, slowly returning to the earth from whence it came, and how would Mr. Bigshot Director explain that one?

He wouldn't have to, not unless Jared could find a way to link him to it.

He grunted as he put out the cigarette.

One other interesting fact gleaned from his brief conversation with Vandergriff: the blood was AB negative. Not exactly unheard of, but far from common.

Yesterday, anticipating the need for such info, he'd called up an old girlfriend at Cedar Sinai, where Katherine Wickersham had been treated after her accident on the Bruckheimer flick. After one not-perfectly-legal file violation in return for the promise of another date, he found out the actress was... yep, you guessed it...Type AB negative.

Coincidence? More than likely. As he himself just pointed out, whoever lost that blood had to be pushing up daisies by now, and Wickersham was still very much alive. In any case, she was also the only person who might know more about where the blood that poured from her character had came from, and he had an appointment to meet her in less than 15 minutes.

He pushed the accelerator of the van down even harder, and careened down the freeway toward the Hollywood Hills at near 90.

# TAKE 5

Katherine Wickersham lived in a high-rise apartment squarely in the middle of the Hills, in a doorman-guarded building where Jared showed three forms of identification and just about submitted to a rectal cavity search before they even announced him. Their attitudes changed almost instantly, however, when Wickersham bade them to let him up.

Her apartment was the penthouse at the very top, on the twentieth floor. No buttons on the elevator; it was all controlled by the desk guard below. Jared stepped out into a short hall leading to only one door. It was partially ajar and, figuring Wickersham left it this way for him, he pushed it open and stepped across the threshold.

The entrance led onto a spacious loft-style living room. The entire far wall was glass. He saw the tops of several of the other swanky high rises around them and, in the distance, the Capitol Records building. It was a modern-day Mount Olympus, designed so that its very rich inhabitant could look down on the masses and decide which direction to send their lives in. Decorated tastefully, velvety blue wallpaper and black leather couches and recliners, a huge flatscreen television, Persian rugs, a large wet bar to his left that ran half the length of the wall, artwork from some of the higher-end art galleries in L.A., a pure white marble bust of passing likeness to its owner on a pedestal by the door.

But the effect of the elegant décor was washed away by the trashed state of it all.

Garbage—bits of paper, left-over food, empty wine bottles and soda cans—was strewn everywhere. The wet bar was devoid of any alcohol, most of the drinking glasses scattered on their sides and one smashed to pieces on the floor. A lamp and table were overturned next to the couch, the bulb shattered on the carpet. He might think he was looking at the site of a robbery if it wasn't so painfully obvious someone lived in this mess.

A cold ball formed deep in the pit of his stomach.

Why did his mind turn immediately to Gross?

"Miss Wickersham?" Dead silence answered him, no TV, no radio, not even the electric background hum of air conditioners. "Katherine Wickersham, are you here?"

"Here," a monotone voice croaked from his right, causing him to jump. A doorway stood to his immediate right leading into an unlit kitchen bigger than his entire apartment, and it was from this direction that the single word had originated.

Katherine Wickersham stepped forward into the sunlight coming from the window wall.

# TAKE 6

Though he would admit it to no one, the woman in front of him was one of the few actresses he was genuinely in love with. Not sexually (though he'd masturbated to her sex scene in *Timberglen Summer* more than once), but in a respectful, school-boy, weak-in-the-knees kind of way. Her performance in *The Tower Outside Cairo* moved him to tears for Christ's sake, (a nice side effect being an earth-shattering blowjob from his date). He'd been sorry to hear about her accident, but after meeting her with Davis, he realized no amount of scarring could hide her natural beauty.

But those opinions shriveled as he faced her in her living room.

She stared at him, or rather, stared *through* him, like someone utterly lost in thought. She wore ratty pajamas, her short brown hair in tangles and knots the size of pennies. Eyes sunken, bags underneath so dark they showed even through the corkscrew snarls of scar tissue. Her jaw glistened with drool, her arms limp, shoulders sagging. She looked nothing like the professional he'd seen last week.

Not a spark of life in her.

*Like Krieg*, he thought.

But that wasn't accurate. Lars Krieg exhibited an emotional void, but the life was bred out of him, like a man dedicated to military service. He showed plenty of energy when excited, and that made him forbidding, but there was nothing at all threatening about the sad creature in front of him. The vitality was *pummeled* out of her, and she resembled something closer to a concentration camp inmate whose spirits were broken.

But she was still in one piece. Whatever conspiracy his subconscious had cooked up about the blood type was obviously defective. This woman may look godawful and been slacking on the housekeeping, but she wasn't physically hurt, and she didn't appear to be missing any teeth.

"Jared Mane," he said. No change in her slack expression. "We met the other day, remember? I'm from the second unit at Trimax? We had an appointment to take some close-ups." He let his eyes wander around the trashed living room. "Is this a bad time?"

He expected her to say she'd forgotten or wasn't feeling well, anything to excuse her appearance and the state of the apartment, but she merely croaked, in her inflectionless voice, "Okay," and shuffled past him toward the couch in the middle of the room. Her feet never lifted more than an inch from the ground, nudging aside a crusty TV dinner tray and a mound of empty soda cans.

Maybe this was just her lifestyle. Just because someone was a big star didn't mean they couldn't be a slob. He heard some actors got depressed after finishing a shoot, and Wickersham seemed enough of a workaholic to fit the bill.

"Miss Wickersham, are you feeling all right?"

She stopped, turned in a ponderous circle to face him. She never turned at the neck or waist, but spun as though her body was one solid, jointless structure.

"I…I don't…know. I haven't been feeling…right."

"Do you need a doctor?"

He counted mentally to twenty and then opened his mouth to prompt her again when she rasped, "Nothing... tastes good. Can't...*feel*..."

He frowned at her. People on heavy drugs were nothing new to him, and this woman appeared doped out of her gourd. Some sort of pain medication perhaps, for the scars?

*Not even all the Percocet in L.A. Quit trying to rationalize this.*

"When did this start?"

She shrugged and let her eyes drift to the carpet.

This was not going as planned. He almost felt a little guilty, as though he were taking advantage of the poor woman and boy, was that a new one for him; he usually *liked* that feeling. Jared stood in the doorway, trying to decide if he should press on or call for help.

Wickersham ran her hand along the back of the couch, giving off a muted squeaking like a fart as she rubbed the leather. A frustrated look wrinkled her brow. She rubbed harder and harder, as if trying to get a stain out with her palm.

"Um, should we...go ahead with the shoot? If you'll just have a seat around the front, where the light can hit you."

She shambled obediently around the front of the sofa, lowering herself into the middle seat slowly, like an old man with arthritic hips. This sad wretch was so different from that crisp businesswoman reading her lines with Cox and Werdner. She stared straight ahead, unblinking, out the window and all the way to China, for all he knew.

Jared brought his mini-cam case over and pulled the strap over his head. He knelt in front of her. "Miss Wickersham, do you remember filming your death scene earlier this week?"

"I...remember..." she said, but from the way she trailed off, he couldn't determine if it was a confirmation. There was a momentary flicker of activity deep in her pupils.

He looked down, checked the remaining battery time on the camera, and adjusted the settings. "Did you happen to see where the blood came from that Gross used for the crime scene?"

"Blood." She gasped, her chest hitching. He felt like he was talking to his autistic cousin, a girl of twenty with the mind of an infant.

So where did this leave him? The cops would be all over him by nightfall, and he'd learned exactly squat from the one person who...

Susan.

The realization hit him hard. *Susan* was there during the filming. If he finished up here fast enough, he could call her before he was dragged in for questioning.

He brought the camera to his eyes, framing the comatose Wickersham's left side in the viewer as she stared off into space and started filming. He slowly swept around to capture her from all angles. "Do you know if—?"

The actress turned her head, looked in the camera at him, and *shrieked*.

Jared's heart rate tripled as he sprawled backward away from her. His first thought was that he'd offended her, invaded her personal space, and she was going to scream rape. But her caterwauling was just as vacuous, primitive and devoid of any rational thought.

Wickersham attacked, leaping off the couch to fall across him. She flailed, most of her blows aimed at the camera but plenty raining down on him. He was too stunned to defend himself. One slap rattled his teeth; another caused a burst of stars across his vision. She wrenched the little digital model away from him and flung it across the room, where it landed in the floor against the wet bar.

Even in the midst of the insanity, his thoughts leapt back to Krieg and his attack on the tabloid cameramen.

Once the device was out of his hands, she rolled off and struggled to her feet. She gave one final scream, her hands going to the sides of her face like Macaulay Culkin as painted by Edvard Munch. She pulled at the scarred flesh until it became a sagging, hollow-eyed death mask, the nails biting into the skin until they drew blood.

And then Katherine Wickersham, two-time Academy Award nominee and once the idol of millions of Americans, charged at the wall-to-wall glass windows of her twentieth-story penthouse.

Jared was sure she would bounce off, perhaps brain herself and fall unconscious, because the glass would be thick enough to prevent the 'accidents' depressed rich folks occasionally had. But the glass *did* break, shattering from floor to ceiling and spreading out on both sides of the actress in a jagged oval. She plunged through in a ragdoll-ish—yet queerly graceful—freefall. Being so in tune with the aesthetics of filmmaking, he saw it all in slow motion, but had no chance of performing the dramatic, last second save.

By the time he reached the edge of the building—almost sliding over the carpeted ledge himself—she was nothing but a red splotch on the pavement below, a brilliant abstract watercolor amid a kaleidoscope of glittering glass.

Still trying to figure out what the flying fuck had just happened, Jared pulled out his cell phone and dialed 911.

Behind him, the camera in the floor continued to record.

# SCENE VIII

(cut to)

# TAKE 1

Trimax managed to hold off the press conference until after the funeral. The police released precious little information, not even committing themselves to the suicide announcement (although rumors ran more rampant than those concerning the contents of Richard Gere's ass), and the media practically foamed at the mouth to break the real story of the death of one of America's biggest former acting talents.

The funeral itself was brief and to the point, definitely not a Hollywood affair, only attended by her small family, a few friends, an awkward Phillip Reilly, and most of the cast of Arterial Slice. Werdner came in a black skirt short enough to see London *and* France, a cigarette jutting from her lips and a cloud of smoke following her around like a miniature storm cloud. Cox bawled louder than anyone and clutched double-handfuls of tissue. Wickersham's ex, Jean du Vaulier—he of the critically acclaimed French film *Le Boutique*—came to pay his respects with his almost-not-legal girlfriend hanging on his arm, and Davis fought the urge to cram a few knuckles down his mouth.

Torsten Gross and Lars Krieg were conspicuously absent.

Davis and Susan spent a few minutes in the company of her fellow actresses making polite small talk, but, as they made to leave, Davis slipped away and doubled back to talk to them once more.

"Did she say anything to either of you before she died?"

"Yeah," Werdner growled, spewing smoke. "She said, 'Hey guys, I think I'm gonna take the new one-way express elevator at my apartment this weekend.' We didn't see anything wrong with it, did we, Sam?" She strolled away, muttering, "Asshole," under her breath.

Cox stayed with him, snorting up snot, mascara running in twin lines down her cheeks. They crossed the graveyard together, angling toward where her little yellow Aston Martin Roadster convertible was parked on one of the weaving cemetery roads. "No, she didn't say anything. We hadn't talked to her since she finished filming."

"Since her death scene," he added, mostly to himself.

"That's right. Why do you ask?"

"I don't know." As he watched, she opened the passenger side door of the sports car, sat down, and popped open the glove compartment. She took out a bottle of prescription pills and shook two into her hand.

"What?" she said defensively. She took the pills quickly, dry-swallowing them, as though he would suddenly leap forward and try to take them from her. "It's not what you think, it's just something to help me calm down."

He shrugged, wanting to ask her what her sponsor would say about that, but keeping his fat mouth shut for a change. He liked Cox, and didn't want the actress mad at him for intruding.

Instead, he asked what he'd approached her about in the first place. "Have you...noticed anything strange going on? Anything at all? With the filming, with...Gross?"

"Everything's strange with that guy." Her voice sounded far away, distant, and it was way too early for her tiny, white, round friends to have taken her there. "He scares me a little." Her eyes grew big and focused on him again. "Wait a minute, you don't think he had anything to do with this, do you?"

"No, no," he said quickly, and excused himself.

Filming continued at a breakneck pace with its remaining cast. The loss of the star humbled everyone at the studio, but not enough to stop them from plowing ahead with production. And Gross…Davis likened him unto cockroaches after a nuclear blast: *nothing* would stop that guy. Wonder of wonders, second unit work was actually needed three more times, always overseen by either Pickerill, who became much friendlier, or Gross himself, who did not. But this work became considerably more stressful, and for a very good reason.

His cameraman was in jail.

Jared's stepmother had called to give him this information after he'd been missing for nearly twenty-four hours, but she didn't know the charges. Davis was too distracted by the blaring news of Wickersham's death in every form of media to notice his partner's absence. Since then, he'd been unable to find out anything. Wherever the cops were keeping Jared and for whatever reason, they'd allowed him no visitors and they wouldn't tell Davis what was going on. He filmed every shoot alone. Otter cried all week.

If death and imprisonment weren't hot enough issues, things weren't much better with Susan. A wall of tension had grown between them after her announcement that she'd gotten the part, and he had doubts it was all the fault of his petty jealousy.

And behind all of this chaos was a common denominator he couldn't ignore: Torsten Gross.

His shadow loomed over all the misfortunes in Davis Lowe's life. He wasn't ready to throw logic to the wind and embrace something as wacky as Jared's theories yet, but the man continued to rub him like a cheese grater, and his skin was getting raw in a few places.

# TAKE 2

The morning of the press conference—held two days shy of a week from when its subject swan-dived out of a plate glass window twenty stories above unforgiving sidewalk—was clouded over, light rains blown through in the night and more promised on the way. Usually this kind of information—casting on a third-rate studio horror film—would be divulged in a simple press release, but the interest in the case was still massive, especially considering the police had released no information. Gross was forced to cancel shooting at the studio's insistence.

Davis wanted to attend. The conference probably wouldn't answer any of his growing number of questions or soothe his mental sore spots, but it couldn't hurt.

He spent the night with Susan, sans sex, and she was up and gone by the time his alarm went off. He didn't know where she went, although they used to keep each other informed of every move. He felt a sudden moment of panic where this one lapse signaled the end, a confirmation he was losing her.

He dressed and ate alone before heading off to the studio.

Trimax issued no mandate about attendance, but Otter begged to go with him. He picked his film editor up on the way, who was, for some ridiculous reason, wearing a black armband he wouldn't take off. They arrived at the studio as the rain picked up, steel-gray clouds forming an undulating curtain across the sky. The press was arriving amidst a flourish of umbrellas and filing inside, a mixture of entertainment columnists and reporters, local news, and national affiliates.

Waiting to the left of the door, water sluicing off his forehead and down the troughs of his face, was Jared Mane.

Davis hurried through the rain to him. He resisted the urge to throw his arms around the man, but Otter was no such slave to inhibition. He wrapped Jared in a bear hug that nearly lifted him off the ground and cried, "I thought they put you in the Witness Protection Program!"

"When did you get out?" Davis tried to hold the only umbrella over all three of them.

"This morning," Jared rasped. He had bags under his eyes, a four-day growth of beard, and sunken cheeks, not to mention a voice full of broken glass. His t-shirt and jeans were dirty and wrinkled; they must be the same outfit he was wearing when arrested. "They waited to have this little shindig until they were sure they didn't wanna indict me for murder."

"*Murder?*" Otter shouted, drawing the stares of several press members. A few of them went for their cameras or micro-cassette recorders, modern day gunslingers ready to draw their six-shooters, but once they decided the three severely underdressed men wouldn't hand them another news story by shooting up the place, they continued past.

"Jesus Christ, Jared, what's going on?"

"Do you think we can get inside first? I haven't slept in four days, I busted my ass getting over here in time for this thing, and I was about to catch pneumonia waiting on you guys." He didn't wait for an answer, and Davis and Otter fell into step behind him.

A line formed in the hallway outside the pressroom so a large gentleman in a suit could check credentials. They got into line behind a waterlogged NBC delegate and his cameraman. Otter tried to question Jared as they waited their turn, but he maintained a bristled silence and told them he wanted to hear what was said inside first.

The NBC man's turn came, and he flashed a press I.D. like a police badge and started to walk through. The large man shot out an arm and stopped him.

"No cameras." The bouncer pointed two fingers at the accompanying cameraman and his shoulder-mounted rig.

"What? It's a press conference!"

"Sorry, studio's orders. No cameras or recording devices of any kind."

The NBC reporter sighed and threw up his hands. "Go wait outside George; the fascists are out in force. I'll get what I can and the anchors can read it as copy." George turned and squeezed past Otter with his camera and retreated down the hall. NBC was allowed in.

Davis nudged Jared with his elbow, who only kept his head down, not looking at the guard, so Davis caught Otter's eye instead and raised a questioning eyebrow. The film editor just shrugged his fleshy shoulders. Davis ground his teeth in frustration. He shouldn't expect anything more from a guy who believed *Men in Black* was a documentary, but this was all too weird in Davis' book, a book rapidly running out of pages.

The bouncer almost didn't let them in either, stating it was press only, until Davis made it clear to him they weren't just studio employees, they were part of Gross' personal entourage, implying they were part of the press conference. He granted the three of them admittance into a wide but shallow room filled with rows of folding chairs and a stage at the front with a podium and several seats behind it. The press took up most of the audience chairs, so they found places to stand at the back. There wasn't one camera or tape recorder in the whole place, only perturbed reporters ready to scribble quotes on notepads or whatever was handy. One unprepared individual attempted to write on a gum wrapper and the other trash from his pocket.

The studio didn't want anything that went on in this room today recorded.

*The studio…or Gross?*

He heard the director in his head, screaming in his clipped, German accent, 'No pictures!' only it wasn't like when Britney Spears or Jack Nicholson got mad at the paparazzi and asked them to turn off the camera, or even when Van Damme and Mel Gibson started getting grabby; this was instant fury, violent rejection, and—

*Panic? Maybe even fear?*

Yes, now that he thought about it, Gross had seemed frightened by the prospect of being captured on film. For the first and only time, he wasn't calm and in control. And he never wanted cell phones anywhere near the set.

Davis glanced again at Jared, trying to determine if he was mulling over the same connection.

About two minutes after they found space to occupy, Phillip Reilly took the stage from the left, followed by Torsten Gross, Katherine Wickersham's publicist…

And Susan.

# TAKE 3

Her appearance onstage was startling, to say the least. Davis almost raised his hand in greeting before realizing how inappropriate it would be. She was dressed in a dark blue business suit he'd never seen, hair gently curled and allowed to hang around her shoulders. She looked like a genuine movie star, and he felt a hard little lump in his throat as she took a seat beside Gross and the other execs, her prom dates for the event. Reilly took the podium.

Now Otter and Jared looked at him expectantly. He shook his head; she mentioned nothing to him about attending today. And it wasn't like when he did the guy thing and she talked and he blanked it out.

"Thank you all for coming," Reilly said somberly, and Davis didn't think he would be spouting any cheesy one-liner's today. "This conference will be brief, but we'll give you the little information the police have released to us. On July 12th, Katherine Wickersham did commit suicide by leaping from the twentieth story of her apartment building."

On his left, Jared snorted.

"I'll take some questions now."

A young black woman on the left side of the room raised her hand. When Reilly gestured to her, she stood and said, "Sarah Smith with *Entertainment Weekly*. Will the role held by Miss Wickersham be recast?"

Reilly glanced at Gross before answering. "The studio was willing to do just that if necessary, but Mr. Gross assured us her work on the project was complete at the time of her death. This film will be her legacy."

*Some legacy*, Davis thought. Like finishing up a five-star meal with dessert at McDonald's.

A middle-aged rocker type with short, spiky hair and horn-rimmed glasses in the center of the room raised his hand and stood without being called on. "Sidney Spitzen, *Rolling Stone*. I'm compiling a short biography of Miss

Wickersham's life. Is there any word yet on the circumstances behind her suicide?"

"Spitzen?" Davis whispered. "Isn't that the guy that called us? I thought he worked for *Variety*."

Reilly coughed once into his fist and glanced back at Wickersham's publicist, a young, prim brunette in tortoise shell glasses. She nodded. "The police provided little details on that, but they have said there was a note found at her residence hinting at severe depression after her recent accident and divorce from Mr. du Vaulier. She was seeking help for clinical depression for some time, and was on prescription medication that she stopped taking prematurely two months ago."

Spitzen wrote furiously on his notepad, but remained standing. "Uh huh, uh huh, not to debate with you, but I've already talked to several members of Miss Wickersham's immediate family, and they say she'd improved a hundred percent, that she showed no signs of depression in quite some time, especially since her return to acting."

Jared leaning forward, listening to the man eagerly.

Reilly frowned and shrugged. "Much like you, my friend, I don't make the news, I just report it." The executive got a mild laugh out of this little gem.

Spitzen muttered something that sounded suspiciously like, "You're no damn reporter, dickhead," and then said aloud, "Considering this isn't the first, uh…'mortal tragedy' Mr. Gross has suffered while filming, is Trimax afraid of what affect this will have on box office?"

Davis happened to be looking at Gross when this question was thrown out. The director's heavy brow furrowed.

"I'm sorry, I fail to see what that has to do with Miss Wickersham," Reilly sputtered. "It's a little bit early to conjecture on what kind of take we can expect from a movie that hasn't even wrapped."

"Okay then, what about the rumor that a Trimax employee was there with her when she committed suicide, and that there's a tape of the entire incident?"

The room of reporters exploded, talking amongst themselves, repeating the inquiry. Davis kept his eye on his partner, and the expression of surprise on Jared's face was one step shy of eyeballs bugged out on stalks.

Reilly laughed into the microphone, a harsh, barking sound. "Absolutely ridiculous."

Shaking his head, Spitzen sat down.

They listened to the rest of the bland questions for about ten minutes, but Davis had trouble following the flow of conversation. He stared at Susan now, trying to catch her eye, but she affected a Stepford-wife kind of pose and stared vacantly at the ceiling in the middle of the room.

When no one else stood, Reilly said, "If that's it, Mr. Gross would like to speak with you."

Reilly once again turned proceedings over to Torsten Gross, who stood glaring out at the press from beneath his thick brow before giving another practiced soliloquy free of any German sputtering. "The death of Katherine Wickersham is not only a sobering reminder of life's fleeting nature, but a staggering blow to cinema itself. I would only like to say that I will treat this, Miss Wickersham's final chapter in her body of work, with the respect it deserves." Gross stopped, and his careful frown reversed itself to become his unpleasant grin. "And, as the show must go on, I also want to use this opportunity to introduce you to the newest cast member of *Arterial Slice*, a rather talented young woman named Susan Campbell."

Susan stood up, grinning like her teeth were greased with Vaseline, and gave an abbreviated curtsey. It seemed like a moment where flashbulbs should be going off, but there were no cameras in the room.

Davis' jaw tightened. He knew now why Susan hadn't mentioned her attendance here this morning. This was nothing but a cheap publicity stunt, a chance to capitalize on a woman's death.

She already had the talent; now she was acquiring that go-getter apathy.

Gross said his goodbyes, denying a fresh volley of questions (including Spitzen, who all but stood on his chair to get the man's attention), and led the troops back out. Davis thought Susan glanced back at him on her way out, but he couldn't be sure. The reporters left in a much bigger rush than they arrived. He noticed Spitzen lingering as he reviewed his notes.

Davis turned on Jared. "All right, you heard it and you didn't like it. Now tell us what the hell is going on."

"Not here. For God's sake, not here. You guys feel like eating?"

"Look at me," Otter answered. "I always feel like eating."

# TAKE 4

The three of them went around the corner from the studio to the Fresh Market Delicatessen. They caught the place prior to the power lunch rush and were able to order quickly and find a quiet table by the front window. Traffic sloshed by, each tire spraying up a fan of water from the gutter. The rain tugged at Davis, dampening his soul and emphasizing the feeling of dread that had been slipping over him since Jared's announcement before the press conference. Davis found he wasn't all that hungry and suspected the same of Jared, who took perhaps two bites of his sandwich the entire time they were there. Otter squeezed himself into one of the narrow chairs and began to wolf down his order.

"Spill it," Davis told his partner. "Right now."

"I don't even know where to start. And none of it's going to make sense." He looked exhausted, and the fluorescent lights of the place made him look even more haggard. He pulled out a soggy cigarette from his jeans pocket and started to light it.

"I thought you quit," Otter scolded.

"It's the only thing keeping me sane."

"Maybe, but you can't smoke it in here," Davis said. "Now, start by telling us why you were arrested. I've been trying to find out for a week and I couldn't get jack shit. Who do they think you murdered?"

"They don't think, not anymore." He dropped the unlit cigarette on the table and turned to the window to watch the traffic. "It was Wickersham. Remember the close-ups she was scheduled for? I was there when she did it. I sat right there and watched her jump…" He shuddered once, hard enough to rock the table, and Davis saw tears welling up in his eyes. "Nothing I could do."

"But they just told the press no one was there," Otter said around a mouthful of corned beef. "They said it was just a rumor."

"Oh, well, if *they* said it then it must be true! Because nobody in a position of power ever lied to the American public before!" The tears dried up, retracting into the depths of his bloodshot eyes as easily as they appeared. He pierced

Davis with a hard stare of the same variety as the one he'd given him at the set last week. Because the memory was at the forefront of his head, Davis knew what the next words out of his friend's mouth would be. "Remember my theory about the blood?"

"What blood? What theory?" Otter asked.

Davis nodded. He wanted to tell Jared to shut up, to stop him before he got ramped up again, but the sickly look on the man's face stopped him. He was so tired of this, so tired of Torsten Gross being the first thing out of everyone's mouth, so tired of having to worry about the people around him.

Jared continued. "Even if Wickersham hadn't pirouetted out that window, they still would've brought me in for questioning. I gave that blood to the LAPD—maybe that was stupid considering what I suspected, but I did it—and they found out it was real and so was the tooth. *Real human tissue*, Davis, just like I told you. And they wanted to know where it came from."

Davis's stomach was suddenly queasy, and that anxious dread was increasing, making his head burn like a bad case of the flu. Otter's eyes went back and forth between them like someone following the ball at a tennis match. "What did you tell them?"

Jared swallowed before answering. All his usual humor, his carefree charm, was gone, replaced by this sullen creature. "What could I tell them but the truth?"

Davis groaned and slapped his forehead. "You told them it came from the set of a horror movie? You're lucky they didn't fit you for a straitjacket. You're gonna get us fired if you go around making accusations like that!"

"All I told them was the truth, man. What was I supposed to do? Lie? I was *under arrest*."

"What are you guys talking about?" Otter whined.

"What did they say?" Davis asked, ignoring the overweight third of their party.

Jared shook his head. "They laughed in my face, same as you did. The fact that I brought this stuff to their attention in the first place was in my favor, but that in connection with me being there when Wickersham died..."

"Why should that matter?"

"Okay, here's the crazy part, the part I don't even understand myself. The blood and the tooth...they ran the full battery of tests on it while they had me in custody. It was *hers*, man, it was Wickersham's, not just her blood type, but *her fucking DNA*, and if you can explain how that's possible, I'd love to hear it."

Davis snorted and shrugged sarcastically. "Why do I even have to explain it? Obviously they did the tests wrong, surely they could see that. I mean, we went to that shoot with the blood on Tuesday and Wickersham was still alive on Thursday when you saw her, with, I'm going to venture a guess, all of her teeth, right?"

Jared frowned but nodded.

"Then how could they accuse you of her murder if she committed suicide?" Davis knew the answer already even if he didn't want to admit it: they couldn't, but it was too suspicious not to pursue.

"I don't know. For just a second, let's leave that weirdness and talk about this 'suicide.' Did she seem suicidal when we met her?"

"I was in her presence ten minutes, during which she said two sentences. I hardly think that qualifies me to work up a psych evaluation."

"Her family didn't think she was. And the studio just said she left a note, and she goddamned well did *not*."

"How do you know? Did you go through her apartment?"

"No," he admitted. "But the woman wasn't depressed, man, she was *dazed*. She wasn't crying over her divorce like they're making it seem, she was acting more like she'd just been to the dentist for a root canal and was so high she didn't know her own name. And she said some seriously weird shit, too."

"So what, Jared? So what if she thought she was the president? How does that fit in with what you want us to believe about Gross? You're missing the fundamental concept of suicide; unless he threw her out of that window, *she killed herself!*"

Anger flared across Jared's face.

"Goddamn it Davis, you weren't there, you didn't see her! It was like she was scared, like she was trying to get away from my camera! She attacked me and then ran screaming out of a plate glass window like 9/11 all over again! Does that sound like a typical suicide to you?"

"What's typical about suicide? I know if it was my last shot at self-expression, I wouldn't do it like everyone else!"

Jared eyed him with brows drawn together. "Don't be funny, this isn't funny."

"Am I laughing, numbnuts?"

"Fine then, go back to the blood. Even if you don't want to believe it was Wickersham's, it was not a prop, it was *real*, real enough to get me arrested. You say Susan was there when they filmed it? I want to talk to her then, I want her to describe it to me, exactly what she saw."

Davis hesitated for the smallest fraction of a second, recalling that undertone in Susan's voice, but the pause dragged too long and gave his partner all the opening he needed.

"She saw something, didn't she? She told you about something. What? Tell me."

"She didn't see anything. Not anything that relates to what you're telling me. No way could that blood be Katherine Wickersham's."

"The cops saw enough of a connection between the two to keep me locked up."

"They let you out, didn't they?"

Jared slammed a fist down on the table. Their plates jumped and rattled. Otter shrank away. "The only reason I'm out is because I got the whole thing on tape. My camera was running when she offed herself, okay?"

Davis stopped, his anger put on hold, and took a breath that he blew out through his teeth. "That was true? Then why did Reilly—?"

"*Think*, Davis! They're covering it up, and they have the money to do it! I don't know if they're doing it for themselves or Gross, but Trimax does *not* want that information disseminating. All I know is that the cops were ready to connect me to her death—no matter how illogical it might be—and then Trimax swept in with bags full of money and I was set free and told to keep my mouth shut if I knew what was good for me."

"Told? By who?"

"Some Trimax legal flunkie."

"Do you have any idea what a tape like that is worth, just for the cult value alone?" Otter muttered.

"And they didn't do too good of a job covering it up if that Spitzen guy found out about it," Davis added.

"Yeah, he did his homework, all right," Jared said. "He must have contacts in the police department. He hasn't seen it or this thing would be blown wide open and I'd have media headhunters crammed up my ass."

There was one other option, and Davis felt it best to lay it out now while the subject was officially open. He braced himself and said evenly, "Maybe he *has* seen it, but it just doesn't show things like you remember. Maybe...you're imagining some of this."

Jared stood, toppling his chair, and shoved a finger in Davis' face. "Fuck you, I'm not crazy!"

"Why tell us all this then, huh? What do you want from us, Jared?"

"A little trust, you bastard! You're my only friends in the world and I don't have anybody else to go to! I admit, it doesn't sound sane, but I don't have all the answers!" He turned and stomped away from them through the restaurant.

"C'mon Jared! Where you going?"

"To find someone that'll listen. Gross is up to something and I'm not gonna let him get away with it!" He left without a backward glance, striding into the rain.

Davis sat watching him and felt like shit.

"Okay, do you wanna tell me what just happened?" Otter asked.

# TAKE 5

Davis arrived back at Susan's apartment late that afternoon, wet to the bone and dreading going upstairs. It felt as though their relationship had aged two decades in the span of the last twenty-four hours, like they'd skipped over all the good stuff, all the frenzied lovemaking and long glances, and went right to where his parents had been near the end of their marriage, where they'd found any excuse not to be in the same room together. The idea of things progressing that far with Susan was unbearable.

Still, he'd avoided leaving work. For starters, Otter wouldn't let him leave the deli until he'd told the entire story. His film editor listened silently, head bowed and eyes squinted behind his glasses. His response wasn't as bad as Davis feared, but not as rational as he would've liked.

"Do you think we should stay on this job?"

"Ot, if we want people to take us seriously in this business, we can't start reneging on contract work. Especially not over this."

"Do you really think Jared made all this up?"

"Tell me what you think, Otter. Do you understand what he's claiming? That Gross killed somebody? Or, even worse, that he somehow killed *the same person twice?*"

"It's possible," Otter said, so quietly Davis almost missed it. Since Jared's explosive departure, they'd drawn stares from other deli patrons. "We just don't know *how* it's possible."

"Sure it's *possible*, anything's *possible*, it's *possible* I'm going to win an Oscar in my lifetime, but it's also pretty damn unlikely."

"I don't know," Otter said, shaking his head. "I just don't know."

"I thought Gross was your hero. Do you think he's capable of something like this?"

"Maybe it wasn't him. Maybe it was Krieg."

"Maybe, maybe, maybe. Are our careers worth riding on maybe?"

The editor was silent, and Davis knew why. To someone like Otter, someone to whom family and friends were the most important thing in the universe, that was an easy question to answer.

When they arrived back at Lowe-Mane, a message waited on the company line. Reilly wanted to see him first thing in the morning. Otter agreed to go with him.

Davis spent the rest of the day bumming around the office, creating work to take his mind off Susan. He kept expecting her to call, perhaps just to tell him she loved him, but there was nothing, and he refused to initiate contact until he had to. He did try calling Jared, but couldn't reach his partner's cell.

"Fuck it," he whispered in the hallway outside her door, and used his key to let himself in. After all, he could speak his mind, but it all depended on how he did it. It just required subtlety and rationality.

Susan, Tonya Werdner, and Samantha Cox were sprawled around the living room, Susan and Cox sitting cross-legged on the floor, Werdner stretched across the couch, open scripts in front of them and two glasses of wine on the coffee table. All of them were smiling and laughing, the television turned to the local news in the background, where the reporter discussed the details of Katherine Wickersham's suicide.

Something in him snapped at seeing them so merry in front of the story of their castmate's death.

"Why didn't you tell me you were going to that press conference today?" he demanded. *So much for subtlety.*

All three heads turned in his direction. "Well, hellooooo sunshine," Werdner slurred.

He ignored the woman and stayed focused on Susan's large, too-innocent eyes. "I'm serious. What's going on with you?"

"What, does she have to let you know when she goes to the bathroom?" Werdner asked, lurching to her feet. "Beg for permission to be let off the leash?"

"Stay out of this," Davis snapped.

"C'mon Tonya, this is none of our business." Cox stood and slipped an arm around the other actress's waist and led her around Davis to the door. "I'll call an car for you, honey."

"I don't need a car, I'm not drunk!"

"Trust me, dear, no one would know better than me."

"I'm sorry about this. I'll see you both tomorrow," Susan called after them.

Davis waited for the door to close before barking, "It was a pretty cheap move, don't you think? Taking advantage of that woman's death to move your career up another notch?"

She stared at him coldly. "Trimax asked me to go and I went."

"You knew it was low and underhanded, that's why you've been sneaking around here the last few days, and why you couldn't even look me in the eye when you were up there!"

"You're one to give career advice!" She leapt off the floor, grabbing her script and tucking it protectively under her arm. "If Phillip Reilly had a sign-up sheet to lick dog shit off his Italian loafers, you'd be at the top!"

"Don't try to make this about me!"

"It *is* about you, Davis!" she screeched, in a voice he'd never heard. A voice he wasn't even aware her vocal cords had the potential for. He gaped at her. "It's *always* about you! Were you ashamed I was on stage at that press conference, or were you just jealous?"

"Jealous? *Me?*"

"Yes you, you shithead! You always have some way to blame everybody else for your inadequacies! 'You lied to me about the part,' 'you went to a press conference,' all that bitching just to hide that you don't have an ounce of faith in yourself! Every time someone else has something going for them you have to begrudge them, or it makes you feel like shit!"

"That…is untrue," he said.

"*Is* it? Is it, Davis? I have done nothing but support you over the entire course of our relationship and the first time I get something you want, you can't do the same for me. If you ever decide to be honest with yourself, give me a call. Until then, I think you better go home and find someone else to bully."

"Yeah, I think I better. That first one, I mean." He about-faced, stomping out the door, and turned back halfway down the hall. She stood in the doorway, with tears on her cheeks. He hadn't wanted it to go this far, he badly wanted to discuss this Jared thing with her, to warn her about Gross, and that was more important than any of this crap. "Aw, Susan—"

She stepped back and slammed the door before he could say anything further.

# TAKE 6

"Everything all right?"

He heard the question as he stepped off the elevator in the lobby. Cox was sitting on a bench with Werdner passed out against her shoulder while they waited for their Uber.

"Yeah, it…I just…" He shrugged, not knowing how to finish the sentence.

"I get it. Relationships are hard." She leaned Werdner against the wall so she could stand up. "I've been thinking about what you asked me, about Gross."

"Did you…did you see something?"

"No, nothing like that, I... Look, I'm trying really hard to stay sober. My doctor says I'm still on the uphill climb. And I don't know, maybe this was really the wrong movie for me to have taken at this point, but...I don't like this anymore." The longer she talked, the more fear stole into her voice, the thicker her Jersey accent became, until all her vowels were stretched to disproportionate length. "I film my death scene in a couple of days, and I'm scared shitless. I want away from Gross and Krieg and that awful set, and I don't know how Susan and Tonya can still be so brave about it all. Is that stupid?"

"No. I don't think that's stupid."

A honk sounded outside as their cab pulled up. Cox swiped at her eyes and went back to get Werdner to her feet. "All I can think about is getting past the next two days and then I'm through. I just feel like I'll be a lot better off once this is over."

Davis said nothing, but watched the two actresses as they made their way outside in the deepening shadows of the night.

# SCENE IX

(night shot)

# TAKE 1

The meeting with Reilly was short but in no way sweet. As soon as Davis and Otter walked into the building, he could feel the change. Instead of the usual indifference, people stared at them, pointed, and whispered, or let their eyes slide off entirely to find other things to land on, like they were prisoners on their way to ol' Sparky. Otter's hands shook as he clutched Davis' arm.

Reilly's secretary sent them right through this time, and as they started down the long hallway toward his office door, he couldn't help but again think of the Wizard of Oz, of the heroes walking down the gothic corridor toward the man they feared would zap them into oblivion.

*That makes Otter the lion, and me the scarecrow*, he thought. *Too bad our tin woodsman is MIA and Dorothy is off having cocktails with the wicked witch of the west.*

They knocked and a muffled voice told them to enter. The office looked the same as he remembered, a Victorian hunting lodge.

"Gentleman," Reilly said curtly from behind his desk. "Come in and take a seat."

They entered and each took one of the high-backed leather chairs. The executive continued to study something on the desk in front of him, and Davis took the opportunity to slap Otter's leg to make him stop fidgeting.

Reilly looked up, a steely expression on his wide features. "One of your crew members has gotten himself in a lot of trouble."

It struck Davis for the first time that Reilly had no idea how small their company was. He'd never been to the office, never asked for details. He might think Lowe-Mane was a miniature little studio, with receptionists, and multiple cameramen. Would they have still been hired if Trimax knew they were three guys working out of a rented office?

"He was arrested for murder," Reilly snapped, his tone making it sound like Davis had tried to argue. "And then he goes around badmouthing our director and, I might add, making the most ludicrous accusations against him. I just want to know, is this Mane guy a killer?"

"No!" This outburst came from Otter, an angry exhalation that brought him to the edge of Reilly's desk. "He didn't do anything! He would never hurt anybody!"

"That's not what the cops say."

"They did let him go," Davis pointed out.

"*We* let him go," Reilly corrected, with a grin that made it clear he believed the person on the receiving end was a first class moron. No more goofball cracking bad jokes; this was the shrewd prick that made millions in one of the most cutthroat industries in the world. "The studio can't afford that kind of negative publicity, so we pulled every string we could and threw money at the problem until it went away. If the movie were wrapped, I'd say go ahead, make whatever kind of crazy claims you want, a bunch of urban legends might get those asses in the seats, but we can't afford to have accusations flying that could get this project shut down."

"Doesn't sound like the police would've been able to hold him anyway. Their evidence was pretty flimsy and, if he's to be believed, Gross is the one with something to hide."

"The blood, right?" Reilly asked smugly. "The blood Mane claims came from the floor of the set? Mr. Gross has no idea about it. He allowed the police to search the premises and they came up with nothing."

"That just means it's his word against Jared's. You asked me to keep an eye on Gross for you. Why aren't you willing to believe he might be hiding something?"

Reilly stood and came around his desk, disappeared behind the Gothic chairs, and reappeared between them. He placed one hand on each of their arms—not gently—and leaned toward Davis. "Lowe," he growled through clenched teeth, "have you ever heard of something called 'money?' You know, it's that green paper I use to buy things and you use to wipe the drool from your idiot chin? This is Hollywood, you stupid son of a bitch, and the dollar is all that matters here. I asked you to keep an eye on him to make sure he was on schedule, not to accuse him of murder. I don't care if Gross fucks five-year-old's while sniffing coke and strangling grandmothers, as long as he finishes on time and under budget. If you're going to stab someone in the back in this business, you wait until *after* you're finished with them, and only when you've made damn sure you don't need them for the sequel. The studio has invested a large sum in this man. Do you know how much we stand to lose if he went to jail? I can tell you, it's a helluva lot more than a hack like you is ever going to see in your short, anonymous career."

Davis took a deep breath, staring straight ahead and ignoring the executive's jaw, which was almost in his eye socket.

Reilly straightened up and smoothed out his suit. "I could waste my time making sure this Jared Mane never works again, but he's done a good enough job of that himself. So what I want is for you to assure me he will never go near this picture or its director ever again."

Otter and Davis exploded in unison. "Mr. Reilly, you can't!"

"It would be impossible, he's our-our…best cameraman!"

"If it's impossible, then your contract is terminated," Reilly said, in a way that implied such an arrangement would be dandy and legalities be damned.

Davis looked back down. "All right, yes sir, he's off the job."

"And if he says one word about this to the press, Trimax will sue your studio so hard and fast you'll be working in the Stone Age. Now get out. I'm done with the both of you."

They stood and walked out of the office.

Otter jumped on him the minute the door swung shut. "How could you do that to Jared? How could you let that—" he lowered his voice to a raspy whisper even though they were halfway down the hall, "*asshole*—accuse him like that?"

Davis stopped before they came within hearing range of the receptionist desk. He heard the words coming, but was powerless to stop it. "Otter, nobody's accusing him. They're the ones that got him off. They're just trying to protect themselves."

"But this is going to crush him!"

"Oh c'mon, *crush* him? Nothing gets through to that guy, and that's the problem. More than likely he'll bang a few more film groupies and forget all about it. Besides, there's nothing we can do to help him. Getting ourselves fired from this job won't do anything for any of us. He'll just have to sit this one out."

"Why do you even want to keep this job? Don't you see, they're never going to make you a director, not after this!"

He was right, so right it felt like a knife sliding right between Davis' ribs and straight through to his heart. "What about the money, Otter? If we want to keep our business, we have to do some things we don't like, and this is one of them." He felt awful, sickened by his own petulance—for Christ's sake, now *Otter* had more guts than him—and he needed to do something to make this right.

Something clicked, an idea popped into his head from whereabouts unknown. It was weak and a long shot, but an effort that showed a little of that faith Jared wanted. "Maybe there is something we can do for him."

"What, put him out of his misery?"

"The only way we can help Jared is with proof. That reporter—what's his name, Spitzer or Spitzen—said Gross had been through this kind of tragedy before. Remember, at the press conference?"

"Yeah," Otter said cautiously.

"Do some research. Talk to some of your internet buddies. Find out what happened the last time somebody Gross worked with died. In fact, find out anything you can on that German weirdo."

"I'll see what I can dig up." Otter continued down the hall. "But don't expect much. If it was anything big, the media here would already have it."

"Maybe," Davis said, but he thought about Jared's claims, that the studio was keeping the real story out of the press. Just how much would a film studio be willing to hide, if the culprit brought in more money than God? Hell, Reilly had given the answer himself: quite a lot. "It's all we can do."

They'd stopped next to a conference room door along the hall to Reilly's office to have this conversation. As he hurried to catch up with Otter, it opened, and Davis looked over his shoulder to find Torsten Gross stepping out. Davis saw his face for only a second before he about-faced and goose stepped down to Reilly's door.

Davis could swear the man had grinned.

# TAKE 2

Jared's van occupied its usual space in front of the office when they arrived. Davis and Otter said nothing to one another as they went inside.

His partner was in his studio, fiddling with a camera and several of the umbrella lights. He glanced up when they came in and shook his head.

"Look, let's just forget about it, all right? I won't say anything else if you won't. The best thing to do right now is just get on with this job and finish it."

Otter's mouth squinched over to one side as he glanced at Davis.

Jared caught the look.

"What? What is it? You two firing me or something?"

"No," Davis said. "Not us."

Jared leaned against the wall, folded his arms across his chest, and waited.

"Reilly doesn't want you working on *Arterial Slice* anymore."

"He can't do that. I don't work for him."

"He'll terminate our contract."

"Davis…this is my company too. We're partners. I let you take jobs without consulting me because I trust your instincts, but you can't just shut me out."

"I'm not shutting you out. You're going to stay away voluntarily, for the good of our company."

Jared watched him, the silence between them stretching out like a soap bubble, ready to burst and spew forth vulgarity and violence. Davis couldn't imagine what a fistfight between the two of them would be like, but he was ready to move if Jared's arms should unfold and come at him.

Instead, the other man stuck out his jaw, shrugged, and turned back to his camera. "All right, then."

Otter tried unsuccessfully to stifle a breath of relief.

"Jared, we're on this job for another two or three weeks, and then we're finished. It's right back to the old days…" But Davis knew that could never be true. The old days for the Lowe-Mane Production Company were just as gone as Elvis and yo-yo's. As gone as Babe Ruth and Nirvana. As gone as—

*Davis and Susan?*

They might make a profit off this job, but it had still cost them more than it was worth.

"It's fine," Jared said, reloading film. "I get it."

"Jared—" Otter began.

"I said it was fine, Ot. Now, as far as I know, this studio is still mine, so unless you guys have anything further to say to me for the next month, I'd appreciate if you'd stay out of my face till *Arterial Slice* is wrapped."

Davis motioned for Otter to leave and followed behind, closing the door gently behind him.

"What are we gonna do?" Otter whined when they reached the front. "We can't break up over this Davis, we just can't! This place is all I have beside Mom! You guys are my family!"

"We're not breaking up," Davis said, feeling silly, but also feeling a twinge of that separation anxiety he'd felt at the climax of his parents' divorce. "Remember what I told you. Just see what you can find on Gross."

"And if I do?"

Davis shook his head. "We're going to the cops and then the media. And we're gonna nail that German son of a bitch."

# TAKE 3

The Lowe-Mane Production Company might belong, in a legal sense, to Davis Lowe and Jared Mane, but the building it inhabited was almost exclusively the domain of Terrence Ottman the Third.

While its namesakes worked on location or shot on a set, he roamed its lush blue carpeting and freshly painted hallways with the pride of a lion in the savannah. Long after they'd retired to their homes, he remained holed up in his editing room, sometimes sleeping sitting up in his leather recliner rather than go home to face his depressingly empty apartment and answer phone calls from his hypochondriac mother; a fact of which neither Davis nor Jared was aware. He knew every inch of the office, every nook and cranny and secret—everything from those porno mags Davis kept locked in his bottom desk drawer to the emergency cigarettes Jared kept hidden in a panel behind his studio door. Well, everything, that was, except for the door just past Jared's studio that led to the dark, stripped-down guts of the building, the area they hoped to expand into one day.

He loved this job, but it was about far more than a job.

He felt safe here, sheltered from a world that took one look at his burgeoning weight (pushing up past 325 now, thank you very much) and then looked away in disgust. Behind his bank of monitors and with more computer power than had been used to put the first man on the moon, there was no one to judge him. With his art, he could express all the emotion he was too shy to exhibit to the world in person.

So he stayed long after Davis left, after Jared turned off the lights in his studio and walked past without saying goodbye. He worked as the noise next door from Chang's Buffet died down and the sun fell out of the sky. When he heard Mr. Chang locking up, he took a break from playing an old version of "Space Quest 5" while he edited last week's footage to go and lock the front door.

The night beyond the glass was still and hot, the rains from the day before already dried in the strip parking lot outside. A shadow-covered Mr. Chang hurried out to his little car and drove away. Otter thumbed the deadbolt and turned off the lights in the reception area at the front. The only light in the suite now was the wan desk lamp in his office and the harsh glow of computer monitors.

He went back down the hall, trying not to look for too long at the door at the end, which never stopped frightening him. The Door at the End of the Hall, as he secretly thought of it; like a 40's era horror flick. The darkness beyond sucked at the crack at the bottom.

Okay, so it terrified him. According to Jared, most things did.

A hollow, musical *ba-lump* from his computer speaker brought him out of his nightly inspection. He peered into his office, squinting through his glasses. A tiny box had appeared in the corner of the monitor displaying his internet activities, an indicator someone had just instant-messaged him.

He plodded into the room and wiggled back into his chair. On the screen to his far left was a frozen shot of the ebullient Samantha Cox as Julie Knight, exploring the room where her fellow nurse had been murdered the day before in the land of *Arterial Slice*. One of the few tidbits of footage grudgingly surrendered by Gross. He was interspersing it with clips Davis had taken of the room itself.

*Poor Julie Knight*, he thought. Her death scene was being shot tomorrow, and then her character would join Nancy Dubose in the fictional graveyard of the mind. He rather liked the character from what he'd seen of the footage; she was written as comic relief, and he likened her death to a cinema tragedy, like when Randy bought it in the second *Scream* movie.

Next to that, his paused "Space Quest" game, in which space janitor Roger Wilco currently learned to pilot a ship. And lastly, on the monitor to which he now turned his attention, was a website displaying a photo of a nude, large-breasted woman spreading her legs and attempting to show off her spleen. He closed this window down and brought up the IM.

From RedDwarfFan970, and only one line—'Is this what you're looking for?'—and an attachment. Before he even clicked it, he knew the answer to that question.

The attachment was a newspaper article from the land of schnitzels and schnauzers. He needed only to read the headline, which was in German but easily translated through a language filter program.

*Actress Perishes in Bizarre Appliance Mishap.*

And below that, the subhead: *Latest in the Gross Curse?*

Otter read no more because it would just be a rehashing of the thirty or so other articles he'd read as they came in all afternoon. He didn't know German and was unable to find anyone in any of the German chat rooms that spoke English, so he was forced to rely on contacts with the AP and various American newspapers—all techies and web-dwellers like himself—to find the material he sought.

And found it they had. He was now enough of an expert on Torsten Gross to write a tidy little book. He might even do so, after this job was finished.

He even knew what the first line would be:

*Every single person that ever died in a Torsten Gross film has died in real life within a month of filming their death scene.*

*Not the first time*, that Spitzen guy had said at the press conference. Yeah, and today wasn't the first time the earth had turned a full circle either.

Not a single one of the twenty-two deaths (twenty-three including Wickersham) were attributable to the director; he was never so much as questioned by the authorities. And why should he? The causes of death were far ranging—everything from a rash of suicides, to car accidents, to other, more strange incidents such as the toaster mortality discussed in the article in front of him (the accompanying picture showed a police officer holding the culprit at arm's length, as though afraid it would explode)—but none of them gave even the slightest hint of murder.

His first film had been a horror movie for Morgen Pictures with a much younger but still brutish Lars Krieg as the killer. Shooting spanned no more than a month, and in the wake of the wrap, one actor and one actress—the only victims in the piece—were dead, she of a three car pile-up on the Autobahn in which she was the cause, and he of a self-inflicted bullet in the brain. The same happened after his next movie a little over four years later, leaving three dead this time. In all cases, death occurred after the thespian in question finished filming all of their scenes.

The deaths were viewed as coincidental at first, because again, there was absolutely no way Gross could be involved. They actually helped the movies sell, pushed them from low-budget slashers into country-wide blockbusters by giving them a spooky urban legend side note, like that supposedly dead munchkin in the *Wizard of Oz*, or the ghost in the background of *Three Men and a Baby*. Then, as the man's career continued to spiral upward over the next two decades, they became a joke. Someone in the German film industry dubbed it the 'Gross Curse,' a title the director stubbornly refused to comment on.

The dilemma was obvious: the foreign press kept a constant eye on him, the film studios were wary despite the fact his pictures brought in money faster than their accountants could count it, and the actors were finally buying into the superstition and refusing to work with him.

Gross needed a way to start fresh.

And he'd found it right here, nestled in the hills of La-La Land.

# TAKE 4

Did Trimax know about the Gross Curse when they'd given him the job? The American media certainly hadn't caught wind of it—all except for Spitzen, if the Curse was even what he was referring to with his question—or Katherine Wickersham's death would've gotten ten times the coverage it received. That in itself wasn't hard to believe, once you saw the big picture; Gross might be a god with stateside geeks and pop culture junkies like Otter, but what average American could name even one actor from the modern mainstream German film industry? A story like that wouldn't be picked up by the AP because their audience wouldn't care, and with Gross only making one film every five or six years, the furor had time to die down in between, making them look like isolated incidents to all but those following his career closely enough to connect the dots. Now that he knew what to look for, Otter had found several conspiracy theory bloggers and indie movie websites that knew all about the Curse.

And of course, the studios were always in the thick of things, squashing controversy wherever they could. In a country where the press was neither as free nor as rabid as America, the Gross Curse became more of a cautionary whisper than an actual, documented phenomenon.

In any case, someone would tumble to it; something this big couldn't be kept secret for long no matter how much Trimax wanted it to, especially with an American actress involved. Otter himself had gone a long way toward putting it on the radar with his online inquiries today. And then let's see Gross try to do to the legitimate press what he'd done to those paparazzi.

Otter brought up another waiting file from his task bar, this one a video clip. He'd watched it twenty times tonight and determined it held no further clues, but he wanted to see it again even now. It was a news clip from Germany more than twelve years old, of the young actress from the movie snippet he'd showed the others. Her name was Helga Schultz, and in the clip she was interviewed by some talk show host four days after filming her death scene in *Kill Now, Die Later* and two days before her real death by stumbling into traffic. It was all in German, but he didn't need to understand the words to get what he needed.

There was absolutely no expression on the young woman's face. She looked like she'd been drugged and propped in her chair. Utterly listless and unresponsive, the talent she'd exhibited in the film evaporated. The host seemed put off as he questioned her. He would have to show this to Jared and ask if it was a fair approximation of Katherine Wickersham's behavior before jumping out her window.

Another odd thing struck him as he researched: he could find plenty of photographs of Lars Krieg and even a complete biography, but no picture taken of Torsten Gross, ever. No school pictures, no family pictures—he'd apparently dropped out of the sky before showing up on the doorstep of Morgen Pictures—and every article on the director was conspicuously free of any recorded image of its subject, which explained why Otter had no mental snapshot before meeting him at the party. He avoided premieres and all social events where press might be in attendance, such as Katherine Wickersham's funeral. Even during the height of his controversy in Germany, the director managed to stay out from in front of the camera.

Honestly, Otter had no idea what to make of any of it. He tried to think about it rationally, the way Spock would, because letting his emotions intrude (mostly just the cold edge of mounting fear at this point) would only distract him from reaching a conclusion.

Unlike Davis and even, to a certain extent, Jared, Otter was not limited by the boundaries of logic, reality, or, depending on how you looked at it, sanity. He could come up with plenty of ways Gross might be doing this, everything from warlock magic to alien mind control rays.

*More pressing matters than 'how,' Otter.* That inner voice belonged to Davis, the person he trusted above all others, and it always served to calm him when he got this worked up. *Like, for example, if this 'Curse' thing is real...*

Otter glanced at the monitor on the left, of the frozen picture of Samantha Cox, her mouth hung askew in that funny way people have when you pause them in the middle of conversation and suddenly a syllable designed to be displayed on the human face for only microseconds stretches into infinity. That was one person who didn't know about the curse, and it was information she might like to have before tomorrow.

A shuddering sigh ripped out of his throat.

He didn't want to be responsible for this any longer. His brain hurt thinking about it.

*And you're scared.* This slightly snide accusation was all Jared.

All right, so what if he was? Sure, a lot of silly stuff scared him—aliens, monsters, the presidency of Donald J. Trump— but this was no longer his imagination, this was an actual Scooby Doo mystery, and everybody knew you didn't leave the investigating to the chickenshit, sugar-addicted canine with a speech impediment.

You got Fred and Velma.

He picked up the phone and dialed Davis' cell, the only way he could be reached when he wasn't at Susan's. He got the voicemail after five rings and left a message, striving to keep his voice calm, saying he'd found urgent information. After a second's hesitation, he called Jared's cell and did the same. If he'd known Sam Cox's number, he might have gotten up the courage to call her, too.

So that was it. All up to him until morning.

He couldn't sit here all night and think about it. Might be good to go home and sleep in his bed, perhaps even call his mother and listen to her latest illness and assure her he didn't have cancer. He powered down all his CPU's and squeezed out of his chair. The desk lamp was the last thing to go, and he got as close to the door as possible before stretching back to turn it off. He was plunged into soupy darkness.

Otter punched the button to lock the door of his office on his way out and then jiggled the knob for good measure. It was pitch dark in the hallway now, the closest light the halogen bulbs in the parking lot and those were too far away to reach into the suite's depths. He turned in the direction of the front door and put a hand on the wall to guide him out.

He'd taken only two steps before a piercing light blazed in his face.

# TAKE 5

It tore through his eyeballs, forcing the lids down, and still he put up a hand for added shielding. The darkness jumped away, scurrying to find hiding places, shadows thrown into stark relief behind him.

Instant fear, clammy and cold, slipped under his skin like a medicinal dose from a syringe.

"Who's there?" He hated the puling edge to his voice. He squinted through his fingers, trying to pick out the source of the light, but it was too bright, too all encompassing. He felt pinned by it, like an escaped con spotted by the searchlight from the guard tower.

"Greetings, *mein freund*," a voice thick with accent purred cheerfully. "You are the one they call Otter, correct?" 'The vun,' it said, and his name became 'Ottah.' Unmistakably German, and Otter needed no other clues to know who stood at the end of the hall.

He felt his heartbeat, under considerable strain most of the time anyway, jump an extra hundred beats a minute.

"Mr. Gross?" His eyes adjusted to the light at last, and he could make out a gaunt silhouette, the source of the brilliance mounted on a large box perched on the thin man's shoulder.

A camera. A movie camera. One of the mobile, battery-operated rigs. It looked heavy enough to crush the old man.

"What-what are you doing here, sir? Davis already left for the day."

"But my boy, I've come to see *you*."

"M-m-me?" he stammered. A month ago he would've been thrilled to be in this man's presence. Now…serious gooseflesh time. "I'm sorry, all I can do is make an appointment for you."

"You're very intrepid, you and your partners, *ya*? One of you investigating me, the other telling wild stories to the police. Yes, you're all very…troublesome."

Otter took a step backward, away from the director.

"Troublesome? Oh, I-I've never been troublesome. My mother always said I was a good kid, never gave her any trouble."

"Good, you say?" He could hear the smile in those words. "In that case, I have a present for you Otter. The best gift one can bestow upon a fellow human being."

Otter couldn't swallow, his throat had forgotten how, and for a moment he thought he would choke. The office, his refuge, no longer felt quite so familiar; that bright light turned it into an alien landscape. He backpedaled further. His heel fetched up against something solid and he realized he was at the Door at the End of the Hall, a feat you couldn't have paid him for an hour ago. "What's that?"

The light at last lowered, freeing the shadows, which crept out like oozing blood, and in the residual glow he could see the director's hawk-like nose and feverish eyes floating in the murk.

"Why, *tod* of course. Death." He smiled, but there was nothing natural about it, it was insane and worse, far from human. That fear, uncomfortable but at least manageable, ratcheted up to wild, eye-popping terror.

A larger shadow stepped from behind Gross, filling the end of the hallway.

Otter gasped.

# TAKE 6

Lars Krieg came forward, and Otter's paralysis broke at the sight of the muscle-bound form bearing down on him, wearing his tan jumpsuit from the movie. The light from the camera swung back up, but Krieg blocked it, throwing his gargantuan shadow in front of him to land on Otter.

He turned, grabbed the knob to The Door at the End of the Hall, and flung it open without hesitation. The terrors were *behind* him after all; any beast waiting for him in the back of the building would play second fiddle to the ones that had come in the front door.

The darkness hit him first; if he thought the office was pitch black when the lights were out, it was nothing compared to what lurked behind The Door. Next came the heat, a blistering wave that leapt out to strangle him. Lastly was the smell, the stink of stale air mixed with something distantly rotten, like fruit gone bad.

Otter plunged in, swimming through the stifling air, and slammed the door shut behind him. The light from the camera disappeared, sealing him into this tomb. He turned and continued running, a line of sweat popping out along his forehead. He again put one palm to the wall as a guide, as he did when leaving for the night. His breath wheezed, though not strictly from fear; this was why his momma told him to haul his big fat ass to the gym every once in a while.

*Ironically, being chased by a crazy German director and his murderous cohort is probably the one thing she* didn't *worry about,* he thought, and suppressed the urge to laugh hysterically. He ducked into the first open door on his left, pressing up against the other side of the wall.

His breath came in sloppy, hiccupping gasps. Everywhere was midnight black, a starless void where direction was meaningless, but he dared not hunt for a light switch.

A deliberate footstep sounded in the threadbare carpet outside. They'd come after him. Or rather, Krieg had; the light from the camera didn't follow. Otter waited, straining to hear, and released his breath only when he heard another noise further down the hall, moving away from him.

A back door to the office existed somewhere, he knew. It stood right next to Chang's rear entrance, meant to allow the owners of the suite access to the dumpster behind the shopping mall.

Otter slipped to the very edge of the door, deliberate and stealthy (or as stealthy as 325 pounds of pure blubber can be), and listened so hard his eardrums throbbed. The silence in the office was far too thick to be genuine; the stillness of too many people trying too hard not to make a sound, like when you played indoor hide-and-go-seek as a kid.

Krieg had passed by and was somewhere between him and the back exit. Should he go toward the front? What if Gross waited that way? No doubt he could take the old man, but one squawk in German and he would never outrun Krieg.

Otter took a deep breath and stepped into the hall.

# TAKE 7

Both directions were equally black, but he turned left, toward the uncharted back of the building. This was *his* turf after all, and just the fact that he knew a back door existed gave him an edge. If he could slip past Krieg in the dark, he was home free.

Otter felt along both sides of the hallway for the next available hiding place. Another door opened onto darkness across the hall and he dove in, sure his elephantine steps were giving him away. He paused, listened again, then popped back into the hall before he lost his nerve, scurrying another few feet.

A hand slid around his wrist in the dark, prompting a high, stuttering scream from his raw nerves. The mitt felt big enough to engulf his arm from the elbow down. It pulled, swinging him around, then let go of him like a shot put.

Otter rebounded off the wall, smashing his shoulder against the plaster. The blinding light from the camera blazed from his left, harsh and intrusive, chasing away the darkness and any chance of hiding in it. Otter didn't try to block it this time. He was caught, trapped between them, and then Krieg's arms encircled him from behind, drawing him into a constrictive embrace. The actor was the only person who'd ever been able to get his arms all the way around Otter's girth.

Gross spoke rapidly in German. He came closer, the three zillion watt camera bulb growing in Otter's face, like he always imagined a UFO light would when he had his inevitable close encounter. He could hear the whir of the mechanism now, and knew it was really recording. "Oh now, Mr. Otter, I don't understand the fuss. You always wanted to work with me, *ya?*"

"Please, sir," he begged. Krieg's arms—one on his upper chest, the other his waist—were like iron, and Otter kept thinking of all the damage his hands had pretended to do, to Katherine Wickersham, to poor Helga Schultz. No one ever murdered by these hands in front of a camera was still above ground these days.

*And Gross has a camera on you right now...*

Even in his terror, Otter saw the implication.

"Please, you don't have to do this, I don't know anything!"

Gross was close to him, just behind that light, and he bent over until his face hovered just above Otter's. "But I only want you to give a message to your friends, one even they can't miss." There was a weird undercurrent in his voice Otter felt sure he must be imagining, an electric, insectile buzzing that pulsed in his temples. Gross purred dramatically in his rolling accent, "Tonight, I make you…a *star!*"

Otter bent his neck, buried his face in the arm across his chest, and bit down hard.

Krieg growled in pain, his grip loosened, and Otter broke free, shoving Gross and his camera out of the way and sprinting for the front of the office. The light disappeared for a moment as the director swung around and then was at his broad back once more.

The hallway ahead was empty, the door back to the land of Lowe-Mane open and welcoming, and Otter chanced one look back to see how close his pursuers were.

When he faced forward again, the door was gone.

In place of the long hallway he'd just seen with his own two eyes was nothing but a dirty blank wall matching the rest of the suite, the corridor ending abruptly, as if the exit had never existed in the first place. His arms pinwheeled, but he had no room to stop. He rammed face-first into the new wall. His bulbous nose crunched painfully; there was an angry crinkling noise as his glasses shattered, several shards of glass slicing into his cheeks hard enough to draw blood. The bent frames dangled from one ear.

Otter sat down heavily in the floor, staring up at where the hall now stopped. He put his fingers to his face, feeling the trickling blood mixed with the tears and sweat that coursed down his cheeks.

He heard Gross speaking to Krieg in German, and then the giant's hands were on him, forcing him to lay back against the floor of the hallway.

*It's only pretend, it's only pretend*, he thought desperately, as Krieg removed a foot long carving knife from a sheath on his belt.

And then the pain started, and Terrence Ottman the Third could only scream.

# SCENE X

(wide angle)

# TAKE 1

Davis' apartment was only two rooms, the front door opening onto a rectangle with bed and couch on one side, dresser and TV on the other. When his cell phone woke him around nine, he discovered he'd missed the bed the night before and was lying fully dressed between it and the couch, on the rock hard layer of padding that served as the carpet; not an easy feat in a space where the bed took up most of the room.

He sat up, a headache pounding at his temples hard enough to make his eyes water. He remembered drinking last night at a bar up the street and almost coming home with company: a brunette with great legs that was all over him until he started whining about Susan.

He searched the floor for his phone, found it almost under the dresser, and pressed the call button just before it turned over to his voicemail.

"Davis?" Jared asked.

"Yeah, what's up?" His own voice sounded fuzzy.

"Did Otter call you last night?"

"I don't know. If he did, I didn't talk to him. Why?"

"Because I have a pretty frantic message from him on my phone. Said he had urgent information for us."

Davis stood, wincing as the room spun. "Aw, shit."

"What?"

"I asked him to look into Gross' background. See if he could find out anything weird about him. Maybe he came up with something."

"You did *what?*" The phone rattled in his hand on the last word. Or maybe that was just the bones in his skull.

"Don't yell! Jesus man, we were doing it for you!"

"You should've stayed out of this, Davis. I told you, just go on with the job. I had things under control. You really shouldn't have gotten Otter involved."

"Oh, quit talking like a fucking spy. You were the one that wanted us to follow you on your damn hunch or feeling or whatever."

"Not anymore. Now I was just looking out for you guys. The wheels are already in motion."

"What 'wheels?' What are you talking about?"

"Just meet me at the office. We've got to find Otter."

The phone went dead, and Davis wobbled across the room to find a fresh pair of clothes.

# TAKE 2

He arrived at the office before Jared.

Otter's car was in the lot, parked in its usual spot. Davis sat in his own vehicle for a minute, letting the hangover settle behind his eyeballs. Everything looked perfect and serene, a typical day, birds chirping and sun shining.

So why the flutter of something dark in his chest?

*Because you're letting Jared's bullshit get to you.*

But that wasn't all of it. He'd listened to the message from Otter on the way to the office, and it *did* sound frantic.

He got out and walked to the glass front door, but it didn't budge under his hand when he pulled on it.

Locked.

The front door was *never* locked when he got here. Otter always opened it by eight o'clock.

He dug for his key ring but couldn't even remember which key he needed. He was trembling when he finally got the lock undone and stepped into the building.

The lights were off, as they'd been the day they surprised him with champagne he hadn't deserved, but he didn't think a party waited in the building today. He flipped the switches beside him to turn on the fluorescents in the reception area. They flickered, growing brighter by lurching degrees.

"Otter? Otter, where are you?"

Davis stepped across the reception area and stopped at the opening of the hallway beside the desk. All the doors were closed except two.

The door to Otter's editing room stood wide open.

The door at the end of the hall was open just a crack. He'd never seen it open. He knew Otter was secretly terrified of it.

Davis continued down the hall, heart thudding in his ears. He could sense that wrongness in the air, it wasn't his imagination, and dammit where the hell was Jared?

He stopped at the edge of Otter's door.

Peered around the corner.

And sighed in exasperation.

His fat childhood friend and current film editor sat in his usual spot, hands on the keyboard, staring at the monitors, one of which showed *Star Trek*, the next a cooking show, and the last a porn website he would undoubtedly be embarrassed to be caught perusing. Davis was so relieved at finding him he vowed to not even tease him about it.

"Otter, man, what's up? Why was the door locked?"

The other man didn't answer. He didn't even jump at the sound of Davis' voice and try to click off the porn site.

*He's asleep*, Davis thought.

*No, he's dead*, the cynical critic in him corrected.

But Davis could see him breathing, his back gently rising and falling on the tides of his lungs. Plus he sat bolt upright, and Davis didn't know too many people that fell asleep or died without their head at least lolling.

Davis started forward. "Otter? Hey Otter, wake up, rise and shine, it's mor—"

The computer chair abruptly swiveled around to face him, and Davis flinched away from the horror within it.

His film editor wore a light blue Monty Python shirt, depicting the rabbit from *Holy Grail*. It looked like someone had run the front through a shredder. It was slashed and ripped, the entire area on his bulbous stomach stained a deep burgundy.

Blood.

Blood everywhere, blood so dried it had stiffened the material.

"Jesus Christ, Otter," he whispered. "Are you okay? What happened?"

Otter again stayed silent. His initial appearance had jarred Davis so much he hadn't noticed the slack-jawed expression on the man's face, the half-open eyes and hanging jaw, and, dear God, was that a runner of drool about to leak from the corner of his mouth?

"Otter? *Terrence?*" he asked, using the name for the first time since junior high. "Talk to me. What happened, huh? Where did all this blood come from?"

"Da...vis?" He sounded out the two syllables as though speaking an alien tongue.

"Yeah, it's me Otter. What happened? Where are your glasses?"

Otter slowly turned back to the computer bank and raised a hand as if to point. But the wrist was limp, and he ended up jabbing his arm in the direction of the monitors. "No," he said, the single word like the communication of a baby, limited vocabulary attempting to convey leagues of meaning. "Feel not...good."

What did that mean? He was sick? What did that have to do with the monitors? Why was he acting so sluggish, so...

*Drugged? So doped he doesn't know his own name?*

The sudden connection to what Jared had told him was like a mental slap in the face. Davis retreated quickly, away from Otter, out of the room, his brain racing, fear rising like a bubble in his throat...

A hand fell across his shoulder.

# TAKE 3

Davis spun, ready to start throwing punches at the demon his mind conjured, but Jared pushed his arm down. "Hey, man, it's me, calm down." He watched Davis for a second, saw his wild eyes, panting breath. "What happened?"

"Otter. Something's wrong with Otter."

"Let me see him." He pushed past Davis into the studio. Davis waited in the doorway while Jared tried to talk to him, then spun him around and pulled up his shirt to examine the smooth, unbroken skin beneath. The only response Otter made was to groan and gesture to the porn website and ask, "Pretty?"

Jared's hair fell over one eye, but the other was sufficient to convey his anger when he looked up at Davis. "Gross fucking got to him."

"That's stupid." Almost an automatic response, like an out-of-office reply email.

"Katherine Wickersham acted just like this before she… died."

"Yeah, but you still haven't convinced me Gross had anything to do with her either. I mean, first of all, there's the question of *why?* Why come after Otter?"

"Maybe he found something out on the little expedition you sent him on. Or maybe it's retaliation for me sticking my nose where Gross doesn't want it."

Davis started to answer, but the words caught when he thought of Torsten Gross stepping out of the side passage on the way to Reilly's office, the man's narrow face stretching into a knowing smile.

"But…does he have some sort of drug? Something that makes them act like this?"

"I don't know," Jared said. He straightened and strode past Davis and into the hallway. "But I'm gonna find out."

"How?"

"Do you know what today is, Davis?"

He almost said Thursday, but the idea of trying to joke right now made him physically ill. He shook his head.

"They're filming Samantha Cox's death scene today. Which means in a matter of hours she could be a vegetable just like Otter here. So I'm going to the set to stop them, and I'm going to hunt down Gross and beat the answers out of him if I have to." He turned to walk out.

Davis ran after him, grabbed him by the shoulder. "Hey, woah man, you can't go down there! You go near that set and Reilly is gonna come down on us with the wrath of God!"

Jared spun, fury blazing in him so bright it was like an aura standing out from his body. "Don't you get it, Davis? This job is over. We're talking about Otter's *life* now. He is going to die if we don't get some answers."

"Die? You don't really think…he'll *die*…do you?"

"Listen, I know some stuff I haven't told you, and I don't have time to explain it right now. If all you're concerned about is your precious contract and your shitty company, then fine, I quit, I'm no longer an employee here. Otter means more than that to me." He grabbed Davis by his upper arms, and pulled him close until their eyes had no where to look but in each others. "But understand me, you shit, you've got to *watch* him. Don't let him out of your sight, don't let him near anything dangerous until I find a way to reverse this. Tie him down if you have to. It's the least you can do."

Davis nodded, burning with guilt and fear. "Call the police then. If it's as bad as you think, call the police."

"We don't have time. They won't believe us, and no doctor is gonna be able to help him. Gross has gotten away with whatever he's doing for too long." Jared released him. He hurried toward the front of the office and shouted, "Watch him!" over his shoulder before he disappeared through the door.

Davis turned back to Otter. He stared from one monitor to the next, touching the keyboard like he'd never seen one before.

"I should call the police," he muttered. He should, even if Jared said not to, and what would it hurt to have a doctor examine Otter? He could sense his thoughts speeding up, panic taking over, but didn't try to stop it.

*Susan, you have to call Susan.*

That seemed right. He had to tell Susan what was going on, she would want to know.

*And you have to warn her.*

That too, warn her away from Gross like he should've done after their fight, because she had a death scene too, and if he lost her…

The thought of her sitting somewhere, slack-jawed and drooling, sent him into overdrive.

Davis scrambled in his pocket for his cell phone, turning away from Otter, then stepped out into the hallway so he could talk without the other man hearing.

Then a keyboard came down on the back of his skull, and all Davis knew for a while was darkness.


# TAKE 4

The van had filled with cigarette smoke before Jared even got halfway to the warehouse set for that piece of trash *Arterial Slice*. It hung in the air like a miniature smog cloud, its own ecosystem.

He had no plan, other than what he'd told Davis; he would find Gross and beat the man if he had to, torture him until he divulged his secret, until he told him exactly *what the fuck was going on*. He didn't care if he went to jail afterward; he believed—*knew*—Otter's life was at stake, that if they didn't reverse whatever had been done to him, their film editor would find an equally tall building to practice high-diving from, or cross the freeway during rush hour, or commit some other form of grisly hara-kiri.

Just like all the other poor schmucks Gross had worked with over the years.

Jared had gotten a top flight education in Torsten Gross 101 from his new friend.

He arrived at the warehouse on Crenshaw twenty minutes after he left Lowe-Mane. The building looked deserted, but that told him nothing. He picked up his cell phone, considered calling Davis, but anger stopped him. He didn't know where things would go between the two of them, but suspected that after this weird business was through, there would be a parting of ways.

He knew his friend had been trying to sell out for a long time despite Jared's every attempt to steer him straight; maybe he just needed to see how lonely it was at the top.

For a brief moment, he held the phone and considered calling his new friend, the only one willing to believe his story. He didn't know what he would tell this person either and besides, Cox might already be inside shooting. He stowed the phone in his breast pocket instead, for easy access if the police were needed after all.

Jared got out of the van and tied his hair back in a ponytail with a rubber band from the ashtray. He opened the rear door, searching through months of accumulated fast food wrappers for a weapon, like an archeologist sifting through layers of earth. Under a pile of Taco Bell wrappers, circa eight months ago, he came across a hollow steel bar he'd used to steady a camera on a shoot he and Davis completed two years ago. Filming some inserts for a low budget war film, both of them stoned, and they ended up laughing so hard they couldn't stand up for half an hour.

Thinking about that caused a sharp pain in his stomach.

He hefted the bar in his hand; short, not much longer than his forearm, but heavy and solid. Should do the trick even on Krieg.

He crossed the parking lot and entered the building through the same door they always came through on trips to this godforsaken place. His heart sent spikes of adrenaline through him, urging him to run pell-mell into danger, but he forced himself to stand still and wait. He heard what he wanted almost instantly, the sound of a door slamming somewhere deep in the building.

And then a scream.

Now he took off without hesitation, slamming through entrances at random, heading in the direction his ears placed the commotion. He passed through the last of the completed sets, and ended up back in the rough parts of the building.

Jared had just entered the middle of a narrow, darkened hallway, corrugated steel on both sides, when a shriek of terror came from right in front of him, on the other side of the wall. He recoiled from it at first, the metal bar almost slipping from his fingers, and then charged forward. He pounded on the wall with one clenched fist.

"Hey!" he shouted. "Hey, who's there?"

He sensed the hesitation from the other side. "H-hello?" A female voice. A familiar one. Jared looked up and saw the wall ended in a small gap between where the support struts joined the ceiling; their voices only had to pass over the steel, rather than through it.

"Samantha? Samantha Cox?"

"Oh God, *yes!* Help me, please, you've got to help me!"

"What's going on?"

She was in tears when she spoke again, the chipper, upbeat rhythm to her words gone, that Jersey accent showing through. "Krieg is crazy! He's trying to kill me!"

His grip on the bar tightened. "Where is he?"

"I don't know, he keeps chasing me, and Gross won't call

a cut!" She halted while she fought her way through a sob. "I don't even know if this is in the script!"

None of this had been in the script, not for a very long time, and people were just beginning to wake up and smell the bitter coffee he'd been drinking. "Where are you?"

"I don't know, in some kind of hallway! I'm not even on the set anymore! I'm…I'm lost!"

"Keep heading forward and try to find some way to get to me! I'll do the same!"

"Okay," she cried.

He turned left and moved quickly forward. This section of hallway held no inlet to get to her side, so he opened the door at the end of the passage, where a short room sat empty of everything but dust and grime. Another door on the right, and he went through it. He could hear her clattering footsteps somewhere close by.

From farther off, a door opened, squealing on rusted hinges.

Cox screamed, her voice echoing in the building. "*Heeeeelp, heeeeeelp, he's coming!*"

Jared ran faster, pushing through rooms and hallways, the gray walls a blur. This place was a maze; he had real trouble believing its original design had such labyrinthine construction. Several times he could swear he came full circle, but when he entered the next room, it was always different.

How much of this place did Gross *really* rebuild? Not just the clean, sterile, gleaming hospital sets, but how much of the *building?*

*It's all one big set*, he thought. Even here, in the parts that were supposedly abandoned for God-knew-how-long, it all felt fake, like bad stage design on an old Doug McClure movie, *The People-Island-Dinosaurs that Time Either Forgot or Didn't Like Very Much.*

He burst into a passage only minimally better lit than those previous, aglow from flickering fluorescents in the ceiling. A long, rectangular room stretched out in front of him, split lengthwise by a sturdy floor-to-ceiling chain link fence on his right that made absolutely no sense, the kind of contrived situation that always showed up in horror movies. Three other doors led in this room, two on the other side of the fence, unreachable through the obstruction.

"That's…that's just *retarded*," he muttered. His jeans and shirt were drenched in sweat from his run, his hair unraveled from the rubber band in a sweaty tangle. "There's no reason for a room like this." The sense of being herded like a rat in a maze—and even more, of being watched—was thick.

He waited, panting, trying to figure out what to do now. The only door on this side of the fence would take him away from the actress's general direction.

Jared was still debating his next move when the door to his right burst open and Cox ran into the room.

She sprawled to her knees, weeping, and spun around to slam the door. She wore her nurse's uniform, minus cap, and bled from a gash on her forehead. He knew special effects, goddamn it, and this looked *real*. She caught sight of him on the other side of the fence and stumbled forward, twining her fingers through the metal links. "Oh my God, you're from second unit! Please, please help me, he's coming!"

He went to her, leaning down until his face was right on the other side of the fence from her ragged breathing, and as he did, he noticed something curious. Something that explained the sensation of being watched.

On her side of the fence, in the far corner of the room, tucked up high under a steel crossbeam where it was virtually invisible, was a camera. A red light like a tiny eye indicated it was running.

Gross had wired the whole fucking building.

He looked back at Cox, meeting her gaze directly. "Is this real?" he demanded.

"Huh?"

"Are you acting right now, or are you serious?" He was aware of slipping into the same doubt he'd warned Davis about, but he could suddenly see all of this being some radical, in-character, single-take technique Gross insisted on (or just another drugged out episode of Cox's life) and he needed to know he wasn't making a fool of himself.

She looked at him with shocked disgust. "No!" He had trouble believing anyone was a good enough actress to fake such outrage.

"All right, tell me what happened."

She glanced back at the door she'd come through, shaking hard enough to rattle the chain links. He closed his fingers over hers on the fence. "God, I need a drink." Her Jersey accent came out strong, turning *God*, into *Gwad*. "I picked a great time to hop back on the wagon, huh?"

"Tell me," he repeated.

"We were running my death scene and Krieg…he-he just starting beating me! Really hitting me! And Gross let him do it! That son of a bitch told me to go with it! Go with it, can you believe that?" She spoke fast and Jared let her ramble this time, so long as she was on topic. The answer was close, he could feel it, like a man searching for a light switch in the dark, the mystery almost solved. "I managed to get away, and I thought he would call cut, but Krieg just kept coming after me. Even after we were off the set!"

"We're not off the set yet," Jared said, looking back over her shoulder at the camera. The red light stared at him balefully. He was beginning to understand, some of this was coming clear when cross-referenced with the information from his new friend. If they could get off the set, away from the cameras…

"We have to get out of the building. Keep moving ahead until you find some way to me or—"

The door beside her crashed open.

# TAKE 5

Samantha Cox shrieked, a torturous noise from deep in her throat. She ripped her fingers away from his and pushed off from the fence, stumbling backwards and working her way across the room.

"Run!" he shouted. She may die, but he would be damned if he'd let it be because she slipped into a horror stereotype. "Don't look back, just *run!*"

She turned and fled through the door at the far end.

Krieg tore into the room with a single-mindedness that was terrifying for its animal simplicity. Now he carried a butcher's knife.

"*Hey!*" Jared bashed the steel bar against the chain link fence, jarring his arm all the way to the shoulder and creating a jangling racket. "*Leave her alone, you motherfucker!*"

The behemoth stopped, turned ninety degrees to face him. And smiled.

Cold ribbons wove through Jared's skin. He stopped rattling the fence and froze. Some part of his own sanity dropped away as he stared into that mad smile with its perfect white teeth and pitted lips.

Krieg raised the knife, slashed at the air almost playfully, and took off after the actress.

Jared ran through the door behind him, back into the dim maze of hallways. He moved without any direction this time, totally at random, panic overriding his better judgment. He no longer knew if he sought a way to save Cox and Otter, or merely to find a way out of this madhouse.

Time passed. He tried his phone while still moving, found it lacking signal in the bowels of the cavernous warehouse, and slipped it back in his breast pocket. A minute later, he burst into another room so hard and fast he came close to vaulting over the railing in front of him. He leaned against it to catch his breath, rivers of sweat flowing off his forehead. He now stood on a narrow catwalk that ran around the top of this square room.

This place was some kind of electrical room; ancient wires ran in bundles all over the walls, junction boxes set at irregular intervals. A ladder built into the other side of the catwalk led down to a bare concrete floor. He could see cameras in here too, one mounted on the ceiling and at least two from the underside of the catwalk. Through a pair of double doors on the bottom level, he thought he could see daylight.

Motion and sound below him. Cox came into view from under the catwalk and sprawled across the dusty floor in a pathetic heap.

He yelled something, a wordless noise of recognition, and then moved fast to the ladder on the opposite side. When he was halfway around the room, he stopped to look back.

Krieg entered and set upon her before he could even shout a warning. She lay frozen in his shadow, black hair in a puddle around her head, reduced to a shell by the knife hefted above her.

"*Get off her!*" Krieg didn't spare Jared a glance as he reached the ladder and started down, looking over his shoulder the whole time.

The butcher knife descended with a whistle as it split the air.

And it was no goddamn special effect as the blade cleaved crosswise into her neck, just above the pristine white collar of her nurse's uniform, sinking into the vulnerable flesh with a meaty *thunk*. She tried to scream—a jerking, thrusting movement of her head and gaping mouth that was like… well, as disgusting as it sounded, like she was giving head—but that first stroke had hit something vital, and she made a bubbling, choking noise, then coughed a scarlet mist into the killer's lumpish face. Her hands batted weakly at him. Krieg wrenched the knife free and drove it in again, in nearly the same damn spot, creating a divide in her delicate neck that looked as big as the Grand Canyon. The life went out of her in a rush as a the torrent of blood gushed from the wound.

Jared heard himself babbling as he came down the last few rungs of the ladder, weeping at the violence and his own failure. He held the metal bar in two sweaty, trembling hands. Everything else was forgotten now, and the world seemed much simpler, reduced to the single act of murder he'd just witnessed. He reached the cracked concrete floor of the room and turned to face Krieg over the body of his victim.

"Get off her," he repeated. Some of the strength came back to him, and he swung the bar as he would at a mad dog. "*Get off her or I'm gonna bash your head in!*"

Krieg stood mechanically, grinning, and pulled his weapon out of Cox's flesh with a thick, slurping sound. His dead eyes never left Jared's. Blood covered him across the chest of his jumpsuit from the arterial slice the movie promised. The maroon pool from Cox was still spreading around her.

He couldn't take Krieg, he knew that now, not with a metal bar, probably not even with a fucking *bazooka*, and he doubted the man would let him walk out of here after what he'd just seen.

They might've stared at one another until the angels played the earth's swan song, if the door behind Krieg hadn't opened again and admitted the man of the hour himself, Mr. Torsten Gross. He strode in, ever the parade marshal, and came to stand by Krieg.

"Mr. Cameraman," Gross said, giving his title the usual treatment. "You aren't supposed to come here anymore. You almost ruined a perfectly good scene. Not to mention, you accused me of murder."

"You *are* a murderer." Jared nodded at Cox. "We both know it, and now I have proof. Let's see you get rid of that body before I get the cops here."

"Body?" Gross waved a hand at Cox's prone, still form. "You mean this body? My dear man, you must be confused."

Jared opened his mouth to refute this also, and closed it with a snap.

The torn, bleeding figure on the floor was stirring.

# TAKE 6

He watched in amazement as Samantha Cox got unsteadily to her feet, looking like a nature video of a fawn's first shaky steps. She faced away from him, but as she spun he could see that blood still poured from her partially decapitated head in a river, flowing down her nurse's uniform and spattering around her feet in droplets the size of quarters.

Cox's cranium flopped backward on her new elastic neck, increasing the size of the ragged hole in her throat. Jesus Christ, it looked like very raw steak in there, the artery still squeezing out blood with each visible pump of her heart and, oh God, was that white bit her fucking spine—?

"Oh, you…you bastards…"

Gross came forward to stand beside his slaughterhouse ragdoll. "You see, cameraman? We're making a *movie*." The director extended a bony middle finger and ran it through the red mess still brimming around the edge of the hole in her neck. "Or did you never learn the difference between real—" he popped the finger in his mouth, sucking it clean so thoroughly his already sunken cheeks bowed in, "— and make believe?"

Jared bent over and retched, spilling the soupy contents of last night's dinner onto the concrete.

He recovered quickly, wiping his mouth on the shoulder of his shirt. Thankfully, Cox's head had flopped back forward, closing the gap, and she only stared at him with eyes half closed and a dreamy smile on her lips.

"No, no, you killed her."

"I have done nothing. She is an actress, a great one. See how she has fooled even you with her performance?"

Jared shook his head. This wasn't like in Wickersham's apartment, or even when he'd seen Otter this morning; this transformation had happened right in front of his eyes. He'd seen her die, he was sure of it, and now she was up and walking around like a much sexier version of Lazarus.

"Samantha," he said, speaking slowly, "Are you hurt?"

She didn't answer, only stared dully. If she was alive, in whatever form, it was very different from the way she'd acted minutes before, a total personality overhaul. The blood flowing down her chest had diminished, but the skin of her throat still hung in a gaping flap.

"Samantha, do you remember what you just told me, that Gross was trying to hurt you? If you can understand me, come away from them. Come to me."

She took a half step forward, like a drunk walking the line at a traffic stop, and then stared curiously down at her foot, as if it had moved without command.

Gross reached out and took her hand. "I think this nice man wants to make sure you all right, *liebchen*. Let us go to him, my dear." He walked forward and she came this time, leaving Krieg to pant by the door.

Jared backed up toward the double doors, matching their pace, keeping the distance between them the same. Now that she'd changed, her essence—*everything that made her Samantha*—scooped out like ice cream, he found himself as scared of her as he was of them. He tore his eyes from the lackluster expression on Cox's face to look at Gross. "What is it, man? Just tell me what you did to them."

"Look at her!" Gross shouted, still advancing, giving Cox a vicious shake as he spoke. "See her with your own eyes! She is right in front of you, walking on her own two feet!"

"Don't give me that bullshit! Frankenstein over there just turned her neck into sliced salami! What did you do to her? *What did you do to Otter?*"

He sensed another set of eyes on him, so tangible it was like a hand on his shoulder. He jerked his head around to make sure no one was sneaking up on him. A camera mounted on the underside of the catwalk stared back at him. Whatever the key to Gross' (trickery, hoax, fucking *magic??*), he still suspected it was based in those cameras.

He took another step back, away from Gross, while he watched the device.

The camera followed him, its red eye tracking.

As he turned back, a splash of orange on the wall beside him caught Jared's attention.

The director stood only two feet away, advancing quicker

than Jared retreated. "Come dear boy, you're obviously confused. Drop that silly weapon and let's get you someplace where you can lie down. The heat of this city has fried your brain, *ya?*"

Jared only pretended to listen; he had no doubt if he surrendered to these two, he would need to be fitted for his own drool cup before the day was out. Mostly he thought of that familiar splash of orange he'd glimpsed behind him.

He just had to make sure.

Jared risked another glance over his shoulder.

A large orange hazard tag hung from a much newer bundle of cables, the kind the electric company put on newly installed junctions. Gross might've redesigned this building from scratch, might be working some kind of voodoo Jared didn't entirely understand, but he still needed electricity for his precious cameras.

Gross took advantage of his distraction and leapt forward.

Jared swung the bar, felt the jagged end tear across flesh.

Gross fell back from him, attack abandoned and smile replaced by shock. Krieg growled and started forward. The front of the director's sweater flopped open where Jared's swing had torn it, and from within…something was *glowing*.

Soft and blue, and it appeared to be shifting.

*Like static*, his mind told him. *He has a fucking TV screen in his chest.*

"You're…you're a goddamned German Teletubby," he said in horror.

Gross covered the hole with one liver-spotted hand, blocking out that unnatural light, and snarled in German to Krieg. The massive actor started past Cox with knife held ready.

"Cameraman…" Gross hissed.

"Film *this*," Jared said, and swung the bar again.

It smashed against the flimsy tin door of the junction box.

A miniature explosion of sparks showered out from the wall like fourth of July fireworks, and he waited to be electrocuted. The lights in the room didn't ebb or flicker but blew out like candles, and before they did, he saw the red light on the camera—right above his head now—wink out.

And one other thing he glimpsed as well, although it must've been his imagination.

Just before plunging into darkness, the walls of this strange room faded like a mirage, until he could almost see right through them...

Gross' enraged howl brought him back to what passed for reality.

Jared turned toward the door behind him, a tiny sliver of daylight at its edges, and ran.

He pushed open the door, stepped through...

And ran into a large bulk directly in his path.

"Otter?" he asked, squinting in the sudden light. He saw the fist coming toward him just before it struck him dead center in the forehead.

Jared wasn't aware of Otter ever hitting anything in his *life*, but he did so now, a punch worthy of the greats, rattling his brain and laying him back out across the floor where he bopped the other side of his head against the concrete. As black spots swam through Jared's vision, Otter came to stand over him.

He kept his eyes open long enough to see Krieg appear with the knife and hear Gross screaming behind him.

"Don't, you fool! We'll have a body on our hands!" He sneered down at Jared. "Clever boy, aren't you, Cameraman? No matter. I'm sure we can find another way to solve our... 'casting problems.'"

This time it was Krieg's fist that descended on him, and Jared went out like the lights.

# TAKE 7

He felt dull throbbing on both sides of his head even before opening his eyes. Movement also, the minute jostling of his body and sense of force indicative of locomotion. Jared peeled his eyelids open to take in his surroundings.

He saw blurred green—tree-dotted landscape flashing by on the other side of a pane of glass. He looked blearily around, his head as heavy as a bowling ball, and tried to get the gist of his situation.

Jared sat in the passenger seat of an unfamiliar car, something low, small, and sporty. And *moving*. The trees whipped by outside at a rate that must be well above the legal limit. The lush countryside, however, was only on his side of the vehicle. On the driver's side, his hazy vision picked out nothing but empty air and sky, a drop off so deep and abrupt the city stretched out below all the way to the ocean.

He even recognized the area. Somewhere up near Mulholland, one of the roads that wound along the cliffs on the east side of L.A. He tried to bring his hands up to hold the aching coconut atop his shoulders and found he couldn't move.

The seatbelt was strapped across him, although its necessity was in doubt after the other measures taken to keep him in his seat. The black belt disappeared against his chest beneath a duct tape girdle binding him to the seat back like a cocoon. The silvery adhesive was pulled taut just below his shoulders, barely giving him room to breathe. His waist and lap were similarly bound to the bottom of the seat, arms at his sides, tucked under layers upon layers of tape.

A wave of claustrophobia gripped him. He fought it off by taking in the rest of the vehicle.

Samantha Cox sat bolt upright beside him at the wheel. She gripped it with tightly curled fists. Her eyes were as wide and unblinking as a doll's, jaw unhinged. Her throat, he was both surprised and not surprised to see, was once more a smooth, unbroken expanse of tender flesh, her head firmly attached once more.

"Samantha," he croaked. She turned to him, but there was nothing in her face to indicate she even recognized him. Even the bruises and forehead gash were gone; she was complete and whole once more. The only evidence of the violent trauma was her bloodstained nurse's uniform, now more red than white.

Jared twisted his head as far as he could and caught sight of Otter crammed into the back seat of this tiny vehicle, which could only be that sleek little Aston Martin of Cox's. The film editor's belly was up against the backs of their chairs, and he stared straight ahead in equally stupefied fashion.

What the hell was going on? Had Gross let them go?

The car jostled over some uneven bit of road and a clinking noise came from his left. He looked down, at Cox's feet, and discovered enough wine and liquor bottles to keep a small army well soused. They rolled around her feet and the pedals of the vehicle, sloshing the liquid inside onto the interior. And her foot, he saw, was duct taped to the accelerator.

His grogginess slipped away.

Without cameras, Gross couldn't kill him—or whatever he did to his actors and actresses to turn them into lobotomy patients—so the best he could come up with was to frame the recovering substance addict for their deaths in a stunt so contrived it was more like the setup for an after-school special. With Cox in this addled state, it was no more difficult than placing a straight razor in a baby's hand and then waiting for nature to take its course. The resulting explosion when they flew off the cliff *Thelma-and-Louise* style would get rid of the duct tape for all but the most thorough investigation, which would never be performed anyway. The cops would take one look at the remains of those alcohol bottles and her checkered past and probably wouldn't even check Cox's corpse for blood alcohol level.

And he and Otter were just along for the negligent ride. Anonymous passengers in the celebrity death report. Not even worth mentioning by name on the evening news.

"Oh God," he moaned, thinking of Wickersham's plunge. He thrashed in his seat to no avail; the tape held him down so tight he couldn't even jiggle an ass cheek. "C'mon guys, snap out of it! Otter, get me outta this, and I'll buy you the biggest cheeseburger you've ever seen! WAKE UP!"

Jared looked out the front windshield and saw a sharp curve to the right. Nothing ahead except a short shoulder of rocks and then a big nothing. The cliff side rushed at them like an L.A. bum asking for change.

"Uh, you might wanna turn that wheel, honey." He struggled, trying to just yank one arm up and out of the tape. He felt several hairs rip out by the roots, but overall, he couldn't budge an inch. "Turn!" he shouted. "Turn, goddammit, *turn!*"

He screamed, but at the last second Cox turned the wheel with halfhearted slowness, unconcerned by her impending death, perhaps acting out of some dim memory of her past life. The ass of the car slid around into the oncoming traffic lane and bounced over the rough shoulder before squirting back onto the road. Cox flopped in the seat, her foot pressing down on the accelerator, and they shot off in a burst of speed.

During the few seconds the car tossed them around, something bounced against Jared's chest. It was just enough of a distraction from his present situation to make him look down.

His cell phone.

It was still in his breast pocket, jutting halfway out of the top of the tape. Gross hadn't even thought to search him for one. He might be totally in control with his cameras, but he made a lousy crook when he had to think things out for himself.

Jared checked the road. A long straightaway and gentle curves ahead.

This would take some patience. He tossed his hair out of the way and then leaned his head forward. The tape actually helped him for this part, holding the phone in place so he could slide it out with his teeth, lay it on his shoulder, and capture it with his cheek.

Who to call though? He doubted the police could do anything to help them. And, he suddenly realized, there was only one voice he wanted to hear right now.

Even if the guy had been a dick lately.

Shit, when you were staring straight down death's hungry gullet, lots could be forgiven.

"Hey Siri," he said, "Call Davis."

# TAKE 8

For the second time today, the unharmonious tweeting of his cell phone dredged Davis up from the depths of unconsciousness. This time the waters were tougher to swim through; his remaining hangover combined with the blow to the back of the head almost kept him down.

He stirred, aware of something sticky coursing down the side of his face, but had no idea what it was until he put his hand there and held it in front of him.

Blood on his fingers. And pain like a rotten tooth at the back of his skull.

He sat up amid a litter of keyboard keys and the broken plastic remains of one of Otter's keyboards. A glance at his watch told him he'd been out for almost an hour, more than enough time for the drugged film editor to abscond.

The phone continued ringing. It lay a little ways down the hall, where he'd dropped it while trying to call Susan. The screen was cracked, and something rattled inside when he picked it up. He checked the caller ID before answering.

"Jared, man, I've got a problem."

"Can't be half—bad as mine." The phone crackled, either with the threat of bad reception or its fall to the floor, but he could hear the urgent tone of his partner's voice.

"Otter knocked me out, he's gone, I lost him."

"Don't worry—that. Otter's here with me."

"With you? How'd he get with you?"

Jared got out about two syllables of an answer, and then screamed, "Oh Christ, turn, *turn you stupid bitch!*"

"What's going on?"

"No time for that. Let's just say the world's about to get real lonely for you, my man."

"What?"

"Oh shit," Jared moaned. He started to speak so fast Davis could barely follow the flow of his words, the reception increasingly torn with static. "Listen man, I'm sorry for everything late—you gotta believe—now, this is not—be an accident, *Gross* did this to us, he's not hu—, he's—you gotta stop—eep Susan—him, whatever you d—talk to—porter—"

"Jared, I don't understand!" Davis shouted into the phone.

And then one perfectly clear phrase, bursting through the static: "The power, Gross still needs POWER!"

"Jared!" he shouted.

The phone went dead in his hand.

# TAKE 9

Jared spotted the hairpin curve sign just before he started into his rapid explanation. At the speed they were going now—better than 100 with Cox's leaden foot—they wouldn't be able to turn even with a fully conscious driver at the wheel.

He finished, giving Davis the most important part last, the info on his new friend, the only person that might be able to help now, and then the end of the road was in sight, the end of *his* road, and all he could do was scream. The movement caused the phone to slip off his shoulder, bounce from his lap, and drop into the floorboard, out of sight.

Cox did try to turn at the last second, and the back end of the car slewed around once more, pointing them at another section of the cliff's endless edge.

Except this part had a tree planted on it.

One lonely tree rooted to the rocky shoulder, fighting for life for who knew how long, waiting for this moment when an actress' sports car would slam into it at 108 miles per hour.

The Aston Martin collided head on at the front driver's side, the tree ripping through the metal like tin foil. He had a fraction of a second to watch Cox and Otter launch forward past him like human-shaped missiles. Jared saw the humor in the fact that Gross had at least secured him in place and then the car disintegrated around him.

# SCENE XI

(voice over)

# TAKE 1

Davis barely knew who he was, much less how he arrived at the hospital.

The phone call from the police felt like a dream, slow-motion and blurred around the edges. The words 'car accident' and 'critical condition' stuck out at him.

So did 'dead.'

He arrived at Cedar Sinai and stumbled through the hospital, ghostly visions of the *Slice* set superimposing over this one.

"M-Mane," he stammered to the overworked nurse at the front desk. "Jared Mane, what room please?"

The nurse checked a list on the desk and then looked up at him. "Your name?"

"Davis Lowe."

She grimaced, looking back down at the list as if to avoid his eyes. "Well, sir…"

Before she could continue, a tall man in black slacks and a white polo stepped out of the crowd in the waiting room. The nurse looked relieved at the sight of him. He laid a hand on Davis' shoulder.

"Mr. Lowe?"

"Yes," he said without turning around. To the nurse, he pleaded, "Please ma'am, where?"

The tall man didn't give up. He moved his hand to Davis'

upper arm and pulled him firmly away from the nurse's desk. "Mr. Lowe, I'm Detective Bert Garbin with the LAPD. I've been waiting to speak with you. Could you come with me, please?"

"No." His mind kept returning to what he'd been told over the phone, but he couldn't believe it was real until he'd seen it with his own two eyes.

Poor Otter and Samantha Cox dead, and Jared soon might be.

"No, I have to see my friend."

"This will just take a moment, Mr. Lowe." The man was really tugging now, and Davis had no strength left to fight. "If you'll step this way."

He led the way through a door and into a private hospital conference room. Davis still felt distant, outside himself, watching all this through a peephole in the fabric of reality.

"Have a seat," Garbin told him, and Davis did so without question, dropping into a chair at the conference table in the middle of the room.

"What's this about?"

"I was hoping you could tell me that."

"I…I don't—"

"Was this part of some movie? A stunt or something that your studio was rehearsing?"

Davis stared at him blankly. The conversation flow was too convoluted for his addled brain to follow.

Garbin stared back, perhaps searching for evidence that the ignorance was genuine. He pulled out a small notebook and rifled through pages. "These two employees of yours—a Terrence Ottman and Jared Mane—were involved in a severe car accident with the actress Samantha Cox. They were up in the hills and would've flown right off a fifty-foot cliff if the driver—that was Cox—hadn't hit a tree. She and Ottman were killed instantly. Mane is upstairs in surgery—"

"How is he?"

The detective studied him again over the notebook. His eyes were calm but very hard, pieces of quartz flashing in his skull. "In bad shape, from what the docs say. Broken ribs, arms, a leg. Internal bleeding. They say…well, maybe you should wait and get it from them."

Davis closed his eyes before the vertigo could induce vomiting and put his head between his knees in case it did anyway.

"I'm sorry," the detective continued. "I hate to do this to you now, but I need some information, and I need it immediately. When was the last time you saw Mane?"

"This morning, when he left our studio."

"And where was he going?"

"To…to speak with Torsten Gross. That's the director of the film we're working on."

"The studio said they'd forbidden Mane to be anywhere near Gross or his set. Why was he going there?"

Davis faltered, unsure what to say, how much to explain. Garbin was snapping out preformed questions he already knew the answers to. "He believed Gross was responsible for Katherine Wickersham's death. He thought that Samantha Cox was also in danger and that…that Gross had done something to Otter."

"Otter?"

"That's Terrence Ottman. Otter." Something broke in him at having to explain Otter's nickname to this cold interrogator, and the first tears escaped him. He squeezed his eyes shut again until they were sore.

Garbin gave him a minute. When he spoke again, his voice was soft but no more yielding than before. "Where did you get that blood on the back of your head, Mr. Lowe?"

His eyes popped open. He'd forgotten all about it. He put his hand there and winced at the fresh round of pain the contact brought. The wound was crusted over, leaving his hair in a matted tangle. "I-I was hit."

"With what?"

"A keyboard."

"By whom?"

He sighed, wishing he'd said he was mugged. "By Otter. Just before he left the studio."

"Why? Did you have an argument? A fight?"

"No, it wasn't like that. I don't know why he did it. He was acting strange this morning…and…"

"Strange how?"

"I don't *know*," Davis moaned in frustration. "That's what Jared was worried about, why he went to Gross. None of this makes sense to me, so how can I possibly make it make sense for you?"

"I am fully aware of what Mr. Mane believed and his involvement with Katherine Wickersham's death. Everything Gross said about that incident checked out, and nothing Mane said did. I think he would've been arraigned, if not for….well, some compelling evidence."

"The video."

Garbin confirmed nothing, just held up his notebook. "Now let me tell you what Gross said happened today. He claims that Cox—a known recovering substance addict—showed up for work this morning drunk. Mane and Ottman came barging in, making more accusations, took her and left. Both of their cars were left at the set out on Crenshaw, so that checks out. Gross says he knew nothing after that. Cox was behind the wheel of her own car, and there were plenty of alcohol bottles in her vehicle to support his claim. What do you make of that?"

"I don't know, goddammit! I was lying unconscious on the floor of our office, okay?"

"And yet a quick check of Mane's cell phone record shows he called you just before the accident. Shows that you and he had a conversation of fifty-two seconds. What did he tell you, Mr. Lowe?"

It was the first time he'd really stopped to think about the call. He was so groggy after getting it and the call from the police came so soon afterward, there was no time for analysis. He thought back now, letting his gaze drift away as he concentrated, but could make no sense of the garble. Except that last phrase about Gross 'needing power.' Sad to think Jared wasted what could've been his last words on an insult. "The reception was really bad. He was screaming most of the time. I think he called me just before…they crashed."

Garbin nodded. "Mr. Lowe," he said, choosing his words carefully, "Do you know any reason why Mane would've been duct taped to his seat?"

Davis looked up at him. Garbin's face was unreadable, betraying nothing. "*What?*"

"Mane was found strapped in the passenger seat of Cox's car with a hell of a lot of duct tape. Ironically, that's the only thing that kept him from being killed on impact, and I have no idea how he managed to call you. Now, I'm no Columbo, and there's a lot of this case that—pardon my French—makes no fucking sense, but it seems to me the last thing anyone would expect is for them to hit the only tree on that cliff side. If they'd sailed over the edge and erupted in the fiery explosion they by-all-rights should have, there wouldn't be any need to investigate when the cause of the accident was so readily believable. Cox's blood alcohol is being checked by the morgue now, but I have a lot of faith it will come back negative."

"I...I don't understand. You think they were murdered? By who? *Me?*"

Garbin smiled at him for the first time. "That's one theory. Or maybe Cox and Ottman did it, some kind of weird love triangle thing. But I can tell you this: it would've taken quite a while to duct tape Mane into that seat, and Gross didn't mention anything like that when he gave his version of events. In fact, when I told him there was a survivor, he looked ready to explode. I'm guessing that guy ain't the greatest poker player."

It took Davis a minute to digest all this, and another to believe it. "Thank God," he whispered.

"We're going to get those toxicology reports back in a few days, and then I think Torsten Gross is going to have a lot of new questions to answer, don't you?"

Davis nodded. He wanted to say more, wanted to babble out the whole story, but they could investigate and arrive at the facts without him. He knew the crazy parts of the tale, but they were going to find the *answers*, the string of truth that would explain it all away.

"We'll talk more a little later." Garbin held open the door. "But for now, go see your friend. And take care of that head wound."

# TAKE 2

Jared was moved to ICU by the time Davis could find the correct floor. Everything the detective had told him was put on the back burner of his mind along with Otter's death, his problems with Susan, everything, as he hurried down the white hallways in search of the proper room. He met a doctor coming out and asked him for an update. The man listed injuries in cold, clinical terms that made Davis want to scream in his stethoscope until the man's ears bled, ending with the fact that his partner was stable but in a coma and they had no idea how long it—or he—might last.

Steeling himself, he stepped into the room.

Jared's father and stepmother looked up when they saw him. His father, a high-priced attorney with several clientele of the acting persuasion, nodded and breezed out of the room without a word…but not before Davis saw the tears in his eyes. His stepmother came over and hugged him, whispered something consoling, and then followed her husband out. Davis let his eyes wander the tiny white room before allowing them to land on his friend.

The thing on the bed was unrecognizable only because there were so many casts on its body, misshaping, disproportioning, turning it into a Picasso work of art. Everything up to the neck seemed to be dipped in plaster; Davis thought things like that only happened in sitcoms, when the protagonist was strung up in traction at the end of the episode, but here it was, happening to his best friend. They'd shaved off half of his long hair on the left side of his head to suture a finger-long wound there, and he couldn't help thinking the man would be more pissed about that than anything.

The rest of his face was scratched and bruised, the upper right half swollen outward and the closed eyes puffy. Tubes ran in and out of his nostrils, his mouth, through the casts on his arms, sensors attached to his forehead and neck.

Davis would never again be amazed at the man's ability to pick up any girl, at any time, in any place. He would never laugh at him speaking Spanish in an exaggerated Texas accent. Jared Mane would lie in this bed and waste away, a corpse without a grave.

Looking at him, Davis expected to feel unbearable sorrow.

Instead…a sudden rush of anger came.

No, not anger. *Rage.* He wanted to take it out on something, needed to take it out on someone.

And he knew who.

Gross had done this. The man was a murderer. Nothing more supernatural about it than that. He'd killed Otter and Cox and Wickersham, and put Jared in this hospital bed, and for what? A movie? A fucking shitty *horror* movie?

But the police were going to link him to it, and that German fuck would pay.

*If that helps you sleep at night.*

Davis ignored the comment from that eternally cruel side of himself, and curled his hands into fists at his side.

*Ignore me all you want, but you can't ignore the fact that you had a hand in this. If you'd just listened to Jared…*

"No," he said aloud. That wasn't true, he wouldn't accept responsibility for this.

He waited for this voice to say more, to argue with him until the nurses came in and pumped him full of something to put him out, but nothing came. That bitter-sharp rage subsided without anything to take its place, leaving him hollow.

Davis made it to a chair next to the door before his legs gave out.

# TAKE 3

The following three days passed somehow.

Davis slept when his body collapsed, ate when it begged. He took shifts with Jared's stepmother, but never left the hospital. The only thing marking the passage of time were specific incidents, the two or three conversations that rose out of the monotony.

A nurse came in to clean the wound on the back of his head that first afternoon, swabbing the shallow cut with antiseptic and lecturing him on proper care of the surrounding bruise. There was a near miss on the morning after the accident when Jared's heart stopped and the doctors came blazing in to bring him back to life. He would always remember running into Otter's short, dumpy mother in the hospital hallway, trying to tell her how sorry he was, and receiving a slap in the face before she told him she always knew he would get her boy into trouble, and that he was a very bad person. Reilly called him on his cell phone—which was still acting hinky—to offer his condolences and then told him the studio thought it best if they terminated their association. Davis could recall reporter after reporter sneaking in to the room for pictures or a quote about Samantha Cox's death, and being turned away by the nurses.

On the third day, he sensed a presence in the doorway and looked up to find Susan there.

She was crying and wringing her hands. Her eyes couldn't decide which of them to land on, him or Jared, and eventually settled somewhere in between. Davis stood but didn't go to her, the protocol for these situations lost over the time they'd been apart.

Finally she came forward and gave him a stiff, awkward embrace that he didn't return. "I'm sorry about Otter. And Jared, of course. I would've come sooner, but...well, the show must go on."

He nodded.

"Do the police know what happened?"

"Not yet."

They stood looking at one another, not knowing where to go. When he could take it no longer, when the pressure built and he could sense her getting ready to leave, he blurted, "I love you."

"I love you, too." There was relief in the words, as though she were only waiting for him to say it first. "Listen Davis, we wrap up shooting on Wednesday. Really there's just the last scene with me and Werdner and Krieg to film, but Gross gave us a few days off. The reporters have been… awful. When we get finished, why don't you and I have lunch and talk about…about where we're going."

"That sounds good," he agreed, although he really didn't know if he could wait that long. He'd been so worried about her that day, with Otter zoned out and Jared going crazy, so eager to be her rescuer, her knight in shining blue jeans, but that sense of urgency was gone now. He still wanted to tell her about Gross, what the police suspected, but he was too scared to break this tenuous bond by spouting off and trying to get her to quit. No, if this business with Torsten Gross was all going to be over by Wednesday, then just let it end without further uproar from him.

"I'll see you later. I'm going home to shower and sleep for a day straight." She rose to give him a quick kiss on the lips. "I love you so much Davis. Keep an eye on Jared."

"Trying to."

She smiled, glanced at the patient one final time, and turned to leave. He watched her go all the way down the hall, wait for the elevator at the other end, and give him a tiny wave before the doors slid shut.

Several hours later, as he paced the waiting room, he noticed a man sidling too-nonchalant past the nurse's station, a tall guy with short, choppy blond hair and narrow frame glasses, He was dressed hip, like someone in the business. He also looked naggingly familiar.

The man came down the hallway and stopped outside the door. "Davis Lowe?" he asked. "My name is Sidney Spitzen. I'm a reporter."

Now Davis placed him; the trendy *Rolling Stones* guy with all the inside information at the Wickersham press conference. Or was it *Variety*, looking for quotes about Gross? Davis came forward, waving his hands. "I'm sorry, no comment. I don't know why they let you up here, but you have to leave now. Nurse!"

Spitzen stood his ground. "Wait, wait Mr. Lowe, I'm only here because your friend Jared came to *me.*"

The nurses looked up from their station, and one of them, a big bruiser that resembled a man in drag, came around the counter and started their way.

"What are you talking about? And you better explain fast or Nurse Ratchet here is gonna drag you out by your hair."

"Jared came to me two days ago and told me an incredible story, and I told him one in return. He was trying to keep you and your friend Otter out of this, but with him, well, incapacitated, I figured I better come and speak with you. Can we go somewhere and talk?"

The nurse arrived. "Is this gentleman bothering you, Mr. Lowe?"

Davis eyed Spitzen for several seconds before answering. The man's eyes were honest behind his glass frames. "No, it looks like Mr. Spitzen and I have something to discuss after all."

# TAKE 4

Davis didn't know what to make of the rock n' roll reporter as they stood next to one another in the elevator. He looked like someone on one of those insipid teen dramas, with spiked-up hair, dressed in dark blue suede pants and a white dress shirt with the sleeves rolled up, and a messenger bag over one shoulder. The man had to be around Davis' age, but he exuded the calm assurance of someone much older.

Spitzen remained silent on the trip down, staring straight ahead. Davis opened his mouth to speak at one point, but the elevator doors slid open to let in a flood of patients and hospital crew.

The reporter didn't stop in the lobby, but continued through the revolving door exit. It was late afternoon, the first time Davis had been outdoors in three days. They made it to the sidewalk before Spitzen finally spoke.

"C'mon, there's a coffee shop on the next block. We need some privacy."

Davis shook his head before the words were out. "I'm not going any further until you tell me what this is about. Why did Jared come to *you*?"

Spitzen sighed and rolled his eyes, still somehow looking terminally hip in his exasperation. "Because he wanted to know how I found out about the video recording of Wickersham's death."

"So how *did* you know about that?"

"I grease the right palms in this city, and it was only sheer luck I caught wind of it. I didn't really believe it at first—it sounded too much like the million other urban legends crawling around this city—but once I saw Phillip Reilly's reaction, I knew I was on to something. Thanks to the power of the studio's green, this thing is a better guarded secret than Michael Jackson's plastic surgery records."

Davis sneered. "And it just happened to fall into your hands, a reporter for *Rolling Stone?*"

Spitzen shook his head with a tight grin. "First of all, I don't work for *Rolling Stone.*"

"Or *Variety?*"

"Ah, you remember that, huh? I've been trying to get in touch with you for a while, ever since I heard you were working with *the* Torsten Gross. No, I'm actually freelance. I just used some old credentials to get into the press conference. And the story I'm writing isn't on Wickersham, it's on Gross. I've been working on it off and on for the past three years, but I never thought I'd have a chance to get so close to him."

"What did Jared tell you?" Davis demanded. The idea that this might be a trick occurred to him, a ploy to get him to talk.

"Everything he told you. I know you don't trust me yet, and I'm not asking you to. Jared Mane just happened to be in the right place at the wrong time, and was privy to a piece of the Torsten Gross puzzle no one's ever gotten before. Probably because he's never worked with a second unit. Now Mane and your other friend have paid for it with their lives."

Davis felt a rush of guilt at this and wondered if it was what the reporter intended. He remembered Jared stomping out of the restaurant, declaring he would find someone that believed him. This man was apparently the 'wheels in motion' he'd mentioned on the phone just before they found Otter. "Jared's not dead yet."

"I know. I just want you to see that the fact Gross went after them—which is obviously what happened here, no different than the mob rubbing out witnesses before trial—just proves Jared was on to something."

"Okay then, what did *you* tell Jared?"

"The history of Torsten Gross…and the Gross Curse." Spitzen sounded somehow like Vincent Price as he said these words, relishing their impact a bit too much. All he needed was a goddamned echo effect and a light under his chin.

"What curse? What do you mean?"

"Lowe, were you aware Gross made twelve films in Germany before *Arterial Slice*? And that every last actor and actress that ever died in one of his films is now dead in real life, without a single exception?"

"I—I don't understand." But he thought perhaps he did. Too well.

"Just like Wickersham. Just like Cox, who, I'm told, finished her death scene just an hour before her actual death. Convenient she was able to do so, being 'drunk' and all." Spitzen quieted as a man in a wheelchair was wheeled out of the hospital's revolving door in front of them. "Everyone who ever filmed a death scene for Torsten Gross ended up on a slab within a month. Strange accidents, suicides, things like that. They started calling it the Gross Curse. The studios cleaned it up, kept it from becoming too public, and the fact that he only made a movie every four or five years let the story die in the press. But in the business, it got bad. People started refusing to work for him, so when Trimax came sniffing around for talent, he jumped ship and defected to America."

"How does that explain Jared and Otter? They were never in one of his movies."

"All of the victims exhibited unusual behavior after filming their deaths. Like a depression, an emotional drain. Either one of them act like that?"

"…just one."

"Ottman, right?"

"How did you know that?"

"Because he was in the car voluntarily. There has never been any circumstances in any of the other deaths that looked suspicious in the least. Suicide was always verifiable, no foul play involved in the accidents. But Jared was *strapped* in that car. That says to me Gross wasn't able to do to him whatever he does to the others, including Otter, and he was forced to improvise. If he'd've done the job himself, he'd have a body to account for."

Davis was uncomfortable with the fact that this was making sense. "But *how?* How does he do it? What makes them act like Otter acted?"

"Nobody knows. Everybody really thought it was a curse, you know, a coincidence. There's no logical reason why a director would want his stars dead, and even when the authorities considered looking at him or Krieg, they always had firm alibis. Even I was ready to admit it might just be some cosmic joke, but Jared disproved that. He's the first person to come up with real, hard evidence linking Gross to a death, but in a way so insane no one believed him. And Gross tried to do away with him after that and slipped up. I think he's running scared."

Davis could say nothing. He thought about Susan. Susan getting ready to film a death scene, excited to be acting in her first real movie.

A movie that, if this man could be believed, might be her last.

"There's more," Spitzen went on. "Nobody knows who Torsten Gross is."

"Isn't he Torsten Gross?"

"Yeah, but who *is* that? There's no record of his family, or his birth, no school records, not even any pictures of him as a boy. No pictures of him at all, in fact, even after he became famous. I didn't even know what the guy looked like until that press conference, where, I'll point out, no cameras were allowed. He just showed up on the doorstep of Morgen Pictures one day, and impressed them enough for them to let him make a movie."

"Okay, I can understand why you talked to Jared, but why come to me? I mean, as of yesterday, I don't even work for Trimax or Gross anymore. I can't give you anything else, so what are you after?"

"The final piece of the puzzle," Spitzen said, his words speeding up. "This story is a ticking time bomb, and it's about to explode. The police are circling and gathering enough evidence to go after Gross. It's gonna happen any day now. The media is already in a frenzy over this, but right now they just think Cox and Wickersham are a coincidence. Sooner or later someone else is going to put together the big picture; it's just below the surface of *everything* Gross is. I've gotta break this story now, or it's gonna get buried under a ton of other coverage. And I need help anywhere I can get it."

Davis had trouble drawing breath. "You know my girlfriend is playing the final victim in *Arterial Slice*."

"I'm aware. I'd say you have as much reason as I do for wanting to take down Gross."

Susan was suddenly all he could think about, he wanted to hold her and touch her and insure she was safe, even though he'd seen her just a few hours before. If he presented her with what Spitzen had told him, she'd have to see the danger, wouldn't be able to accuse him of petty jealousy. His career was over, so what did he care?

His career was over. That fact hit home even in his growing panic, as he stood on the sidewalk with Hollywood's answer to Hunter S. Thompson.

And he was surprised to find he really didn't care. Only Susan mattered now.

"Listen, I'll help you, whatever, but first I have to talk to Susan. I have to tell her about this and convince her to leave the movie." He pulled out his phone, dialed her number, and got voicemail. Goddamn it, if she was already asleep, she would've turned off the ringer. Davis sprinted up the sidewalk, heading toward where he'd parked in the hospital garage three days before.

"Lowe, wait!" Spitzen called after him. "Gross might be after you too!"

"I don't care! I've gotta tell her!"

"We need to come up with a game plan!"

"Later!" He left the reporter staring after him by the curb and got to his car after jogging up three flights of stairs. The only way he could keep his panic at bay was by reminding himself that she wasn't in immediate danger. She wouldn't film her death scene for days and by then, Gross might even be in jail. Rather than rush over, he could go by his place, shower and shave so he didn't smell like a hobo when he crushed her dreams, and then he wouldn't leave her side until this was finished.

Darkness had overtaken the sky by the time he arrived back at his apartment. He scrambled out of his car, left the door open, went back to shut it, dropped his keys twice, and finally got into the converted motel room.

He couldn't resist trying her cell again. Voicemail.

A knock came at his door as he wrang his hands in frustration.

In the four years he'd lived here, no one had ever knocked on his door. It had to be Susan.

Davis threw the door open.

And found himself staring down a dark hole five meters wide and without a bottom. It was only after his perception widened that he understood it was the barrel of a pistol.

"Greetings, Mr. Lowe," Gross purred from the other end. "May I come in?"

# SCENE XII

(quick cuts)

# TAKE 1

The sight of the director on his doorstep didn't inspire the terror he was sure the man would've liked it to. He actually looked comically out of place away from the set in his black turtleneck and slacks. And somehow, the gun (Davis knew little about firearms, but it was large and flat black in color) didn't darken his stature any. Everything about the director had always felt so ominous, so…evil…that it was more than a little anticlimactic to see him now as no more dangerous than the common mugger.

If this *was* a movie, Davis would be calling shenanigans on the lazy writing about now.

Gross gestured with the gun, flipping the barrel tip upward quickly and then re-centering it directly in the middle of Davis' chest. "Inside. Now."

Davis went, backing up, hypnotized by the weapon. Just because Gross didn't look scary with the pistol didn't mean he wasn't still frightened. Gross followed him into the room, watching him with his cold eyes. He shut the door without looking.

"Have a seat, Mr. Lowe. On the bed."

The back of the bed was against his knees, and Davis gave in to his natural inclination and let them fold, spilling him backward. With the gun unwavering, Gross managed to grab the only chair in the room, swing it around to face the bed, and ease himself into it.

"What are you doing here?" The question took incredible effort to force through his lips.

"I would think that fairly obvious, even to a cretin such as yourself." Gross' face was hard, each wrinkle set in stone, his bald pate shining in the room's light. "I'm here to kill you."

Davis found he'd made this assumption, so he didn't gasp or cry or beg. He merely sat there and stared at Gross.

And tried to think of anything to draw this encounter out until he could escape.

"Why did you do all this?"

"It is my art, my duty to my beloved public—"

"I'm not talking about the movie. I mean *us*. Jared and Otter. They weren't part of your movie."

"I never should have agreed to work with a *second unit*." Gross spit out the last two words like bites of rancid meat. "Nothing but a cheap means to put out a less-than-perfect product. You Americans. Everything is go, go, go, quick, quick, quick, finish as soon as possible so you can sell it and go buy your 'Kentucky Fried Chicken.'"

"I can't tell you how odd I find it that you think KFC is the American goal."

Gross bared his teeth. "You people have lost all sense of art."

"Since when is murdering people art?" Davis allowed his eyes to dart around the room, searching for a weapon, a fork, a shoe, *anything* he could use in his defense.

Gross threw back his head and laughed. His speech, though still accented, held no more of the pauses or German words thrown in, and Davis wondered if the bumbling had all just been an act. "My boy, it is the *highest* form of art."

"You killed one of my friends. Put the other one in the hospital."

"Then you should have stayed out of my way!" Gross snapped, switching the gun to his other hand, "You and the studio both! I do *not* work with other people! It was never questioned in Germany, because Germany is a country that allows its artists the freedom to maneuver within the realm of their imagination! You goddamn Americans make any censorship in Nazi Germany look like a public lending library!"

"Bullshit," Davis barked, becoming more interested in the argument on its own merits rather than as diversion. "You won't find more freedom anywhere else in the world than you will right here."

"Oh yes, Mr. Lowe, complete freedom, provided you follow the beliefs of the moral majority! Every parent blames everyone but themselves for anything aired in any medium that they do not want precious little Billy and Sally to see! The MPAA gives an R rating to any film where a character smokes a cigarette! Even now your FCC seeks to impose regulations on cable broadcasting because these imbeciles pay to watch television and then want to complain about what is on it!"

"I didn't say we were perfect, I said to compare."

"By all means, compare then! Compare your nation's creative exports to those of Europe or Asia, most of which you never see, because this country's restrictions do not even allow them within its borders! My films are a prime example!"

"Yeah, and most of their leaders steal their food and tell them where to go to church. It's a tradeoff. Now get to your point."

Red coloring had crept into his otherwise pale face, but now he calmed and stared at Davis with eyes that seemed unnaturally steady, abysmally black, and brimming with hate. "All art is an illusion, but especially film, and the magic of it is only sustained if the artist places a curtain over himself and everything he does to create it. I never work with others because I never allow my masterpieces to be viewed while in creation. I have survived as long as I have because no one ever looked behind that curtain. Then your company was forced upon me, and look what happened. Your cameraman stumbled upon something he shouldn't have, you put your fat friend onto my trail, and I was forced to take steps to protect myself. In hindsight, they were…ill-advised…but that is what happens when you are forced to conform yourself to the expectations of others."

"Who do you think you're fooling with this crap? You came to this country because nobody would work with you in your dearest Germany anymore. You ran them all off with your *art*."

Gross turned his head down to the threadbare carpet. The gun arm swooned, dropping the business end down at the ground between his legs. He looked his age in that pose, just a tired old man with too much on his shoulders, but Davis had no doubt he could get the gun back up in a hurry.

"You are correct. Eventually the 'Gross Curse' overshadowed my genius. America was to be a new start for Lars and myself, where the off-camera body count wouldn't matter so much."

"How?" Davis slipped to the edge of the bed, tensing to leap. Again, thinking in film conventions, this was just about the point where the villain usually revealed his plans before attempting to vanquish the hero. "How did you kill all those actors? What did you do to Otter to make him act like that?"

Instead of answering, Gross pulled his head up, raised the gun, and fired.

# TAKE 2

Susan fell into bed almost as soon as she walked through the door, slept a few hours, then stumbled into the shower. As she toweled off, she heard the buzz of her cell from the bedroom and ran to answer. Werdner's throaty voice waited on the line. Susan had decided the woman wasn't as bad as the image she worked to maintain. Since news of Cox's death had reached them, the last remaining headlined actress had become a bit more melancholy, losing some of her bitchy, defense-mechanism edge.

They talked about the film's finale, about Cox, and gradually worked their way to the rumors circling about Gross, but Susan got the idea they were headed there all along. One of the extras had a cousin to a friend to a roommate that said the cops were investigating him in connection with the car accident. Werdner had come to the same conclusion as herself: finish the damn thing and get out of the destruction zone before the nuclear bomb of bad publicity went off.

"Still," Werdner said in her ear as Susan went about shutting her apartment down for the night, "All that publicity might be good for us, you know? Being the last actresses to work with Torsten Gross before they throw him in jail?"

"Yeah," Susan answered noncommittally. Her mind wandered near the end of this conversation, reminded of poor Otter, who never wanted anything more than for people to like him, and Jared in the hospital bed looking like a piñata with all that plaster covering him. Working with Gross hadn't done much for either of them. Then she thought of Davis and how haggard he'd looked at the hospital.

She missed him so much.

What would she do when this gig was over? She still didn't have an agent, didn't even have any other work lined up. She was going back to her old crappy life, and if she didn't make up with Davis soon, she wouldn't even be going back to it with him.

But if this was her first and last shot at the big screen, if she was going the way of those girls from countless campy, low-budget horror flicks, just a nameless blip on the radar of cinema—not a BIG BREAK! after all, more like a BIG FAKE—she was going to do it to the goddamn best of her ability. She just needed a clear head until it was over, and then she and Davis would work this out.

Susan could feel tears coming, tears for all of them, and she didn't want Werdner—who she suspected didn't have the ability to cry—to hear her.

A knock at her door gave her just the excuse she needed.

"Hey, I gotta run, I got someone at my door."

"Okay, great, I got my yoga lesson anyway. Can't keep Master Tony and his rock hard *pecs* waiting. See you soon, sweetie."

Susan hung up, tossed her cell on the coffee table, and started through her apartment to the door. It was just past eight, so it could be a solicitor or Mormon at the door, but she kind of hoped it was Davis. With heart fluttering, vowing to do things to him that would make his toes curl, she pressed against the door, looked out through the peephole and saw...

Nothing.

At first she thought the bulbs in the hallway must be out, then realized that the person on the other side had their thumb pressed against the peephole. If she pulled her head back and allowed in light from her side, she could see the swirls on their fingerprint.

The knock came again, heavier, and she realized she hadn't slipped the chain when she came in earlier. She reached out, trying not to notice her tremble, and moved the little gold piece as quietly as possible toward the sliding mechanism.

She had it halfway across the slot when the person on the other side of the door thudded against it hard enough to shake it in its frame. She let out an involuntary squeak and dropped the chain.

As if the other person had been waiting for a sign of her presence, they began to hit the door hard, over and over again. The door actually *bulged* in its frame.

Susan stared at it, trying to figure who was out there, and found her imagination entirely too eager to supply an identity.

She spun, running back to get her phone, and had it in her hand, actually felt the plastic against her palm, before she realized she hadn't moved from the door, and that her mad dash was only wishful thinking.

As per her usual reaction to terror, every muscle in her body was locked, frozen solid with fear.

# TAKE 3

The report of the pistol in Gross' hand was deafening in the enclosed space; another thing the movies simply couldn't teach you. Davis jumped and winced, partially turned his head in anticipation of the flesh-tearing pain of the bullet, but even as he jerked he realized Gross hadn't fired at him.

The director had raised the gun in his left hand, but only to an angle that would send the bullet into the floor at Davis' feet. He'd then placed the palm of his right hand in front of the barrel before pulling the trigger, all in a motion so quick Davis had no time to react until it was all over.

"*Jesus!*" he exclaimed, more horrified by this than if the crazy bastard had unloaded a slug in him. There had been no hesitation, barely any pain across his face as he mutilated his hand. Davis scooted back on the bed, attempting to put distance between himself and all that blood and lunacy. "What the fuck are you—?"

The words died.

The wound hadn't splattered blood and skin and bone onto the carpet. The bullet had passed all the way through, left a small hole in the carpet a foot from the bed, but the exit wound on the backside of his hand reminded Davis more of a good-sized firework placed inside of a paper bag. Shreds of flesh-colored material hung in ragged strips around the opening.

And from inside—

From inside that tattered hole, something *glowed*.

Gross raised his hand to his face and examined both sides of it. As he turned his wrist, swiveling the injured hand, Davis saw that same glow pulsing from the hole on both sides. It was dirty gray in color, but took on shades of blue from its pulsing luminescence.

It was the dull radiance of light projection, the kind used to transmit images to the human eye. The cold glow of a television in the dark, the ambience of a movie screen in the theater.

The hand, Davis noticed, was the same one he'd shook upon first meeting Gross in Reilly's office, two months and a thousand years ago. His first impression had been a rubber glove pulled over a skeletal frame and that didn't seem far from the truth, with the exception that the skeleton was something like a giant cathode ray tube.

"What are you?" He didn't mean for the words to come out tinged with horror, but they did.

Gross let the wounded appendage fall into his lap, where it continued to emit its wan glow, but the hand holding the gun never moved from Davis, despite the fact that Gross' eyes did, rolling up to the ceiling as he lost himself in his words. "With your limited range of experience, nothing about what I am would make the least bit of sense, so I will not waste breath explaining. Suffice to say, I escaped from a place that makes your human ideas of hell seem like a child's party. I came here to create what I love—art—in one of the last bastions on any plane of existence where it is still allowable. You humans have no idea how fortunate you are in this respect, and yet you throw it all away in favor of your technology, your rationality, your science and logic. You are losing your emotions, the one thing that can save you from the coming darkness...and you don't even see it."

Something happened to his voice as he spoke. It first shed the German accent, slipping into a dialect of perfectly unaccented English, and then lost its tonality to become higher, laced with a tight humming. "But I digress. In any case, I have played the role of Torsten Gross in this human disguise for nearly three decades, and when they stopped allowing me to give birth to ideas in Germany, I came here. A mistake, to be sure."

That sound in his voice. Not humming. More like buzzing. It cut through Davis' head like an arrow.

"Krieg," Davis said, taking advantage of a momentary pause to halt that voice. "Is he—?"

"Quite human, I'm afraid. One of the few I have found on this godforsaken planet that shares my vision."

Davis wanted to smile—after all, the man really was giving up his secrets like a Bond villain in the third act—but that voice…God, that voice was *killing* him, giving him a headache so bad he could feel his heartbeat at his temples.

"You asked me how I did this. How I weave my magic. I must first counter that with a question of my own. The German word is *seelc*, but you Americans say 'soul.' Do you believe in the concept of a soul, Mr. Lowe?"

"I-I don't know. I don't go to church, if that's what you mean."

"It doesn't matter. Nevertheless, let me assure you that there is *something* that powers the human body, some bit of animus that goes beyond the flesh. Something that allows you to experience the full range of emotion that art is meant to evoke."

"You're going…" He stopped to collect his thoughts after the pressure of that electric buzzing mercifully lifted. "You're going to tell me this is about heaven and hell?"

Gross sighed. "My dear Mr. Lowe, matters of heaven and hell are what happens to your soul *after* you die, and not even I know that. My only aim is to convince you that every human possesses one, an inner being more attuned to the world around you than your five senses. Will you agree with me on that?"

"Yes, yes, absolutely." He would've agreed to anything to get Gross to stop talking.

"Are you aware there is a belief among many primitive, aboriginal tribes—and even some Native Americans of the western world—that a camera has the power to steal that soul, and, so believing, never allow their picture to be taken?"

Davis kept silent, but he felt like he *did* know that, had heard it in a movie or read it in some book.

"My movies are so visceral because they record actual deaths." No grandeur in this statement, just fact. "Deaths of the *soul*. All of the wounds sustained are to this incorporeal inner being, though it manifests itself in flesh and blood until the cameras are turned off. What is left afterwards, as you have seen, is mere shell. They become listless, unable to take any joy in the simplest of actions, unable to *feel*, because the soul is central to that which gives you humans emotion. Their minds become malleable and controllable for one that knows how to use them, as I programmed your friend Otter to return to me if your company moved against me any further." He opened his eyes to look at Davis, and the same glow was in them, obscuring the pupils, creating a halo of muted light around his head. "But the human body cannot survive long in this state, Mr. Lowe. If not disposed of…they find a way to dispose of themselves."

Davis didn't know if he believed in a soul, but he'd seen Otter with his own two eyes, pawing at his beloved keyboards as though not understanding them. He recalled what Jared told him about the conditions of Wickersham's apartment. They'd been trying out the things that once made them happy—booze and food and computers and all the insignificant minutia that made life tolerable—and finding no comfort in them.

A soul. Perhaps not something that went up or down when you died, but something that allowed you to feel, to experience…the thing that allowed even himself to create and appreciate art.

He found it an idea very easy to agree with, so easy it seemed ludicrous that everyone in the world hadn't accepted it as much as the fact that gravity causes things to fall down.

"So you killed them," he said, unable to tear his gaze from that unearthly glow coming from the director's eye sockets. "You killed them for your art."

"*Our* art." His eyes returned to their normal pits of black, for which Davis was thankful. "After all, we are in the same business, you and I."

Davis didn't even bother to comment on that. "So, what happens now? You're over, you're finished. The police are going to arrest you before you can finish *Arterial Slice*, and Susan will be safe."

"Oh, your authorities couldn't detain me. If the Incarnates couldn't, then no dim-witted human with a pair of metal bracelets stands a chance. But you're quite right about my time as Torsten Gross being finished. I will either change identities and start over, or leave this world altogether. However," here he paused, his awful grin returning, "*Arterial Slice* must be finished. It is the concluding chapter in my body of work and *nothing* will stop it. The film is all that matters now, and shooting commences tonight.

"As for your dear Susan...my associate should be collecting her right about now."

# TAKE 4

Everything was frozen except Susan's eyeballs, but she left them rooted to the door anyway, which shook with each thud from the other side. She imagined Krieg out there, bashing his massive shoulder into it over and over again.

Why? For God's sake, what did he want?

*C'mon move, please move,* she cried at her frozen limbs.

*Even if this was a horror movie, none of those stupid bitches ever got caught because they froze and let the killer hack them to pieces!*

They remained stubbornly still.

She needed to calm her racing heart before she could unlock. She closed her eyes, trying to think of something, *anything*, besides what was coming through that door.

Davis leapt to mind.

And with a completely undramatic snap, she was loose, stumbling at first, and then moving swiftly to her phone. She chanced another glance at the door, afraid it would lock her up again, but needing to see.

At the next collision, a jagged crack appeared in the thick wooden door around the lock, a half-circle that ringed it completely. Several splinters of wood flew out to skitter across the floor.

Susan picked up the cell and dialed 911.

Busy.

Just another night in L.A.

The door cracked open, the lock and knob left hanging on the frame, but it only opened as far as the chain would allow. An eye peered in the slot at her, bloodshot and maniacal, and a huge hand with knuckles the size of half-dollars curled around the edge of the door and pushed, pulling the golden chain taut.

Susan screamed and dropped the phone.

Krieg increased his force on the door, and now she could see the individual links on the chain straining and bending out of shape.

She turned and ran further into the apartment, a voice in the back of her mind reminding her that the only exit to this place was the one her attacker was breaking down.

Susan flew into the bedroom, a room whose only window had a cheerfully vertical drop of four floors to the pavement. *The Katherine Wickersham Special*, she thought against her will, and for a moment shame surfaced in the midst of her terror.

She looked around desperately, trying to find a weapon. Then again, unless she had a tank in the closet she'd forgotten about, perhaps concealment was the better option.

She heard the chain snap, then heavy boots on the floor, coming for her.

Susan dove under the bed, half-scooting, half-rolling under. So expected, so clichéd. She only needed to be in her panties to make the stereotype complete. She lay pressed against the carpet, gasping, straining to catch the sound of his approach.

Silence.

A hand closed around her ankle.

Susan screamed as she was pulled from under the bed so fast she got carpet burns on her stomach. She flipped over, squealing and slapping, but Krieg only smiled his dumb lunatic smile as he pushed her arms away. His monstrous hands found her neck, such big bear paws that only three of his fingers could fit around it.

He found her windpipe and squeezed, gently but steadily applying pressure.

Her air supply trickled and then cut off entirely, and, though she pried at those large, lumpy fingers, she knew it would do no good. Black spots blossomed like cancer in a diseased lung in front of her eyes.

Susan slumped.

# TAKE 5

When Lars Krieg released her, she had not so much as a red mark on her neck. The man hunched over her felt for the artery there and found it beating steadily. Krieg was good at what he did—had been since he was eleven and murdered his entire family in Munich—and he followed his orders to the letter, issued by the only person he took them from.

He grabbed the actress by one arm and lifted, muscling one shoulder into her side so she was slung across his neck, like a caveman carrying away his bride of choice.

Yes, he had his orders, and as far as he was concerned, this girl was the most important person on earth at the moment. He couldn't hurt her, couldn't leave a mark on her, and certainly couldn't kill her.

All of that would come later.

# TAKE 6

"Oh my God," Davis whispered. The need for action was a burning coal in his brain. "If you hurt her…"

"Don't worry, she'll be just fine when we're through," Gross said in that droning voice, smiling even wider at his empty threat, and Davis felt that rage from the hospital building in him again. His hands clenched against the sheets on his bed.

Gross raised his damaged hand from his lap, and held it beside the gun. That interior glow was dampened now, the papery, fake skin growing back over it even as he watched.

"See? Everyone is in one piece when my interest in them is finished." He laughed, and the current of electricity in it was enough to make Davis' eyes roll back in his head.

"I'll kill you."

"No, you won't. You are the only loose end plaguing me, and that is why I came to take care of you personally." He raised the barrel of the pistol to Davis' eye so that he was once again staring down that black hole at the bit of metal which would terminate his pointless existence on this planet.

"Hey, hey wait!" Davis cried. "Where's the camera? You can't kill me without a camera, my body will still be here! It'll look like murder!"

"But my boy, none of that matters anymore. By the time your body is discovered, *Arterial Slice* will be finished. Besides...I want to make sure there are no further mistakes when it comes to your death."

"But...but..." Davis sputtered, looking for the perfect last line.

"Goodbye, Mr. Lowe. You've been quite a thorn, and it shall be a pleasure to remove you."

His finger tightened on the trigger.

Davis closed his eyes.

There was another knock on the door.

# SCENE XIII

(moving shot)

# TAKE 1

"Who is that?" Gross hissed, beady eyes squinted in suspicion. His German accent returned flawlessly and fluidly, the sudden loss of his buzzing drone like a dramatic change in atmospheric pressure to Davis' aching skull.

"Gee, I don't know." The sarcasm sounded flat in his quavering voice. "Maybe any one of the hundred people that just heard that gunshot. Maybe the police."

Gross' eyes widened a little at the mention of the fuzz, and Davis realized something amazing: this guy might be a maestro of death with celluloid, but for all his talk and posturing, he wasn't exactly a mastermind in the real world, where there were no cameras to hide behind. The director looked nervous, totally shocked by the idea the police might actually show up during his antics. He might not be scared that they could detain him, but he was certainly afraid they could stop him.

Gross quelled the betrayal of emotion, then moved to the door and pressed his ear against it, keeping the gun on Davis.

The knock came again. And then, on its heels, "Lowe? Davis Lowe? Listen, I'm sorry to bother you again. It's Sidney Spitzen. I think we need to talk a little more about Gross."

Gross moved from the door to the window.

When he did, he switched the gun to his other hand.

Davis leapt.

He dove through the air, jumping so high he was fully airborne when he struck Gross. He felt his shoulder burrow into the man's gut, and if he'd actually been human and as old as he looked, that hit surely would've snapped bone. Instead, the director issued only a curt chuffing sound, and Davis' weight bore him into the wall with an earthshaking crash.

But the hand holding the gun didn't open.

Davis managed to get his knees under him before he hit the floor, jarring him the length of his spine, and grabbed for the pistol. Gross snorted with effort as he tried to pull away, and Davis pushed into him, forcing the arm out and away from them. They struggled briefly, the barrel of the gun swinging wildly across the room.

"Lowe?" Spitzen called uncertainly.

"*Help!*" Davis shouted. There was a thud and the door rattled in its cheap frame beside them. Davis groaned as he struggled with the director. "It's unlocked, genius!"

The knob turned, the door flung open, and Sidney Spitzen flew into the room. He paused when he saw the two of them, the gun pointed at his chest.

Davis felt Gross' finger jerk the trigger.

Spitzen leapt out of the way, landing on the floor at the foot of the bed a split second before the pistol went off again. The bullet shattered plaster as it punched into—and probably all the way through—the wall.

Instead of continuing to push the gun, Davis pulled, just once, a short, sharp tug. Gross, unprepared for the reversal, fell on top of Davis and then over him, spilling onto his back. Davis saw the gun hand finally pop open but couldn't catch the pistol before it tumbled across the room.

Gross flipped over and was on his knees with the speed of a cat. He snarled at Davis, like the night of the party when he'd been so mad at the paparazzi, then kicked out with one of his polished wingtips, missing Davis' jaw as he jerked away and grazing his shoulder instead.

The director crawled across the room for the gun.

"C'mon!" Davis shouted, but Spitzen didn't have to be told. He was already up and offering Davis a hand on his way through the door.

Several of Davis' neighbors had ventured outside for front row seats to whatever nine o'clock news story was in progress. He bet none of them had bothered to call the police, and he returned the favor by not warning them about the inhuman maniac in his apartment.

"Quick, in my car!" Davis was parked right in front of the door to his apartment, but they'd crossed only half the distance before they saw all four tires were flattened. Courtesy of the creature from Channel 12, no doubt. An insurance policy in case things went bad.

"Mine's over there!" Spitzen pointed at a green Toyota sedan a row away.

They ran, Davis chancing one look back. Gross hadn't emerged from the apartment yet.

Spitzen was parked perpendicular to the strip of motel, the passenger side facing Davis' apartment. He unlocked the doors with a remote and Davis hopped in, waiting while Spitzen raced around to the other side.

The reporter started the car, paused, and then, instead of throwing it into gear, he twisted around in his seat and dug in a pile of trash behind them.

"What are you doing?" Davis demanded.

"Give me a second!"

Davis looked out his window. Gross appeared in the door of his apartment, materializing out of the gloom. He gnashed his teeth and waved his arms, like a kid in the middle of an angry tantrum. The little crowd outside Davis' apartment scattered as Gross raised the gun and fired. A flash of orange exploded from the barrel, and Davis heard the slug thunk into the body of the car somewhere beside him.

"*Spitzen!*" Davis roared. "*Get us the fuck outta here!*"

"Hold on, I've gotta find it!" The man was half in the front seat and half in the back.

Gross fired again. The rear passenger window exploded inward in a spray of safety glass.

Davis reached over, threw the car into gear, and tromped on the accelerator. They lurched forward, nearly sideswiping an Escort, and Spitzen abandoned his search to drive the car, cursing under his breath. They squealed out of the motel parking lot, dodging another bullet as they went. Davis looked back and saw Gross running to his own car, the dark blue Mercedes from the party.

# TAKE 2

"He's fucking crazy!" Spitzen exclaimed. The car gave a squeal of tortured rubber as he sped out onto the road toward the freeway, jumping a curb with a bark of protest from his shocks and dodging two lovebirds making out in the process. "He's completely nuts! I mean, he's shooting at people in public! His...his career is over!"

Davis stifled a hysteric laugh at the seriousness with which the reporter said this. "Trust me, he's not crazy. I wish it were that simple."

"What do you mean?"

"You really want your scoop, newsman? How about this: Torsten Gross ain't even human." Spitzen gave him a sharp, questioning look, but before he began the inevitable list of questions, Davis snapped, "What the hell were you looking for in the backseat while I was being used for target practice?"

"My camera. A picture of him on a rampage would've been worth a mint. What do you mean he's 'not human?'"

Davis sighed and ran through his conversation with Gross, telling him about the gunshot and that soft interior glow beneath his fake skin, realizing how idiotic the entire episode sounded when described with as few words as possible.

When he was done, the reporter's mouth was pressed into a thin line. "Well, that's definitely the most amazing story I've ever heard. I'm sure they'll love to hear it while they're fitting you for your strait jacket."

"Now I know what Jared felt like," Davis muttered.

"You expect me to believe that? Gross is up to something—*obviously*—but c'mon..."

"Does it make sense of all those things you told me about this afternoon?"

"Yeah, but so would saying, 'A wizard did it.'"

"I can't help how it sounds, but that's your final piece of the puzzle. And it's a bigger story than you even imagined."

"Okay, I'll reserve judgment. What I can say for sure is, he's at the end of his rope. He made his first overt action against someone in thirty years, and then managed to let you escape. All you have to do now is call the cops on him. With me as a witness, he'll never finish *Slice*. Girlfriend safe, friends avenged, I have my story... all our problems solved."

"Not yet. We'll go to the police, but I have to make sure Susan is safe first. She's coming with us until this over. Do you have a phone I can use?"

Spitzen removed a cell from the car charger in the ash-tray. Davis dialed Susan's number and got voicemail again.

"Oh God. What if they've got her? They could be taking her to the set right now."

"That's all the more reason to call the cops."

"We don't have any real proof!" He could feel himself slipping over the steep abyss into full-on hysteria. "I can't risk them having to question us for hours or sitting on this too long while they wait for warrants!"

"Not enough proof? You said you know where they're taking her. With me backing you up, the cops will at least go to check it out! If she's been kidnapped, we'll have him red-handed!"

"Yeah, unless he kills her before they get there. Hell, she might've gone with him willingly if he told her they were filming tonight." Davis slammed his hand against the dash hard enough to make his bones ache. "Dammit, I didn't say one word to warn her when I had the chance."

They lapsed into silence. The car whipped through traffic, heading north toward Hollywood. "He won't kill her though," Spitzen said slowly. "Not if the movie's as important to him as you say. Not until she's filmed her part."

"The movie." An idea snapped into his head like a popped rubber band. He spoke excitedly, "Her final scene is the climax of the movie! The only other actors in it are Krieg...and *Tonya Werdner!*"

Spitzen nodded, getting the idea immediately. "If he doesn't have Werdner, he can't film the scene."

"Of course not! Her character is the hero of the movie!"

Spitzen grabbed his phone back from Davis and placed a phone call of his own. Within five minutes he had Davis write down a telephone number and address on paper from the back seat. "The benefits of doing a few publicity pieces on the right up-and-comers," he said, in response to Davis' raised eyebrow. "I'll head towards her house, you give her a call."

All Davis had was a home number for Werdner. He told the person that answered it was an emergency that he speak to the actress. The voice, vaguely reminiscent of Pickerill's faux accent, informed him she was in the middle of a yoga lesson and did not come out for anyone. No amount of cajoling would bring the man to budge from this. At last, Davis hung up the phone in frustration.

"A yoga lesson! A fucking yoga lesson!"

"That's all right. If we can't call ahead, neither can Gross. He's gonna have to go to her house just like we are." Spitzen pushed the accelerator to the floor and wove through traffic.

# TAKE 3

Werdner lived in exactly the sort of palatial estate Davis expected. It sat on the southern edge of San Fernando, on roughly a zillion acres of lush, green hillside. A gravel driveway lit only by occasional electric lamps made to look like tiki torches carried them uphill through verdant shrubbery and thick foliage for at least half a mile until the road was lost behind them and dead-ended at a looming steel gate with speaker boxes on both sides. Through the gate, they could see her brownstone three-story, two-wing mansion. A fountain stood in the middle of a circular driveway on the other side of the gate, with a wide, curved set of stairs leading up to the massive front door.

Davis saw no sign of Gross' car, but there was no way he could've beaten them here unless he possessed another supernatural power he hadn't divulged in his diatribe.

"Let me try," Davis said. He reached through the window and clicked the speaker box on his side of the car. This time a Hispanic voice answered. "I need to speak to Miss Werdner, this is an emergency! I'm...I'm part of the crew working on her new movie!"

"I-I don't know... She's in her yoga lesson...and I'm not supposed to..."

This cookie wasn't nearly as tough as the one on the phone. "Sir, go and get her now, or I assure you, you will be out of a job before morning." As he spoke, he thought he heard the sound of a well-tuned engine growling in the distance behind them.

"Okay, *Señor*, but if she's angry, I'm not taking the blame."

"Let me worry about that." It *was* an engine. Coming up the driveway. Davis slid back into the car and looked at Spitzen, who frowned and checked in the rearview mirror.

"I feel like I just landed in the *Cannonball Run*."

Davis opened his mouth to claim the Burt Reynolds role, when they heard, "*What do you want?*" This came from the speaker box so loud and shrill that the phonics of the device ascended into static for a moment. "This better be good, asshole, or I'll shove my foot so far up your ass, I'll be wearing your teeth as toenail polish!"

Davis leaned back out, thinking yoga wasn't doing this bitch much good. "Miss Werdner, I'm Davis Lowe, you know my girlfriend Susan, I work on second unit for *Arterial Slice*—"

"What the *fuck* is second unit doing at my *house?* I'll have to get the driveway torn out and replaced! If Gross sent you, I'm gonna tear that fucker's head off!"

"Miss Werdner, this is urgent! If we could just come in and talk to you—"

But it was her that did the talking, and right over him. "I mean, you come to my house, tell me you have an emergency—oh, and Javier, darling, you're fired—and you pull me out of my yoga lesson just when I was about to reach... *Nervosa* or whatever...."

At the last bend of the driveway, about a hundred yards back, Gross' Mercedes shot around the corner. It squealed to a stop when its driver spotted them, then angled toward them and peeled out, spraying a plume of dirt and gravel behind it.

Werdner babbled on about her ascension to a higher plane. "...and I just can't believe it, I've never had my privacy invaded like this. If you think I'm ever going to—"

Spitzen leaned out the window to the box on his side. He pressed the button and said, "Miss Werdner, my name is Sidney Spitzen and I'm with *Entertainment Tonight*. Got time for an interview?"

Her squawking fell silent, and the gate in front of them slid smoothly open.

# TAKE 4

As Sidney Spitzen waited impatiently for the gate to open wide enough to grant his trusty Toyota clearance, he couldn't help but try to puzzle out how his life had gone from reporting the story to *being* the story. He liked Lowe, who seemed like an okay guy, and he liked Mane even more, who had seemed like *his* kind of guy, but he didn't know either one of them well enough to get shot.

He gunned the engine as soon as the gate was wide enough to admit them, glancing in the rearview at the same time. The director (or whatever he was; he hadn't had time to figure out if he believed the story Lowe had fed him after their escape) barreled toward them with as much speed as he'd been able to gain from the far side of the driveway. Spitzen could see him in there, rage on his face as he prepared to ram them.

Coming out of a dead stand still, they would never escape.

The gate reached its maximum width and was trundling back closed just as quickly; Tonya Werdner was prepared in case her masturbatory fan base ever mobbed her home. Instead of pulling all the way through, Spitzen stopped the car in the middle of the retracting gate.

"Hold on!"

Gross struck them at roughly forty miles an hour, throwing them forward another five feet, and bouncing them first back in their seats and then forward onto the dashboard. Spitzen's chin struck the steering wheel with a grunt, bringing his teeth together with a clack. He saw Lowe slam his nose into the dash and bring a geyser of blood flooding over his lips.

The car had come to rest with its rear end stuck in the middle of the gate. The two sides of the wrought iron were now pressing into his trunk, their motors whining as they attempted to close, but the entrance was blocked with them on one side and the director on the other.

"C'mon." Lowe dribbled blood as he opened the door and stumbled out onto the driveway.

Spitzen straightened his glasses and turned in his seat again, digging through mountains of trash and paperwork until he spotted what he'd been looking for earlier.

His brand new Nikon, still in one piece. He intended to have a picture to go with this story. Spitzen grabbed the strap and wobbled out of the car, nearly falling to his knees. His legs didn't want to obey him; they'd turned to useless strands of wet noodles from shock.

"My car," he moaned. Gross' front end was meshed with

his rear, so much twisted metal and glass between them it was impossible to tell where one ended and the next began.

"Forget it!" Lowe shouted back as he ran for the house.

"*Forget it?* Being freelance means I can't exactly call this a business expense, you know! Gross is gonna pay for this!"

A bullet screamed in the night as the man in question shot at them through the gate.

Lowe was halfway to the steps of the mansion. Spitzen started that way before he turned (ignoring the way everything blurred as he did), raised the camera, had just enough time to turn on the flash, and started shooting like mad.

As soon as the first bright pop went off, Gross screamed and leapt for cover behind his accordioned vehicle.

Spitzen lowered the camera, staring at the spot where Gross had stood.

For just a second, when he looked through the viewfinder…

"Did you just see—?" he began, and then Lowe grabbed him and pulled him toward the house. He put the camera strap over his neck and let the device dangle across his chest so he could use his arms for balance. The fog was clearing out of his brain, but he still felt like he was moving through molasses.

Tonya Werdner came out of the house, dressed in a tiny little black skirt and matching midriff blouse, blond hair pulled back in a ponytail. She smiled broadly, no trace of the harridan screeching at them on the speaker.

"Welcome to my home," she said warmly. Then she saw the blood on Lowe's face and the tangle of cars at her gate. "What the hell happened out here? Is that…Gross?"

The director scrambled over the hood of his car and onto Spitzen's trunk, trying to climb through the gate. He raised the gun and fired two more rounds which went…God knew where. The man really was a terrible shot.

"Hi, Gross!" Werdner said with a dopey grin and raised her arm to wave.

"Are you crazy?" Spitzen shouted. "He's shooting at us!" But it wasn't insanity; he knew actresses like this got so wrapped up in the delusion of their career that the whole world became one continual, ongoing movie.

"Get inside," Lowe growled, ushering her the other direction.

Spitzen opened his mouth as another shot rang out, and then pain like a branding iron seared his shoulder. He grabbed at his left arm, and his hand came away cov-ered in blood.

"Jesus, are you all right?" Lowe asked.

Spitzen couldn't answer. It felt like he was missing a hamburger's worth of flesh off the back of his arm.

"Spitzen?"

He managed a sickly smile. "I...I think it's a flesh wound. Do those actually happen in real life?"

"You'll live." Lowe grabbed him by the other arm, latched on to Werdner, and yanked them both into the mansion.

"I *demand* to know what's going on!"

Lowe closed and bolted her front door without answering. In front of them was a foyer with a grand staircase splitting in two directions and a chandelier whose worth could feed all of China for a year. No way did she make this kind of scratch from her cable porn *oeuvre*.

"Lady, with all due respect, *shut up*," Spitzen told her. The look she gave him could've started a forest fire.

"Is there a back way out of here?" Lowe asked, plugging his bleeding nose with two fingers. When Werdner hesitated, he said, "Tell us."

She frowned, pursing her luscious set of lips. Spitzen remembered catching one of her seedier flicks on Showtime After Dark just a couple of weeks ago, and he knew what those lips were capable of. "The garage on the back of the house has a service road."

He grabbed her arm and pulled her further into the house, towards the staircase with its banisters of gold, before she could argue. Spitzen followed on their heels, one hand clamped to the bleeding hole in his arm.

A butler—an actual butler, in a tuxedo complete with ascot—descended the staircase toward them, and asked in a stiff, completely unpanicked tone, "Madam, shall I call the police?"

"*Yes!*" Werdner screamed. "I'm being kidnapped!"

"No!" Lowe shouted over her. "It's all part of the movie!" With this senseless excuse, he dragged her through an archway to the left of the stairs and further into the house.

Spitzen shrugged and winced at the pain unleashed in his arm from the motion. Behind them, he could hear pounding at the front of the house. "You know how some of these directors are."

Mr. Belvedere raised one fuzzy eyebrow. "No sir, I'm afraid I don't."

The archway led them into an obscenely large kitchen, and a muscular Italian man wearing nothing but a towel stepped out of a room on their right. Spitzen suddenly understood why the yoga lesson was so important.

"Are we continuing then, Miss Werdner?" His dim wits kept him from reacting to the two blood-covered men dragging his student away.

"Don't you *dare* go anywhere, Tony!" she shrieked over her shoulder.

"Where's the garage?" Lowe barked at the actress.

She pointed to another door just ahead. "Don't think you're taking one of *my* cars!"

"We're not. You're coming with us."

Lowe opened the new door into darkness and pushed Werdner through. She either hit a light switch somewhere on the other side or the room had motion-activated sensors. The overheads illuminated a row of high-end sports cars that would make Jay Leno jealous. The closest one was a stark yellow Ferrari.

Lowe pointed at it. "The keys."

"You guys are *not* getting blood in my Ferrari!"

"The keys," Lowe snarled.

"Fine, but I'm driving." She removed a set of keys from a peg on the wall, which Lowe promptly grabbed from her. "Hey!"

They went to the car, and now Spitzen was sure he heard yelling in German from somewhere in the house behind them. Maybe they should've taken Tony and Belvedere, and poor unemployed Javier with them.

Lowe started the vehicle and raised the garage door in front of them. Werdner stood beside the open passenger door, waiting for Spitzen to cram in the middle.

"Ladies first," he said.

"You guys are assholes," she muttered as she crawled in, giving him a generous and heavenly view of her outfit's matching panties.

"Hey, I'm a wounded man."

"You're gonna be!"

Lowe throttled the engine, and the three of them roared into the night.

# TAKE 5

"I want to know what's going on." Werdner said, for the thousandth time.

She had been mostly quiet (and what a rarity that must be) as Davis raced them down the narrow service road. He'd doubled back to the freeway, then pulled over at the first gas station they came to. He needed to think, needed to figure out what came next. They'd been so intent on grabbing Werdner, at foiling Gross' plans, he hadn't stopped to think what they were going to do with her, or how she would help them get back Susan.

"This *is* kidnapping, you know," she said, and Davis felt sorry for anyone that would try to hold this woman for ransom. She paced back and forth on the edge of the parking lot by the freeway onramp like a hooker waiting for her john, her clothing only aiding in the image. Apparently he wasn't the only one who thought so; three cars had already slowed until she gave them the finger and waved them on. "You took me from my home and now you're holding me against my will."

"We saved your life back there." Spitzen slumped in the passenger seat with his feet hanging out. "Show a little gratitude."

It wasn't entirely accurate. Davis knew Gross wouldn't shoot her, or the movie couldn't be finished. But let her think that if it stopped her whining.

It didn't. "Yeah, uh, *why* did you have to save my life again? Who was going to kill me? It looked like Gross was after you two, and I can't say I blame him, having been in your company for more than five minutes!"

Davis wiped at his blood-crusted nostrils as he paced in front of the vehicle and then turned to Spitzen. "How's your arm?"

"Not too bad." The entire shoulder of the reporter's white shirt was stained crimson. He was still awake and alert, but had gone a shade of white a corpse would envy. "I think he just tore a chunk out. Hurts like a bastard, but like you said, I'll live."

"Why was he shooting at you anyway?" Werdner chattered on. "Why was the director of my movie at my house in the middle of the night, shooting at a guy from second unit and…whatever you are?"

Spitzen exchanged a look with Davis. "She's not going to stop until you tell her. Or cut out her voice box. Personally, I'm game for either."

"See, *now* you're threatening me."

"Quiet," Davis snapped. "Gross was coming to kidnap you. To force you to film the rest of the movie tonight."

Panic spread across her narrow features. "*Tonight?* There's a cast call *tonight?* Shit, you have to get me there!"

Spitzen groaned. "This is your show. What do we do now?"

"Go to the cops. At long as we have her, he can't film."

As if on cue, low, tinny music started playing from somewhere. Davis recognized the bouncy style for what it was immediately: porno music.

"It's my cell." Werdner took a tiny phone from a pocket on the back of her short skirt. The two men stared at her with raised eyebrows. "What? I always have my cell on me." She answered and said, "Hello? Oh hi, Gross! I'm—! What? Oh. He wants to talk to *you*." She held the phone out to Davis, with a sulky frown.

"Explain it to her," Davis told Spitzen as he took the cellular. "Tell her everything."

"Yeah, that'll go over well."

Davis put the phone to his ear. "Hello?"

"Mr. Lowe." The director was cool and completely in control again. "It appears you have something I want, and vice versa. I'll make it simple, so that even you may comprehend. You and your new friend bring Werdner to the set, or I kill your girlfriend."

"If I bring Werdner to you and you film the ending, Susan dies anyway. You better think up a better incentive than that."

Davis expected the man to placate him, to promise not to kill Susan in the finale, but Gross didn't even bother. "Yes, but if you come, you have at least the chance of saving her. Of defeating me. If you go to the police, as I'm sure you're considering, you know for certain she will die."

"I don't think so. You can't kill her. You may not be afraid the police can imprison you, but you're damn sure scared they'll put the kibosh on *Arterial Slice*. All we have to do is go to them and keep Werdner away from you."

"Oh, poor Mr. Lowe." Davis didn't like the sarcastic pity in that. That tone suggested Gross was ten steps ahead, and Davis wanted him two behind. "The film *will* be finished, it just may have to be at some indeterminate point in the future. Miss Werdner is the only indispensable element, and I will get to her eventually. Miss Campbell, on the other hand, has already filmed all of her key scenes, and all of her lines. If need be, I can replace her with a double in the finale without serious loss of continuity, but I would rather not. If you go to the police though, I assure you, I will kill her long before they get here, if only to have my revenge on you. Of course, when they get here, they'll find her alive, although she will be a bit...lackluster." Davis could hear that terrible smile in his words. "I don't think the sex will be quite as good either."

"You bastard."

"You might even be able to keep her safe for some time, but, sooner or later, Miss Campbell will choose to end it all rather than go through life with a dead soul. Not even loving you will be enough to motivate her."

The director had him, whether it was bluff or not, it was too big of a risk. Davis' throat locked, but he had to force something out. "How…how do you know I haven't already gone to the police?"

"Because I know *you*, Mr. Lowe. I know you from your work if nothing else. You agonize over each shot, but not for the same reasons I would. You are the most self-doubting, indecisive, and insecure man I have ever met. You look too far to the future, and not enough at the next step you must take, and it freezes you. You see, you would not take such bold action, even if I waited another few hours to contact you; you are incapable."

Davis swallowed. The comment cut him to the bone so succinctly Gross might've known him his whole life.

"What do you want?" All the bravado he'd worked up abandoned him.

"I told you. Bring the girl to the set. Just drop her off, if you and your friend choose the cowardly path. Or, if not, come in, and we shall have ourselves a little…ol' west showdown. Isn't that what you Americans love?"

"We'll…we'll be there." Davis ended the call and looked at his companions. They'd just finished their own conversation and Werdner stared at Spitzen with her mouth open and brow drawn together in horror. "You tell her?"

"As much as I even understood. What'd he say?"

"We can't go to the police. We have to…take her to the set." He jerked a thumb at Werdner.

"What? No way," the actress said. "Look, I don't know what kind of game you two are playing, but I want out."

"It's all true."

"Yeah, I don't believe for a second some shit about Gross 'stealing souls,' but it wouldn't suprise me in the least that he'd murder somebody to finish his fucking movie. I *told* my agent I shouldn't take this goddamn part. I'm done! You hear me? Done! Breach of contract, whatever, Trimax can see me in court!"

As she continued to rant, Spitzen said, "Lowe, I know you're worried, but wasn't the point of grabbing our amiable friend here to keep her *away* from him? The only reason he wants us there is so he can kill us too."

"But if I don't go, he's gonna kill Susan." Davis' eyes burned. "I don't intend to just hand Werdner over; I know the only option is to fight him. I...I don't expect you to understand, but...I've failed. I failed Otter and Jared; I'm responsible for what happened to them. I've failed Susan more times than I can count, but I can't fail her this time. If you two wanna leave, I won't stop you. I stand as much chance alone."

Spitzen struggled up from his reclined position. "Don't think for a second you're getting out of my sight until this thing is over, Lowe."

Davis smiled. "Thanks."

"Ha, thanks nothing! You think I'm doing this because we're buddies? Gross owes me the story of the millennium and wherever you go, he seems to follow. I wouldn't miss this for the world."

"Huh. Well, I guess I'll take what I can get."

"And I suppose this is the moment when my concern for Susan breaks me down and I realize I have a heart of gold and decide to help," Werdner said in a sweet, high-pitched voice. It lowered nearly a full octave as she growled, "Well, the two of you can go butt fuck each other for all I care. I'm not going."

"Of all of us, you're the only one that's safe. You don't die in the film, so he can't harm you."

"I said I'm done."

"You bitch," Spitzen said.

"Leave her alone."

"No, I won't." The reporter staggered to his feet using one arm so he could look her in the eyes. "Lady, I said it once and I'll say it again: we saved your miserable excuse for a life."

The actress snorted. "And I'm supposed to repay you by throwing it away again?"

"No, you aren't." And then, with a growing grin, "but what do you think your fans and the media are going to say when they hear you allowed a woman—a colleague, a *friend*—to die?"

"You honestly think anyone would care?"

"Fine, I won't defame you; I'll make it my personal mssion in life to see that you're *forgotten*. Once I get the word out to the journalism community, you won't see another piece about you, period. Your press junkets will be empty, the paparazzi will scatter. In a month, your name will forever be followed by the question, 'Who?'"

Werdner seemed about to argue, but looked away instead, toward the freeway, and then sighed. "So what's the plan? Do either one of you guys even have a weapon? Preferably a gun?"

"Even if we did, it might help against Krieg, but it wouldn't do any good in Gross' case," Davis said. "I just watched the man shoot himself in the hand and then it healed in seconds, so I don't know if anything we can come up with is gonna hurt him."

"Hold on," Spitzen countered. "Did you see him when I took his picture?"

"Yeah, he..." Davis' jaw fell open. "He screamed and jumped away."

"But did you see him what happened to him? During the flash? I was looking through the viewfinder and I could have sworn I saw..."

The statement stretched out until Werdner prompted, "What? What did you see? I *hate* dramatic pauses!"

"It…it was just a blur because he was moving so fast, but it was glowing, just like what you described. Only all over his body. Like he was made of light. It was like I could…see through his disguise when the picture was taken."

"Gross had Krieg beat up some paparazzi that tried to take his picture." Davis pointed at the camera around Spitzen's neck. "And he wouldn't allow any cameras or recording devices into the press conference for Wickersham."

"And, like I told you, I didn't come across any pictures of him in my research. The question is, does he avoid them so that nobody finds out his secret, or does it actually hurt him?"

"Either way, it's the only edge we've got against Gross. That only leaves Krieg."

"Who, despite being human, is probably the bigger threat."

"We'll just have to handle him somehow. There's three of us. Surely we can beat him up or knock him out or something."

"Are we talking about the same eight-foot tall giant here, Lowe?"

"Okay, let's get one thing straight," Werdner said. "You may have kidnapped me and blackmailed me into going with you, but I didn't agree to help in any sort of rescue."

"You can be the bait then," Spitzen told her.

"And you can kiss my ass."

"We don't have time for this." Davis moved back toward the car. "Let's get going."

There was no more argument as they crammed into the Ferrari. Davis was left wondering how it had come to this, him charging into battle against a supernatural creature with two people he barely knew.

And it started out to be such a normal life.

It was nearly nine o'clock, and a very full moon was on the rise in the L.A. sky.

# TAKE 6

When Susan opened her eyes, she didn't recognize her bedroom. She blamed it on the cold she must be getting; her head ached and her throat felt scratchy and raw. Then she realized the ceiling above her was constructed of corrugated metal and that she wasn't in her bed, but on a cold metal slab.

Memories returned as she spotted a camera almost directly above her, one of the small innocuous boxes that Gross favored. It clung to a steel rafter, staring down at her with clinical disassociation.

She tried to sit up, but her hands were bound to the table by leather straps above her head. Her legs were similarly attached at the bottom and a fifth, larger strap stretched around her waist. She wasn't in the clothes she'd been wearing at home, but a plain white garment that stopped just above her knees, an outfit she'd worn a lot over the last month.

Denise Hutson's duds. A patient's outfit. Someone had put her in wardrobe while she was unconscious.

She shuddered, then raised her head, straining her neck to get a look at her surroundings.

Susan recognized the warehouse, but this was a part of the set she'd never seen. She knew it anyway, from its detailed description in the *Arterial Slice* script: a large, square room that smelled of forgotten abuse. The medical table she was strapped to stood alone in the middle, under a single bulb shining down from above like a spotlight. No windows, and most of everything else was just shadows, but if she squinted she could see the sides of the room were littered with rusty antique medical equipment.

A dingy medical dungeon in Chesterfield Hospital where the climax took place. Hutson was to be tortured and murdered while the killer and Nurse Terry Yancy battled it out. Gross had told both her and Werdner they wouldn't be allowed to see it until the final take of the film, since neither of their characters would be familiar with it.

All fake, all pretend, all just acting. And yet she'd been choked to the point of unconsciousness by the actor that was supposed to be doing the murdering, and brought here in the middle of the night.

What was *real* anymore? She felt her muscles start to lock and forced herself to calm.

"Hello?" It hurt her throat to talk.

In response, one of the shadows on her left moved, and she clamped down on a scream. Krieg lumbered out of the darkness. His eyes glittered with sick amusement as he examined her. She remembered the feel of his hands around her throat and swallowed just to make sure they weren't still there.

"You're awake, my dear." This came from her right. She looked over to see Gross emerging from the darkness outside the little ring of light her world had been reduced to. "I was afraid Lars perhaps choked you too hard. We wouldn't want you to sleep through your big performance."

"Gross...what's going on?"

"Shhhh, no questions, my dear. It'll be so much better for the film if you're left in the dark to scream your lungs out. Soon your boyfriend will be delivering the final component we need to begin, and this movie will have its…what do they say here? 'Martini shot'?"

"Davis?" She was relieved at the idea of seeing him, but Gross' slightly mocking tone told her it might not be the healthiest thing for him.

"Oh, yes, he'll be here. And when he comes…I'm going to kill *all* of you." Gross nodded, something fatherly about the motion. He put a dry, unpleasant hand on her forehead. "I'll kill you and him and the other meddler. Even Werdner, once she's delivered my denouement. I might even hunt down Reilly in whatever rat nest he calls home and kill him for good measure."

Susan gaped at him. It was too difficult to even attempt speech now, and not because Krieg had given her throat the Homer Simpson treatment.

*Well, at least your part's been elevated. From victim to bonafide damsel-in-distress.*

"Rest now," Gross said, turning to leave. "You'll need it."

# SCENE XIV

(enter stage left)

There are certain prerequisite qualities for the dwelling/hideout/fortress of the villain in any horror movie. The place in question should be dark in composition and surroundings, with a healthy layer of fog to give it a necessary dose of isolation.

The only thing the dead warehouse was missing from the list when the three of them arrived was that smothering ring of fog, but that had never stopped the day-to-day monsters of Los Angeles. Nevertheless, Davis kept expecting hidden machines to start pumping it across the parking lot as they pulled to a stop in Werdner's Ferrari. The moon overhead cast a wan light, and the building reached out with invisible hands to gather it right back in.

"Should we park somewhere else, try to sneak in?" Spitzen leaned forward in his seat, staring at the warehouse as he spoke. Davis wondered if it was the first time he'd seen the place, and felt very sorry for him if it was.

"I don't think it'll matter. He'll know we're here no matter what we do."

They were quiet, even Werdner, as they digested this.

"We should try to avoid Gross and Krieg entirely. I only care about finding Susan and getting her out of there."

"That's all well and good for you, but *I'm* the one he wants. What are you gonna do about protecting me?" Werdner looked genuinely scared, perhaps the only words he'd ever heard her say without her trademarked snide tone.

"We're all leaving here together. And going straight to the police." He leaned around her to look at Spitzen. "Keep that camera handy."

Spitzen moved one hand up to insure the strap was tight around his neck. "It's staying right here. Although I'd still rather have a gun, or a knife, or something."

Davis nodded. Even a flashlight would be nice. If they'd had more time to plan, they might've come up with something, but he didn't want to risk Gross thinking they went to the police.

They got out of the car. Davis waited for Werdner to comment on the fact that they were leaving her $250K automobile in the middle of grand theft auto territory, but she was staring at the warehouse too hard to gripe. This place exuded evil like the smoke that must once have billowed from its smokestack. It wasn't something one could put a finger on, just some whispered undercurrent in its aura, so intangible the only part of the body that could sense it was…was…

*The soul?*

They crossed the short stretch of parking lot between them and the main door, Werdner flanked by the two men. The night was deadly silent, the closest sounds that of traffic on the surrounding streets, but not so much as a single person crossed by the corner where the set was located, by car or foot.

But wasn't that the way showdowns always happened in the movies?

*It's not a movie*, Davis told himself for what felt like the thousandth time.

*Oh yes it is, it's all just one big movie, and Gross is directing. Hell, he might be* God.

They reached the entrance and Davis pulled open the door.

# TAKE 2

Davis expected darkness to come spilling out, but weak fluorescents lit the path in front of them from the ceiling. Gross didn't want them falling in the dark before he had his fun.

But he also expected to see the short stretch of hallway that led to the main suite of sets—the hospital room and inmate row and the others—but instead, a longer corridor lay in front of them, opening onto some dim chamber far on the other end.

"This isn't right." Davis swung the door back closed and glanced at the outside to ensure it was the same one.

"Yeah, this is all changed around." Werdner poked her head tentatively inside.

"What do you mean 'changed around?' Are you saying he remodeled the interior?" Spitzen asked.

"No, we're saying he fucking *rebuilt* the place. This hallway has never been here. How is that possible?"

"It's here now." Davis stepped inside. He had to agree with the actress. This wasn't a matter of redecorating. The interior structure had been entirely reconstructed, a job that would take weeks, and yet Davis had been here only five days ago.

And the place *still* looked a hundred years old.

What was that Samantha Cox had told him, about the director hiring 'outside set designers?' Perhaps Gross hadn't given up his whole palette of secrets after all.

The other two followed him inside. He felt a tense moment when the door clicked shut behind them, akin to claustrophobia but far more primal.

That unease continued to grow in him like a beanstalk, from his chest up his spinal cord to his brain, and it was more than the mere fact that they were walking into a creature's lair.

A sensation as light and gossamer as a spider's web fell across the back of his neck, but he couldn't pinpoint its source.

So Spitzen did it for him.

"Big Brother is watching you," the reporter said quietly. He pointed at the junction of wall and ceiling on their right. A camera posted there spied on them, its small red eye hateful, reminding Davis briefly of HAL from *2001*, a film that nearly made him piss his pants once upon a time. It turned to follow them as they went by. "So much for the element of surprise."

"It would've been the same no matter which door we came in."

"I feel like I'm entering CIA headquarters. Should we break them?"

They were both looking at Davis, waiting for him to make the decision. It was his idea to come, and he supposed that made him the leader of the expedition, but he felt weighted down to know a further two lives were on his head if he fucked this up. In this case, however, he had a good answer.

"Wouldn't do any good. Look." He pointed at another camera just ahead, placed so that anyone coming down this corridor would be in its range of vision before they exited the last camera's. And another after that.

"Smile. You're on Candid Camera," he heard Werdner mutter to his right. "How do they know to follow us like that?"

"They might be motion-sensitive."

"Or Gross might have a booth somewhere," Spitzen said. "Those look like closed-circuit jobs. Either one of you guys ever seen a room like that in the building?"

They both shook their heads. Werdner whispered, "How do you know he doesn't control them with his mind or whatever? You said he wasn't...*human!*"

"Power," Davis muttered.

"Huh?"

"Jared. He said, 'Gross needs power.'" That last hurried phone call came back to him, not the shouted and static-torn gibberish, but that last phrase, the one he'd thought was a final insult at Gross. Now, in context, he understood his friend's last words had been an attempted warning, and he felt guilty all over again. "I think the cameras are the only real thing about him. He might be able to work some sort of magic with them, *through* them, but they still require a power source just like any camera. And he needs someplace to record whatever they see."

"That makes sense," Spitzen said. "We know something went wrong when Mane showed up here a few days ago; it's the only explanation for why Gross was forced to try killing him the old-fashioned way. If it has anything to do with those cameras, that's a weakness."

"Exactly. The only problem is, he's watching every move we make. If there *is* someplace he controls the cameras from, he'll never even let us get close to it."

There were no other branches or exits from the corridor before they reached the chamber at the end, a small niche where the hallway opened up and then dead-ended in front of three doors. Here again, a scenario so classic it was straight out of a fantasy epic: the hero faced with three doors to puzzle out the correct one. All looked the same, old and rotted wood, not even any writing to distinguish them from one another.

Davis went to the one in the middle and reached for the knob.

"No," Werdner said sharply.

"What?"

"Too predictable! Never pick the middle one, it's what everybody expects!"

"That's ridiculous!"

"It's the one *you* went for, isn't it?"

"Actually, statistically speaking, I think the one on the left is most likely," Spitzen said.

"And in a situation like this you always want to do what the villain doesn't expect, even I know that!"

Davis gave them a glare and went to the door on the right. He turned the knob, not bothering to say that if Gross wanted to herd them in a particular direction, he would have already arranged the building to do so. It was unlocked. "You both satisfied?"

"I'm being used as bait for two killers while you rescue some other damsel. I'm pretty far from fucking satisfied." Werdner strolled through in front of him in her slinky dress. Davis followed, holding the door open for Spitzen.

The edge was jerked from his hand. The door slammed shut.

"Spitzen!" Davis spun…and blinked stupidly.

The door was gone. There was nothing where they'd entered but blank metal wall, not even the slightest outline of an entrance. Davis put his hands against it, disbelieving his eyes by feeling for the seam instead.

Nothing. Not a single imperfection in the smooth wall.

Suddenly it wasn't such a big surprise that the building was so drastically changed.

Davis pounded on the wall, succeeded in hurting his hand, and then put his shoulder to it with one short, swift hit. It felt as solid as it looked, but on the other side he could hear Spitzen knocking as well, so muffled he might be a mile away.

"There goes our camera," Werdner said cheerfully. "Could've picked up a couple of disposables, you know."

"I hope he leaves. He can't go wandering around by himself."

"What makes you think the door we came in didn't disappear too?" She frowned and looked away. "What makes you think he's gonna let *any* of us out of here alive, no matter what the script says?"

Davis turned to study the room they were now trapped in. It was another short chamber with only one other door, but to their left was a row of metal lockers. They looked old and rusted, but in Gross' playground, looks meant nothing.

Werdner's name was labeled in small, neat print on one.

His was on another.

"*Greetings!*" The voice was metallic and loud, booming all around them. Davis spotted the camera in the corner, set at an angle to record everything that went on in here. A loudspeaker was mounted beneath it. "*I'm so glad you were smart enough to come! Miss Campbell's been so lonely.*"

Werdner gave the camera the finger.

"*Now, now, Miss Werdner, you should to be cautious about your actions on film. This could end up as a blooper on YouTube.*"

The actress swallowed and lowered her hand.

"*Excellent. If you will open up the lockers with your names, you will find everything you need to get on with to-night's scene.*"

Werdner flashed Davis a look, one that said she wanted to open that locker like she wanted a flaming dose of gonor-rhea. Or another one, in her case. They went together, put-ting their hands on the small, flat handles. Davis cringed as he pulled the release.

He couldn't make sense of what was inside at first. Not until Werdner said, "It's my nurse's costume," did he real-ize the bundle hanging in the back of his locker was doctor scrubs, made of the standard blue-green material worn in every hospital known to man.

*"I know the union requires me to give separate dressing rooms for little boys and girls,"* Gross said over the PA system, *"but I'm sure you two can still provide a modicum of modesty."*

"I don't understand." Werdner looked into his locker. "Why do you have a costume? What's he doing?"

Davis continued to stare at the scrubs as he pulled them from the locker. "He's doing what any good director does when unexpected situations arise. He's rewriting the script."

*"Mr. Lowe is correct,"* Gross said. The director could do more than see them; there must be a microphone hidden somewhere too. *"Mr. Pickerill would be quite upset, but I feel this is the best way to finish the film. Miss Werdner plays out her role, and Mr. Lowe, I'm afraid you will just be a nameless doctor aiding her in her quest."*

"Goddamn it," Davis whispered in what he hoped was a low enough tone for even Gross to miss. "He doesn't have to separate us. Once we're in costume, he just hunts us down and captures it on film."

"But what about the script? What are our lines?"

*"It doesn't matter, my dear. You two just do what comes natural: fight for your lives."* Gross paused to let that sink in, always the dramatist. He should've tried to make it as an actor rather than a director. *"Now put them on, or Miss Campbell dies right now!"*

Davis looked around for someplace to go so they didn't have to change in front of one another, but Werdner already had her tight little black skirt and midriff on the floor. She wasn't wearing a bra, only black thong underwear.

She caught his look. "Like it's not something you can't see on Showtime any night of the week."

"Yours maybe, but not mine."

"Oh, Jesus, most men would pay to take off their clothes

in front of me." She spun around. "There, you big baby, is that better?"

He shrugged and began changing.

The scrubs were a bit too big, but he would be able to move fast in them. Werdner was in costume, placing her ridiculous nursing cap on last of all.

*"Very good. Now you both look the part. Go through the door on your left, and we can get started."*

This time the look they gave one another was mutual. They were playing into his hand, going right along with everything he asked, but as yet, Davis could see no alternative. Gross had planned this extremely well even on short notice.

Davis opened the door, and the two of them went further into Chesterfield Hospital.

# TAKE 3

The door swung shut on Spitzen, but he actually watched as it melted, running like hot wax, dissolving into the same uniform metal as the rest of the room. He stood outside for a good five minutes, pounding on the surface and shouting. When he stopped, he thought he could hear a muffled talking on the other side, but amplified, like listening to a bullhorn from a distance.

One thing for sure: he believed Lowe's story unreservedly now. Between what he'd seen when he snapped a picture of the mad director at Werdner's mansion, and having wood transmogrify into metal right in front of his eyes, he refused to be the one holdover idiot in the movie that never accepted the supernatural, even as it was devouring them.

Spitzen stood for a long moment considering his options. Three other doors to choose from: the remaining two in this chamber, and the one behind him, where they entered this voyeuristic funhouse.

The middle door would keep him closest to the other two, if he should decide to press on. However, if he wanted to slink away into the night…

Spitzen sighed. He couldn't just leave them. Besides the fact that his story currently had no ending (not to mention proof of any of this insanity) he also had the camera, the only weapon they'd brought with them, and he was cursed with a conscience that would never let him forget leaving these two to die. Or Lowe, at the very least.

He tried the knob on the middle door. It opened smoothly. Spitzen stepped through and allowed it to close behind him, then waited to see if would vanish. It stayed in place, which gave him a small measure of security.

He was now in an oddly circular room, the shape of a silo. The ceiling was five or six yards above him, capping the smooth, curving metal walls. It was like being inside a giant cigarette. There was only one other door, on the extreme opposite side of where he entered. A metal railing in front of him created a tight inner circle around to the other exit, and when he looked over the edge, he saw another floor at least ten yards down. The room yawned open down there, stretching out to an entire level beneath this one, some kind of concrete dungeon, but wherever it led to was hidden by the platform he stood on. There was no ladder or any other means for accessing one level from the other.

"What the *hell?*" He couldn't think of any practical use for a room like this in the building's original construction. It must be one of Gross' remodels, meant to look dramatic on film. Spitzen looked up, searching the rounded walls of this room, and found what he was looking for.

A camera placed at about shoulder height, attached to the wall by a V-shaped bracket. Watching him patiently.

He went over and stood beside it, pressing his back against the cool metal wall, careful to keep his injured shoulder from jostling. From this angle, it was impossible for the camera to turn and follow him. It didn't matter; there were two more on the high rafters of the ceiling that he couldn't escape no matter where he went. But concealment wasn't his intent anyway.

Movies; Gross' abilities were all about the movies. It just didn't make sense that he could change reality itself at a whim.

Spitzen raised one hand and moved his splayed fingers in front of the lens of the camera next to him.

The result was instantaneous. Across the room, where the camera pointed, the rounded walls disappeared in the shape of his hands as neatly as a magician's illusion. It had the same quality as putting one's hand in front of the projection at a movie theatre, and having the shadow interrupt the image cast on the screen, except this image was in perfect 3D. Wherever the shadows of his fingers touched, amplified by their proximity to the source of the illusion, he could see a plain, square office whose dirt and filth made the fake aging of this one seem laughable. He could see graffiti on one of the walls, a gang symbol in white spray paint, and dark rust covering the surface like barnacles. And, most significant of all, the railing and pit in the center of the room disappeared, becoming nothing more than a dusty, littered floor.

Gross wasn't reconstructing the warehouse.

He was using the cameras not only to record, but to *project*.

Spitzen made a rabbit with his hands, had it bounce back and forth in front of the lens while he watched its shadow on the far wall, and then pulled his hand back out of the way. The round room reasserted itself.

Gross could do more than just steal souls through a camera lens. He could create whatever set he needed, a perfect three-dimensional projection that made even the most sophisticated hologram look cheap. An illusion so real it was tangible, as his hands told him when he touched the railing. That was another advantage to having so many cameras placed at so many angles: there was always a new projector to cover up each person's shadow as they walked through his world, to keep the fantasy constant. The only way to interrupt the illusion was up close to one of the sources, by blocking out so much of the feed the others couldn't compensate, revealing the real world lurking underneath this meticulously constructed projection.

Smashing them would probably have worked after all, but only on a small scale. If Lowe was right, and the cameras still needed power or a way to be controlled, they had to find a way to shut them down. Clear the smoke and break the mirrors. Otherwise Gross could keep them wandering in here as long as he wanted.

*"Having fun, Mr…Spitzen, was it?"* the German accented voice boomed, echoing off the walls. *"Yes, you were at the press conference for poor Miss Wickersham. I never forget a face. You are quite an unexpected addition to the cast."*

"Yeah, well don't go putting my name in the credits just yet."

*"I don't think that will be a problem. The good news is that you too shall have a death scene, but alas, yours will end up on the cutting room floor. I just couldn't think of a way to write it in so late in the film. So feel free to…improvise."*

The door on the far side of the room opened. Krieg came through, huge, ugly as sin, face like road kill, and even that was being generous. He wore a tan jumpsuit that looked like it had already seen its fair share of bloodletting, stained almost a pinkish color. He strode in on thick legs, flexing hands that could crush puppies three at a time, and came straight for Spitzen without hesitation.

"*Lars has asked permission to finish you barehanded. Since he makes so few requests, I decided to oblige.*"

Krieg came barreling at him, snorting air like a bull. For lack of some better action, Spitzen raised the camera and blindly snapped a picture. The flash lit up the room in a moment of stark, white light, throwing shadows and illuminating every crack and crater in Krieg's scarred face.

Gross' voice boomed, "*That won't work on Lars as well as it did me, I'm afraid.*"

As promised, the flash didn't even slow the giant. He reached Spitzen, swiped the camera out of his hands, and smashed it to the floor.

Spitzen turned to run.

Krieg's hand shot out, grabbed him around the neck, and lifted. For a second he was still running, his feet treading ground but not going anywhere like a bad cartoon, and then Krieg turned him around.

To his credit, Spitzen technically got in the first hit as he dangled an inch off the ground.

He made a fist and swung it at the disfigured face.

It hit the man square in the jaw, snapping Spitzen's two smallest fingers like brittle twigs and bringing an amused smile to Krieg's chapped lips.

"*Oh, JESUS!*" Spitzen howled, the pain in his hand a throbbing agony, overreaching even his awakened bullet wound. Before he could react any further, Krieg set him back on his feet, reared back with a fist the size of North Dakota, and returned the punch.

One moment, Spitzen stood in front of him. The next he was on his back, sliding across the floor toward the railing and the opening in the floor, his glasses gone. The punch left him dazed, but not so much that he didn't register the fact that his nose was now a squashed bug in the middle of his face, blood pouring down onto his shirt.

He struggled to stand. His vision swam with angry black dots, and the agony from his hand and nose was a hungry, alive thing, eating his brain from the inside out, making the bullet wound feel like a mosquito bite.

The man had almost killed him with a single punch. Caved in his face like a paper mache piñata.

He couldn't remember how to make his legs work. His body had taken too much punishment for one night.

Too late for self-preservation anyway. Krieg had reached him again. One sausage-fingered hand encircled his neck and lifted him again, then tossed him as easily as a softball.

Spitzen felt the railing hit his back, the metal nothing but illusion but real enough to hurt like a bastard. His center of balance shifted as he tilted over it, then came the long plunge to the hard floor below…

# TAKE 4

Krieg went to the railing and looked down. The reporter was crumpled down there, blood still spreading from his shattered nose. The killer was disappointed it had ended so soon; he would make the others last longer, but there just wasn't sufficient time to really hurt this man if he still wanted to make curtain.

He had only two orders, both carried out. First, to destroy the camera that could hurt his master. Second, to make sure the reporter died.

As he watched, that broken form below started to move. The limbs jiggled and the body twisted and turned. The eyes opened, staring up at him.

But there was nothing in them.

The reporter climbed to his feet and looked blearily around, as if he didn't know how he'd gotten here.

Krieg smiled, but only because he'd done his job. This part bored him, what was left after the master's cameras had their way. They never screamed no matter what you did to them.

The reporter shambled off, moving out of Krieg's field of vision, and he let the man go. He was needed back on the set.

He had bigger fish to gut.

# TAKE 5

Davis and Werdner—now in costume—wound their way through a meandering path of dimly lit hallways and interior rooms for a good twenty minutes. Not a maze actually; a maze would have choices, and they were offered only one direction to go. He felt sure the purpose of this, besides herding them like cattle, was to disorient, make it impossible to escape. It also made him antsy and increasingly impatient, until he moved ahead faster and faster, shoving doors open and plunging recklessly through.

"Slow down," Werdner told him, pulling down the hem of her nurse's skirt. "There's no reason to *rush* to our deaths! What are you gonna do when we get...wherever we're going?"

"I'll worry about it when we get there. *If* I get there. I'm only an expendable extra, after all."

He pushed open another door at the end of a long corridor, and complete darkness greeted them. He stepped into it, feeling it press back against him, a resistant barrier like a layer of velvet, and then Werdner stepped through and the door slammed behind them.

Dim lights blazed on overhead, and they were able to take in their surroundings.

The room was wide, filled with apparatus that looked like something out of a mad scientist's laboratory. Antique dental equipment, ancient medical lamps on tall, arching poles, old EKG machines that resembled squat, waist-high robots. Some of the equipment scattered around the room looked like the kind used to generate electricity for defibrillators or shock therapy. Cameras were set at regular intervals in the ceiling and several lower down, ready to catch the action from all angles.

In the middle of the room was a swiveling table where the patients would undoubtedly receive their generous doses of head voltage. Strapped to it was Susan, wearing nothing but a white hospital gown.

"Davis!"

He ran to her, leaving Werdner behind. When he reached the table he bent over, sliding his arms around her as best he could. He knew it was a waste of precious time, a classic mistake, but he couldn't stop himself from smothering her with kisses. She managed to lean her head forward enough to do the same, setting his swollen nose afire.

"Oh God, Suze, are you okay?"

"I'm fine, but you have to get out of here, it's a trap!"

"That's not gonna make front page news," Werdner muttered, examining a rusted, foot-pumped medical drill. "You think these clothes were a fashion choice?"

Susan tilted her head down to examine him. "Davis, why are you wearing scrubs?"

"Gross wrote me into the movie! Let's save the exposition for later and just get you off this thing!"

Davis released her, a near impossible task, and then pulled back enough to examine the straps. As he reached out to touch one, the door they'd come through opened again.

When Lars Krieg made his grand entrance this time, he was holding a gleaming chef's knife.

"*Annnd* ACTION!" Gross' voice roared around them.

# TAKE 6

Werdner was closest, and she backed away from the killer in horror. He moved agonizingly slow, taking them in one at a time. Werdner (or was it Yancy now?) reached the table beside Davis, bumped it with her hip, screamed, and turned around to slap at it.

Krieg advanced, rolling the knife in his hand.

"Get Susan off this table," Davis told the actress. "I'll take care of him."

"Davis, no!"

"Do it." If Werdner had argued, he would've slapped her, but the actress only nodded slowly, her mouth gaping. With a final glance at the approaching killer, she went to work on the strap binding Susan's left leg.

Davis moved away from the table, circling Krieg till the man was forced to turn away from the women to keep him in view. He remembered how fast the lummox could move when he wanted. If Davis got within arm's length, it was all over. For a moment, his quarry's attention was split in two, Krieg's eyes flicking back and forth like a dog deciding if he wants the steak or the lamb chop.

"C'mon, you big ugly cocksucker, *I'm* the one who doesn't belong in the script. Can't kill the main characters before the extra."

Krieg turned his maniac's glare fully on him and started forward.

Davis backed away. His plan didn't consist of any more than giving Werdner time to free Susan. Krieg was still a good five yards away, but he was running out of room to back up.

"You know, it looks like you had a real serious acne problem at some point. No Clearasil in Germany?"

Krieg's response to this was to lose the smile, his face transforming as quickly as a storm blowing in to a sunny beach.

"You ever consider a mask? Lots of serial killers wear them, you know. Sure save the rest of us the trouble of looking at you."

Krieg glared, nostrils opening and closing with each heaving breath. Gross wasn't much for comedy—comedy killed the tension, after all—and the actor had probably never experienced his victims talking back to him.

"Yeah, that's a face only a mother could love."

Now Krieg growled like he had at the paparazzi, low and continuous. He squeezed the handle of the knife in his hand until his huge knuckles turned white.

Behind him, Werdner finished up with the legs and moved to Susan's hands. Susan craned her head at an almost unnatural angle on the table so she could watch what was happening.

Davis passed the equipment on the periphery of the room, which meant he was officially out of space. He grabbed a wheeled cart with a generator on it and shoved it between him and Krieg. The killer swept it aside, sending it to crash against an EKG machine.

Davis backed into a thin halogen lamp as tall as he was, with the shade turned upward. He grabbed it around the stalk, moving his hands down to the base, and swung it at Krieg.

The bulb shattered against the side of the killer's face, causing him to grunt and stumble in his advance. When the shade lowered, the right side of Krieg's pitted face streamed blood, but he didn't even seem to notice.

Still gripping the lamp, Davis curved his path to the right before he ran into the wall. He turned the lamp around, holding the thin stalk and shoving the heavy base at Krieg's chest like a lion tamer with a chair. The giant snatched it away and flung it behind him.

Davis risked a glance to the right. Susan hopped down off the table. *Okay, now just leave*, he mentally commanded her, but of course she didn't. She was every bit as willing to lose her life for him, and fuck it all, if that didn't mean they were meant for one another, what did? She grabbed Werdner and pulled her to the far side of the room, searching, he knew, for any weapon they could use against the man who had killed Katherine Wickersham, Samantha Cox, Terence Ottman, and countless others. A puppet for the creature masquerading in German skin, but still the man who committed the actual wetworks, the one that ended their souls—if not their lives—with his own two hands.

While he was distracted with these thoughts and a thousand others, Krieg leapt forward and slashed at him with the knife.

# TAKE 7

Torsten Gross watched the action from his control booth in what had been the upstairs manager's office in the building's original construction, on a console of monitors from which he could switch between each of the thousands of cameras in the building.

As his new cast had surmised, the cameras were real, as was the electricity needed to power them. A minor liability to be sure, and it was a mistake to have let the cameraman reach the room where the power flowed, but it took so much concentration to keep things in order, to generate the illusions, when actors ran around haphazardly through them.

And for just that reason, Gross maintained a booth like this on every set, so he could control the cameras manually if his concentration slipped. Maintaining the illusion of the sets was daunting enough, and this was the only place with a thorough enough view of the building for him to create a whole new construction, as he had just before Lowe, Werdner, and the reporter arrived.

And, of course, he also needed a private place where he could soak in all those delicious deaths.

All for art's sake.

But now this film was almost finished, and when it was, Torsten Gross would simply vanish. A new director would pop up somewhere, far from here. Perhaps Japan, where they still had a sense of culture and no real artistic inhibitions.

America had seemed the perfect place to ply his trade, with its excesses and love of entertainment, but they were just as restrictive; more so, with their family groups and religious groups and political groups. To his race, the concept of restricting films and art for the entirety of the public was utterly mindless, when all the people who didn't want to see it had to do was *turn their Upper-damned heads!*

But then, that wasn't really the source of the censorship, and he knew it.

This country's, this *world's*, cultural death was imminent, soon to be followed by much worse. The nameless, ancient thing calling itself Torsten Gross had no doubt the same forces that had driven him from his home on a plane of existence far from this one—where no one cared if he peeled the native inhabitants like grapes and used their innards on his canvas—were at work here. This smelled of the Bleak Scourge, the Dowser Beast, the Stranger, that fiend from beyond time and space, seeking to exert his dominion, to gain a little more ground in the eternal struggle, and if the lazy, addle-brained denizens of this world didn't wake up and put a stop to him and the other minions of the Filament, they would lose the battle just as countless others before them had.

But that was not his war to fight; he was an artist, not a soldier. Besides, if he dwelled on the future too hard, he would be as frozen as Lowe. For now, he needed to get down to the set to insure that *this* film ended properly, the way his new vision saw it.

If the Stranger took this world, whether or not he, Gross, was taken back into custody with it, he wanted his art to stand defiantly and proclaim that he was here, he existed... and he *created*.

Art was the only true immortality.

He opened the door to the booth, and gave a little grunt of surprise.

The reporter's shell had found its way up here. Gross had lost track of him after his death downstairs, diverting all his attention to controlling the area of the building where Lowe and Werdner tread. The idiot shuffled around in the corridor outside, running into the walls like a drunken buffoon, one arm hanging at a badly broken angle. Drool dripped down his chin, mixing with the crusted blood from his broken nose, and his eyes rolled in their sockets like loose marbles.

Gross shoved him out of the way, sending him sprawling to the ground with a wheeze. He had no time to deal with this one. He would get to him when filming was finished, then reprogram him to go home so he could seek his physical death in whatever way he saw fit.

The director strode down the hall, the walls shifting and opening around him at his will, cameras turning quickly away, giving him a direct path to the location of the action.

# TAKE 8

The knife drew across Davis' chest like a pencil-thin line of fire, and he reflexively jumped backward. He landed in a pile of equipment that rattled beneath him but kept him from falling on his ass. Blood cascaded down his chest from the wound, staining the pristine blue of the doctor scrubs.

It *hurt*. Despite that this was all illusion on some level he didn't understand, the pain was very real now. This is what Otter and Samantha Cox had felt, and the image of his friends in this kind of agony was enough to bring that white-hot anger coursing back through him.

He put a hand to the wound and pressed, gauging severity. No major damage, but half a foot lower and a quarter inch deeper and the swift motion would've left his guts on the floor like a steaming plate of spaghetti.

Krieg stared down at him without a shred of mercy.

Before either of them could act, delicate arms slid around the killer's thick neck as Susan leapt on him from behind. "Leave him alone!" She pounded at his face, one fist bashing against the wound Davis had given him on the side of his head, against his crooked nose, his thin mouth, all of which remained as unmoving as cast iron beneath her blows.

Krieg grunted once either in amusement or annoyance as he grabbed a fistful of hair and slung her off. She hit the concrete floor with a bone-jarring thud and went limp.

At the sight of her laid out, Davis burst into motion. His hand closed on a piece of the flotsam he'd landed on, a support bar from a metal leg brace, and he lifted it above his hand and brought it smashing down on the arm holding the knife while Krieg studied Susan.

His large hand opened. The blade clattered to the floor.

Krieg stared at it dumbly. Davis used the moment to kick it across the room to Werdner, who picked it up with her thumb and forefinger and backed away with it held at arm's length.

"Lose something?" Davis asked. Krieg gnashed his teeth. "Bet that wasn't in the script either, huh big boy?"

He swung the brace again.

Krieg dodged out of its way. His hand shot up to snatch Davis' wrist, and then *squeezed*. Davis felt the bones in there grinding together and yelped in pain as he dropped the brace. He saw Susan sit up on his right, looking around dazedly but not in any shape to help. Which only left…

"*Werdner!*" Krieg was still crushing, basking in Davis' pain as he increased the pressured on the mashed potatoes in his wrist which had once been bone. "A little help!"

Across the room, the actress shook her head vehemently.

Davis went to his knees in front of Krieg, and the giant's other hand encircled his neck. With that in place, the hand holding his wrist released, giving him a moment of relief before it joined its mate at the base of Davis' neck.

His lungs screamed. Davis scrabbled at the fingers holding him and stared up into that awful face. Consciousness fled; his hands dropped to his sides.

Then Werdner drove Krieg's own knife into his back.

"Would you just *DIE* already?"

Krieg released him, and Davis fell back into Susan's arms, gasping for air. The killer stumbled backward away from them, swiping at his back, trying to reach the handle of the knife jutting out. Werdner gave him a wide berth as she came around to join them where they lay bruised and battered on the floor.

"Better late than never?" Davis wheezed.

"Be thankful for what you get."

The injury wouldn't be enough to kill him; Davis saw that already. Might as well try killing a bear with a needle. Krieg was…well, time to face facts, Krieg was just *unstoppable*, and the three of them were only delaying the inevitable. This was a steel cage match, a fight to the death, and they would stay locked in this room until they succumbed. Davis glanced at Susan, and saw the same realization in her lovely eyes.

"You know, I think I love you," he said.

She smiled at him. "Not the most romantic thing you've ever said, but I love you too, Davis."

Krieg backed up against a wall and used its surface to knock the knife out. He advanced on them again, the weapon slick with his own blood now. Only Werdner had the strength to back away, but even she didn't seem too committed. Davis didn't think he could even stand.

The killer stood over them now, but Davis felt only a euphoric calm settle over him.

Krieg raised the knife over his head, preparing to ram it down into Davis' skull.

*This would be the point in the movie where a shot rings out and the killer crumples*, he thought.

But that didn't happen, because this wasn't a movie. No, there was no lone gunshot *deus ex machina* to rescue them.

There were actually *three*.

# TAKE 9

Krieg jerked as each bullet tore through him. Small red circles blossomed on the chest of his tan jumpsuit where the bullets exited. His mouth fell open, but only for a second. It pulled upward into an expression Davis thought he would never see the man make: a contented grin. Blood oozed from the corners, joined by twin streams from his nose. His eyes rolled back, but that grin stayed in place as he listed, toppling facedown at their feet with the grandeur of a redwood surrendering to gravity.

"What the *fuck?*" Werdner demanded.

"That's a wrap!" Gross proclaimed from the door behind Krieg. He held the same pistol he'd threatened Davis with earlier in the night, a thin ream of smoke drifting from the barrel. He was at such close range even he couldn't miss. "Such a shame. He was a good and loyal companion. And a hell of an actor."

"What...what was the point of that?" Davis whispered.

Torsten Gross glanced up from the darkened doorway, at the room's cameras. The devices began to move, spinning away from his side of the room and focusing on the three of them. As the cameras moved, an amazing thing happened, one so optically confusing it almost made Davis ill, like shaky handheld footage.

Gross' side of the room melted away like smoke, first becoming transparent and then disappearing to reveal the long, empty factory floor that must be the true version of this place. A defined line ate up the walls and floors toward them, a ripple in reality that moved across Krieg's body and stopped just short of where they sat, leaving them alone in the basement set of Chesterfield Hospital. Only when the cameras moved away from him did Gross come forward and close the distance between them.

Davis forced himself up, wrist still screaming, and then turned to offer Susan a hand.

"I won't be needing him where I go next, and I can't very well leave him behind. This is better for him. Without me, he would have been a run-of-the-mill serial killer, but I made him into a something grand." He walked up next to Krieg's body and gazed upon it lovingly. "And, as this is my last film as Torsten Gross, I have decided it will end as none of my others have. Happily. The villain has been vanquished—dealt a mortal knife blow by our hero Nurse Terry—and Denise Hutson gets to survive with her new doctor friend. In the final edit, the killer will be finished off by one of the police officers."

"So that's it?" Werdner asked. "We're free to go?"

Gross shook his head sadly. "Miss Werdner, that was the ending to *Arterial Slice*, but no matter how much it might seem like it, this is *not* a movie. And you are no heroes. You are horrid people with no appreciation for true art, people whose death I will take personal gratification in."

"Christ, do you ever stop talking?" Davis asked. "Just end it, already!" Susan slipped into his arms and pulled him close to her.

"I'll take that as a last request." Gross leveled the gun at him for the last time.

The director pulled the trigger.

The shot went wide, spanging off one of the warehouse walls, but not because of his horrible aim. The skin on the hand holding the gun began to sizzle, burning off like tissue paper in an open flame, revealing that nauseating glow beneath.

"*Oooowww!*" he howled, dropping the gun and cradling the appendage against him.

"Davis, what's happening?" Susan stared at Gross, her mouth an 'O' of shock; he realized she was still a few narrative acts behind the rest of them.

Whatever caused the reaction wasn't finished. The fake skin all over Gross' body bubbled off like an insanely bad sunburn, and the glowing creature inside was left wearing a black sweater and slacks that began to sag and slip over his shoulders to land on the floor.

The revealed creature was hard to look at; the glow brightened as more of its skin boiled away. There was no substance to it at all, only that bluish-gray light, and two pinpoints of darkness in the circle of its head identifiable as eyes. Davis saw them roaming the room, and tried to follow their frantic gaze.

"The cameras," Werdner said in wonder. "It's the cameras!"

The machines were swiveling back to face him, moving away from Davis, Susan, and Werdner, but without replacing the hospital room set. Gross held out a hand to them and commanded, in that buzzing voice, "*No! Turn away!*" Susan jumped against him when she heard it, and Werdner slapped hands over her ears.

The cameras didn't obey, only continued to gaze at him, and now the *glow itself* was beginning to smoke and smolder.

"*Turn AWAY!*" he bellowed, the voice like a mouthful of bees.

*"LIGHTS, CAMERA, ACTION, GROSS OLD PAL,"* the P.A. system boomed, and Davis recognized the voice. *"THE NEXT TIME YOU MAKE A ZOMBIE OUT OF SOMEONE—"*

# TAKE 10

"—you better make sure they're really dead," Spitzen said into the microphone in the control booth. It was easy to figure out the cameras' controls, and right now he had all fifteen of the ones in the room with Lowe and the others zeroed in on Gross.

"Let's see how you like being part of the cast." He snuffled up blood and zoomed in further.

# TAKE 11

"NOOOO!" Gross squealed. The glowing light that poured from every inch of him was becoming substantial, turning into some gelatinous ooze. The director looked— not that Davis wanted to run a reference into the ground— like the Wicked Witch of the West after her cold shower. Streams of glowing material like radioactive waste oozed off his hand. He writhed, tried to turn and run, but had lost too much of his mass to maintain his legs.

The room changed around them, the quality of the light dimming, the equipment and remaining walls of the room becoming translucent. Chesterfield Hospital evaporated until they stood on a bare concrete floor lit by pale moonlight coming from a bank of large windows near the ceiling.

Only the cameras themselves remained.

At last the creature that had been Torsten Gross, now only a waist high blob, swiveled back to Davis, those two pinpoints of black pleading.

"Please," it begged in its electric-filled voice. "The movie... My art..."

Davis shrugged. "It was overrated."

The monster shrieked wordlessly; the sound vibrated the tissue in Davis' brain to a degree that threatened to give him his very own *Scanners* moment. Gross was no more than a head floating in a fluorescent puddle atop his clothes now. His light was going out, dampening like a fade out at the end of the movie. His scream still buzzed, but now it sounded gargly.

And then the awful noise was gone, and after a few seconds longer the light faded entirely, leaving a pitch black oil slick on the floor.

"*YOU GUYS OKAY?*" Spitzen asked over the loudspeaker.

Davis gave the nearest camera a salute.

Krieg sat up.

He, Susan, and Werdner all screamed in unison, but the giant only blinked blearily and looked around with a confused look on his horrid face.

Whatever fueled Gross' zombies...that bit of magic hadn't died with him. They watched as the killer got on his hands and knees, stared at the floor for a long minute and then proceeded to lick the layers of dirt from the concrete.

"To each his own," Davis said.

He still had his arm around Susan, and he turned to look at her. They stood in a patch of bright moonlight, and her face glowed also, but far more pleasantly than Gross.

"You okay?"

"No, not even close. I feel like shit and I think you have a lot of explaining to do about what just happened, but I'll live."

"Wanna get married?"

She smiled; his heart pitter-pattered. "Not here, if that's what you're asking."

"I was thinking more along the lines of a beach. High noon. No cameras."

"Before you get too carried away with the future…how about just enjoying when the hero kisses the girl?"

"And…action." He grinned and bent to her, sliding his lips against hers.

If there really was such a thing as a soul, it should be used for moments like this.

Behind them, Werdner leaned against one of the walls in her nurse's costume and watched the couple holding one another in the patch of moonlight.

"I thought the main character was supposed to have the romantic ending. The only thing I ever hear at the climax is 'Do you want it on your face or your chest?'" But an uncharacteristic smile played at the corners of her mouth.

"*I CAN BE DOWN IN HALF A SECOND, YOU KNOW,*" Spitzen offered over the PA.

She started to say something bitchy, reconsidered, and then said, "I'll meet you in the car in five minutes." She left through the same door they entered through barely an hour before, which now hung on just one hinge, leaving the lobotomized Krieg to lick the floor, and the couple to continue their kiss.

# SCENE XV

(fade out)

# TAKE 1

"I don't know about the angle. Readjust it a little, try to bring the focus up higher on her face," Davis told his cameraman. The man swung the tripod mounted movie-camera—a heavy-duty beast provided by none-other than Universal Studios—until the new angle was as Davis had requested.

A stand-in was on the business end of the camera, a perky eighteen-year-old blonde in a toga waiting patiently between two pillars in the spot where the talent would stand later in the day when the real director arrived with his crew. Their job was merely to take some establishing shots. "Am I doing all right, Mr. Lowe?" the stand-in—Brittney or Tiffany Something—asked apprehensively.

"You're doing fine." He heard the sound of a car engine outside the open bay doors of the set, and turned around just in time to see a familiar green Toyota park outside and the driver climb out and then start inside toward them. "That's a half hour for lunch," he told his five-man crew. They began to split up and go their separate ways.

Sidney Spitzen came forward and held out the hand not in a cast, which Davis shook. The doctor said the man would heal well, with only a slightly crooked nose to show for the beating he'd taken at Lars Krieg's hand. "The car looks great. I can't believe they were able to fix it."

Spitzen turned and glanced over his shoulder at the car. "They weren't. That's a new one. Amazing how much money an award-winning news story will bring you. Even if the tabloids are the only ones that will print it."

"So…you actually bought that thing again?"

"What? I like Toyotas."

"Okay. Anyway, has our little problem been fixed?"

Spitzen nodded. "The injunction was a slam dunk. Trimax cannot legally distribute any of the *Arterial Slice* footage. That doesn't mean it's not gonna pop up on the internet, but…what can you do?" He took a look around the set, which had been painstakingly built from scratch to resemble the height of the Greek empire. "So how goes this?"

Davis leaned closer and lowered his voice to a conspiratorial level. "Not bad, if I can get this goddamned cameraman to do his job. What a fuckup, I swear."

"That true, cameraman?" Spitzen shouted over Davis at the figure still fiddling with the controls, with close to the same inflection Torsten Gross had given the word. "You a fuckup?"

"Fuck you both," Jared said, straightening up to face them. "It's kinda hard to work with both your arms in goddamn casts."

"Hey, I sympathize." Spitzen held up his own plaster wing. Jared hobbled over, not bothering with the crutches, his also-broken left leg swinging in wide arcs out from his body as he walked. His hair was no more than bristles on his scalp. "Besides, I don't think it's very politically correct to pick on a coma victim. How ya doin, Spitzen? Heard you saved the day."

"Shucks, weren't nothing. I also heard some interesting news about you guys."

"What's that?" Davis asked.

"That Phillip Reilly and Trimax Studios offered you an obscene amount of money and complete directorial control for a horror film based on our supposed exploits with Gross. And two films of your choosing afterwards." Spitzen raised his eyebrows. "And that you turned him down."

Jared held up an arm at Davis. "Talk to this fine fellow. That was his idea."

From behind them, Brittney (or Tiffany) called sweetly, "Excuse me, Mr. Mane, I was wondering if you could help me with my costume change?"

"Duty calls. I'll catch you later, Spitzen." Jared made his way laboriously across the set floor.

"So why'd you do it?" Spitzen asked after Jared was out of earshot. "The big time, your own movie. If I read you correctly, that's all you wanted out of life."

"And three months ago, you would've been right." Davis sighed. "But revisiting what we went through is not high on my list of priorities, and if I did, it certainly wouldn't be for the likes of Phillip Reilly. I'm through jumping through hoops for people...people like that."

*People who care more about money than art*, he'd almost finished. It was true...but it was also too close to something Gross would say. Perhaps there was a lesson there, but he was too tired to suss it out.

Spitzen frowned at him. "Even if it means you stay on second unit for the rest of your life?"

Davis hooked his thumbs through the sleeves of his t-shirt and puffed out his chest proudly. "Hey, I'm entitled to some self-respect."

"Susan made you do it, didn't she?"

"Her advice was taken into consideration, yes."

"So when's the wedding?"

"Undetermined. She said she doesn't count proposals under duress, so I have to do it for real once she gets back from this shoot in Thailand with Johnny Depp."

"And that doesn't make you feel intimidated?"

"Naw, not at all. I was gonna ask her anyway, even before all this happened. I really was."

Spitzen put a hand on his shoulder. "I was talking about the Johnny Depp part. Anyway, I gotta run. I'm giving a speech to a bunch of cultists in about a half hour. They may worship demons, but they pay pretty well."

He started back toward his car, and Davis watched him for a few steps before calling out his name. "Do you...do you think that's what Gross was? A demon?"

"You tell me. You're the one that got the exclusive on his life story."

"He definitely wasn't human, and he came from somewhere else, someplace no man has ever been, but from what he said...I don't think he was a demon. Sometimes it hits me, just how huge this is, how it proves that there's something else out there, something beyond what we know. It's the find of all human history, and no one even believes us."

"Maybe we'll have to do something about that," Spitzen said with a grin. Then it fell off his face as he added, "And let's hope there are no more of him coming."

"Amen." Davis raised a hand in farewell, and Spitzen returned the gesture before getting in his car and driving away.

Davis turned back to the set. He'd been missing Susan all day, but now the last exchange with the reporter was pervading his previous gloom. It was a good distraction, but it also sent his mind down a terrifying path it had traveled many times before in the last few days.

Because there was something else he'd mulled over since the five of them—he, Spitzen, Susan, Werdner, and Jared, after he came out of the coma—had told their stories to the police, after the drooling figure of Lars Krieg had been carted away to a nuthouse, and no remains of Torsten Gross had ever been found but a gooey black sweater and pants. After they saw that the people in authority were more than willing to believe Gross and Krieg had made an attempt on their lives, but that the idea Gross had been some sort of new-age vampire sucking souls through a camera lens was more than they would even entertain.

It sounded, they said, like a movie too unbelievable even for Hollywood.

But Davis' preoccupation was with a tiny bit of information gleaned from Gross' tale only after reviewing it without a gun in his face, and it was this: Gross had come here in flight to make his art, a pilgrim seeking escape from cultural persecution rather than the religious variety, some sort of inter-(spatial, dimensional, galactic?) refugee.

Which could only mean that, as bad as Gross was, there was something out there even worse.

Davis shivered despite the heat of the set. He'd gotten this sense lately, a vague intuition, that something big was coming, and that Gross was only the harbinger, like animals fleeing before an earthquake.

His cell phone rang, and it was Susan, and when he talked to her, his love bulldozed these thoughts to the back of his mind. If something big and bad was coming, then that was the future. He—they—would deal with it then.

From now on, he intended to be happy with the moment.

Like this novel?


YOUR REVIEWS HELP!


In the modern world, customer reviews are essential for any product. The artists who create the work you enjoy need your help growing their audience. Please visit Goodreads or the website of the company that sold you this novel to leave a review, or even just a star rating. Posting about the book on social media is also appreciated.

# About the Author

Russell C. Connor started writing horror at the age of five, and is the author of two short story collections, five eNovellas, and fourteen novels. His work has won two Independent Publisher Awards and a Readers' Favorite Award. He has been a member of the DFW Writers' Workshop since 2006, and served as president for two years. He lives in Fort Worth, Texas with his rabid dogs, demented film collection, mistress of the dark, and demonspawn daughter.

*Director's Cut*, the second novel of the "Box Office of Terror Trilogy," is available now.